MAGIC MOMENT

With an unreal feeling Michele let Lord Randol take her into his arms. She closed her eyes for the smallest second.

"So you feel it, too," said Lord Randol. His harsh voice caused her to stiffen. "Pray do not go all wooden on me, mademoiselle."

Michele flushed and her lashes swept down to hide her vulnerability. "I apologize, monsieur," she said in a low voice.

Lord Randol smiled, a devilish light in his eyes. "Your tongue betrays you. I have not forgotten your habit of lapsing into French whenever you felt most stirred."

Michele felt him draw her nearer. She knew what he meant to do. "No!" she said urgently.

He glanced down at her. There was an implacable look about his mouth. "For a moment only we shall pretend the magic remains," he said softly.

Born in Kansas, GAYLE BUCK has resided in Texas for most of her life. Since earning a journalism degree, she has freelanced for regional publications, worked for a radio station and as a secretary. Until recently she was involved in public relations for a major Texas university. Besides her Regencies, she is currently working on projects in fantasy and romantic suspense.

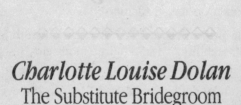

Hearts Betrayed

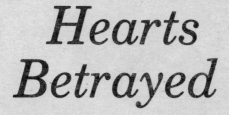

Gayle Buck

A SIGNET BOOK

SIGNET
Published by the Penguin Group
Penguin Books USA Inc., 375 Hudson Street,
New York, New York 10014, U.S.A.
Penguin Books Ltd, 27 Wrights Lane,
London W8 5TZ, England
Penguin Books Australia Ltd, Ringwood,
Victoria, Australia
Penguin Books Canada Ltd, 2801 John Street,
Markham, Ontario, Canada L3R 1B4
Penguin Books (N.Z.) Ltd, 182-190 Wairau Road,
Auckland 10, New Zealand

Penguin Books Ltd, Registered Offices:
Harmondsworth, Middlesex, England

First published by Signet, an imprint of New American Library, a
division of Penguin Books USA Inc.

First Printing, January, 1991
10 9 8 7 6 5 4 3 2 1

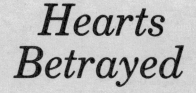

Hearts
Betrayed

1

Lady Basinberry frowned. Her eyes strayed to the ormolu clock on the mantel. "And you say that our niece is to arrive this very afternoon, Edwin? But why ever did you not ask my advice previous to today if you had second thoughts on the matter?"

The gentleman to whom she spoke was rotund in figure, attired in a plain brown frock coat and breeches. His countenance, usually amiable, was just now puckered in an anxious frown. From his position at the grate, where he stood warming his coattails, Mr. Davenport patiently explained once more. "Beatrice, I could not very well turn down such a pathetic communication from Helen and François, could I? I mean to say, it quite wrung my withers to read of their dilemma with their daughter, Michele. Naturally I could do no less than agree to have Michele here for the Season. And too, she is of an age with Lydia. I had hoped Michele would prove good company for my daughter."

Lady Basinberry snorted. "A young woman suffering from a decline is not likely to be good company for anyone, especially for one as flighty as our dear Lydia. You have gone off half-cocked once again, Edwin, and now as usual you have turned to me to bail you out."

Mr. Davenport did not deny the truth of his sister's sharp words. When he had responded to his younger sister's appeal, he had not given sufficient thought to the difficulty of bringing out two young women into society when he was himself a widower and therefore without an established

7

hostess. He sighed and rocked on his heels, causing his stays to creak ominously. "You know that I have never been able to deny Helen anything, any more than you can, Beatrice. Why, even when she was in the cradle, we were used to jump at her every burble. If Helen had applied to you, you would have done no differently than I."

"That is what has me in a puzzle," Lady Basinberry said, pursing her thin lips in irritation. "Why should Helen appeal to you over her elder sister? I find it passing strange indeed. After all, I am well-established in society and could be expected to bring this wretched niece of ours along quite nicely."

Mr. Davenport realized that this omission on their younger sister's part was the crux of Lady Basinberry's ill humor. He was a kindly man, and because he also had an interest in gaining Lady Basinberry's help, he quickly offered an excuse for their sister's laxity. "My dear Beatrice, you must recall that you have until recently been in mourning. Of course Helen would be sensitive to your situation. And perhaps also it was in Helen's mind that Lydia's high spirits could enliven her own daughter's solemnity. I gathered from Helen's letter that she and François are concerned that Michele will dwindle into an old maid if she is not brought out of herself."

"You neglect to mention François's influence on the matter. I am well aware of my esteemed brother-in-law's opinion of me. I have never understood why Helen, as delightful and clever as she was lovely, chose a Belgian over an honest Englishman," said Lady Basinberry sharply. But she was mollified up to a point by Mr. Davenport's analysis. "As for our niece, the young woman sounds an incurable romantic. Other young ladies lost their loved ones at Waterloo, but *they* have not worn the willow for nearly two years! No, they have all since done the proper thing and found worthy husbands. There must be something more to it than what Helen chose to tell you. Is the girl so homely that she cannot engage a new suitor?"

Mr. Davenport's eyes fairly started from his head. He was

aghast at such an unworthy suggestion. "Beatrice! A child of Helen's homely? Surely you jest."

"I never jest over a point of such importance. Grant you, Helen was a raving beauty. But she did marry that quiz-faced little man. He always brought to my mind a bug-eyed frog," said Lady Basinberry with revulsion.

Mr. Davenport looked at his elder sister with the faintest hint of disapproval. "François du Bois is a very good sort, which you would know if you had ever deigned to accept Helen's invitations to visit them in Brussels." There was a spark in his sister's eyes and he realized that he was on the brink of an argument with Lady Basinberry, which would not suit his purposes in the least. He said hastily, "But that is neither here nor there. What am I to do with our niece? Her arrival could not come at a worse time, not with Lydia going on forever over that young captain. How I wish I had never taken her to that balloon ascension! She might never have met the fellow otherwise."

"I suppose that you at once informed Lydia that the young man was ineligible," Lady Basinberry said with a curling lip.

"Of course I did," Mr. Davenport said, surprised that his sister should ask.

Lady Basinberry laughed in derision. "What a fool you can be, Edwin. If you had not done so, Lydia would likely have forgotten him within the fortnight. As it is, you have made of this captain a romantic figure."

Mr. Davenport was driven onto the defensive by his sister's scorn. "I can hardly be expected to understand the convoluted thoughts of a young female. It would have been different if Mary had lived to show Lydia how to go on. Now I come to find out too late that those governesses of Lydia's filled her head with idiotic poetry and chivalric nonsense. What do you think, Beatrice? Not two days ago I discovered Lydia hidden away in the library with one of those cursed romantic novels. She said that it was a vastly pretty tale and she wished very much that she could be carried off in the same manner as the heroine! What rubbish. Then in the next instant a little smile appeared on her face and she began sighing over this Hughes fellow. Why, anyone could see what was in her mind. I tell you, I was never more put out with her in all my life.'' He bethought himself of the impending visit by his niece, and his sense of injury grew. ''Yes, and now I shall have a moping miss as well as my own mooning miss on my hands. I do not mind confessing to you, Beatrice, that I am completely distracted over the entire business.''

''So I apprehend. However, you have done the right thing in applying to me. I shall hold myself ready to guide Lydia's first steps into polite society, and we shall soon see how long she continues to rhapsodize over her soldier. As for our other niece, I hope that she is not one of those who take to their beds at the least thing, for there is nothing I so dislike as a person of weak character. Do not fear, Edwin. I shall see that Michele takes a turn about society, since that is what Helen wishes, even if I must drag the girl from her room.''

''You greatly relieve my mind,'' Mr. Davenport said, speaking with truth. ''I only hope that Michele is able to appreciate our efforts. Helen mentioned that Michele helped to tend the wounded on the streets of Brussels during the battle. I was never more distressed in my life to learn it. When one recalls the tales of shattered limbs and of men expiring of thirst—why, it will be a wonder if the poor girl's sensibilities are not permanently shocked.''

Lady Basinberry shuddered. ''How ghastly! I cannot imagine what Helen was thinking to allow a gently nurtured girl to witness such carnage. It was extremely unwise. I do not in the least doubt that is the true reason behind the girl's refusal to entertain another suitor. She must suffer nightmares at the thought of committing herself again.'' Lady Basinberry reflected a moment, then said, ''Edwin, I fear that our niece will almost certainly be a pale thin creature possessing haunted eyes, quite incapable of getting about in society.''

But when, a few moments later, the butler entered to announce the arrival of Mademoiselle du Bois, Lady Basinberry's grim pronouncement was immediately seen to have fallen short. The young lady that stepped into the drawing room was fashionably attired in a bottle-green traveling pelisse that sported three cape collars and was rather mannishly trimmed with epaulets. The excellent cut of this dashing garment neatly skimmed a figure of pleasing proportions before falling to her kid half-boots, which Mr. Davenport noted at once showed to advantage a pair of well-turned ankles. Her bonnet was trimmed with saucy black feathers and was tied close under the chin, haloing an arresting face. Her large and heavily lashed eyes were her most striking feature, being of an extraordinary midnight blue. Her nose was short and straight, her mouth full.

Mademoiselle du Bois was not beautiful in the usual sense, but her elder relations were instantly struck by the mutual thought that she should have no lack of suitors wherever she found herself. "My word," muttered Mr. Davenport.

The young lady paused just inside the doorway, aware that she was an object of curiosity to the older gentleman and elderly lady who had turned their gazes on her. She put up dark brows and her midnight-blue eyes twinkled. "Have I perhaps torn my hem?" she asked, a thread of laughter in her throaty voice.

Mr. Davenport was shaken out of his bemused state. He surged forward, his portly form creaking in its stays. "My dear niece! Forgive us for staring, but you are not quite what we expected." He surveyed again his niece's lovely face and her graceful figure. There was nothing of the frail invalid in this dazzling creature, he thought.

Mademoiselle du Bois gave her gloved hand to him. She looked around at the elderly lady, who was staring down the length of a prominent nose with an arrogant air. She engaged the lady with a winsome smile. "Am I not, then? I am told that I look a little like my *maman*. But perhaps this is not so?"

Lady Basinberry's mouth curled in a reluctant smile. "You do indeed bear some resemblance to my sister, though Helen is perhaps paler of countenance and her eyes a lighter shade of blue."

Michele nodded. "*Oui*, I have my father's eyes. He says he bequeathed them to me from a pirate ancestor, though I cannot believe this. My father is the most respectable of gentlemen."

Lady Basinberry showed her teeth. "Indeed? How interesting, to be sure. I must be certain to quiz François upon such a flamboyant ancestry." At her dry tone Michele put up her brows in mild surprise.

Mr. Davenport threw a warning glance at his sister and adroitly stepped into the breach. "My dear niece, how delighted we are that you have come. I was just relating to Lady Basinberry the happy news of your impending arrival. She will be playing hostess for us during the Season, you know. And my daughter, Lydia, will be in transports that you will be staying with us. She will have someone with whom to compare notes and to discuss all the grand invitations."

Michele frowned slightly. "I do not wish to sound ungrateful, uncle. But I did not come to London to put myself into society. I shall be content enough to remain in the background while my cousin is squired about."

Mr. Davenport and Lady Basinberry exchanged swift glances. Mr. Davenport cleared his throat. "There is time enough to speak of that later. You have but just arrived! After such a long journey you must be famished. I shall ring at once for the tea tray." He pulled on the bell rope.

"Pray do not trouble yourself on my account. I enjoyed a substantial luncheon earlier, so I shall take only a cup of tea," said Michele.

Lady Basinberry patted the divan cushion beside her. "Come, Michele. Sit beside me and give me all the news of your dear mother. I have had letters, of course, but it is so much nicer when one can hear a firsthand account. She is well, I hope?"

Michele accepted her elderly aunt's kind invitation and gracefully seated herself. She began to draw off her fine kid gloves. "Quite well, ma'am. Indeed, Mama is so energetic that one despairs of keeping pace with her. And as for dear Papa, he has a hand in everything that goes on." She was soon launched on an amusing description of her family's activities in Brussels society.

When the tea tray was brought in by the servant, she offered to pour, which office Lady Basinberry was gracious enough to accede to her. Michele performed the social ritual to a nicety, thus earning Lady Basinberry's unspoken approval. Over tea, Michele gave lighthearted replies to the gentle queries posed by Lady Basinberry. At last Michele expressed herself completely dry of anecdotes. She set down her cup. "And I fear that I must add to my rude manners and inquire where I am to stay. I feel all covered in dust. It was a very long journey."

Mr. Davenport, who had said very little in several minutes, came to himself with a start. "Of course, my dear. How inconsiderate of me, to be sure. You will wish to freshen up before dinner." He rang for the butler and requested that Mademoiselle du Bois be shown to her room. Michele took her leave with a charming show of regret for quitting their company.

The door closed quietly behind her. Mr. Davenport looked at his elder sister. "What do you make of that, Beatrice? I was never in my life more surprised."

"Nor I. That was not the pitiful young woman I envisioned, Edwin. Quite the contrary! Our niece is an extremely self-possessed young woman. And nothing in her conversation would lead one to suppose for an instant that she harbors a debilitating and hopeless passion. I begin to wonder whether dear Helen did not exaggerate the urgency of the situation," Lady Basinberry said.

"And I also! Why, that dazzler could have any number of suitors with but a crook of her little finger," Mr. Davenport said.

"Still, Michele was not at all enthusiastic at the notion of a London Season," Lady Basinberry said slowly. She pursed her lips in her habitual way. "We shall see how things go on before I make any judgments. I venture to say, however, that it will be an interesting Season." She began drawing on her gloves.

Mr. Davenport saw this sign of leave-taking with misgiving. "I say, Beatrice, not going yet, surely?"

Lady Basinberry looked at him. "Of course I am, Edwin. I do have other calls to make."

"I hope that you are not engaged for dinner this evening, Beatrice, for I would like you to come back here. Lydia has not seen you this month past, you know. And certainly your presence must lend ease to what is essentially an awkward gathering,'' said Mr. Davenport.

''I do not deny that my curiosity still runs high. Very well, Edwin. You may expect me to join you for dinner,'' Lady Basinberry said as she rose. She gave her hand to Mr. Davenport, who managed to execute a slight deferential bow to her before she sailed out of the drawing room.

2

Michele was shown by a maidservant to a charming bedroom furnished with solid, graceful mahogany pieces of Chippendale design and accented by rich shades of green in the draperies and carpet. The maid who had traveled from Belgium with her had already unpacked the trunks and portmanteaus, putting away gowns and day dresses in the wardrobe and soft frilly undergarments, stockings, gloves, and nightclothes in the three drawers of the commode. At her mistress's entrance, the maid made a soft inquiry and gestured toward a brass tub that had been set before the fire, along with a screen ready to be drawn in front of it to guard against drafts.

Michele shook her head. "I think that I shall rest first before dressing for dinner. You may draw a bath then," she said. The maid nodded her understanding and quietly closed the door when she left the room.

Michele lay down on top of the coverlet on the canopied bed. She was weary from the long journey but she found that she could not nap. Instead her thoughts wandered. She smiled as she recalled the determined manner in which her loving parents had dispatched her to England and the kindness of relations.

The interview just ended had proved most interesting. Her uncle, Mr. Davenport, was patently anxious to please, so she felt confident that with that gentleman she could quickly establish a comfortable relationship. However, Lady Basinberry was a different matter altogether. Her ladyship had been all that was gracious, with the single exception of that betraying statement regarding François du Bois, but her frosty glance had never warmed and her gently couched questions had been penetrating. Lady Basinberry wore an air of authority, certainly enhanced by the severity of her attire, thought Michele. Her lavender walking dress, though elegant of cut, was conservatively trimmed with ribbons, while her gray velvet poke bonnet had been graced with only a small bunch of black feathers. Michele suspected she would find in Lady Basinberry an exacting hostess of unbending tastes and sense of duty, of which the latter quality could prove uncomfortable for herself if her ladyship had been taken into her parents' confidence. Michele sighed on the thought.

She knew it was her parents' hope that a stay in London would reawaken her former giddy pleasure in society. Her parents could not accept that she had little interest in the social rounds that had once delighted her or that she preferred not to be sought out by the gentlemen who had once formed an admiring circle about her.

Michele had attempted to explain that after seeing and tending those who had been wounded in the costly battle of Waterloo, she found the frivolity of her former life incredibly boring. Though Michele did not touch on it, her mother had guessed correctly that the greatest influence upon Michele had been the loss of her wartime fiancé. She had had a true attachment to the young officer, which afterward had led her to discourage more than one hopeful gentleman.

Though Michele had not eschewed society, she was conscious of a desire to retreat quietly to those pursuits least likely to bring her into contact with company whose pleasures depended upon flirtation. Michele smiled faintly, recalling the gay, naive young girl she had been, who had desired nothing better than to attend the most sparkling functions and to flirt outrageously with as many gentlemen as possible. It seemed a very long time ago.

The bedroom door burst open and Michele sat up in surprise.

A lovely young girl with an abundance of golden curls

flitted across the room toward the bed. Her blue eyes were laughing in expression as her glance met Michele's startled gaze. "Oh, how perfectly lovely you are! I am so glad that you have come. I am Lydia, your cousin. But of course you must have guessed it," she said blithely. She made herself comfortable on the bed beside Michele. "I do apologize for interrupting your nap, but I simply could not wait. I am a very selfish creature, you see."

Michele was amused by her cousin's confiding air. "I am happy to make your acquaintance, Lydia. I do not mind in the least that you visit me."

"What a delightful lilt you possess! It is French, isn't it? Not that you do not speak English splendidly, but you give it such a musical sound," Lydia said.

"In Brussels and in the south of Belgium, where my father's family is from, we speak French because we are so close to France. However, Flemish is spoken north of the capital because there the people are nearer the Netherlands," said Michele. At Lydia's awed expression, she laughed. "It makes for very interesting conversations, believe me!"

"So I should think! I shall want to know about everything, I promise you, for I have never been out of England. I know Papa visited your home once or twice—oh, years ago—but I expect you were too small to recall him," said Lydia, her smile warm. She held out her hand in an easy way. "I do so hope that we are to be friends."

Michele shook her cousin's hand, responding with a smile of her own. Her dark eyes twinkled. "I cannot imagine why we should not."

"Of course we shall be. I shall begin by informing you of all my secrets and pledge you to silence," said Lydia.

Michele laughed outright. "You are really the most engaging creature, cousin."

"Am I actually? How frightfully wonderful! You see how nicely we complement one another," said Lydia, pleased.

Michele learned in an hour of sprightly chatter everything about her young cousin, including the fact that Lydia was desperately in love with a military man. "But Papa will not consent to Bernard's suit, even though he likes Bernard perfectly well. But Bernard is a younger son and in the military, and since the war has ended there is not much hope for swift promotion. I do not care a rush for any of it, except for supporting Bernard in his ambitions, of course. But Papa talks a great deal of rot about supporting me in the manner to which I am accustomed. As though I would not trade my entire closet of gowns for the privilege of marrying my beloved Bernard,'' Lydia said.

''Your beloved Bernard might cavil at the thought of his wife promenading about in only her shifts,'' Michele said, reclining comfortably upon her pillows.

Lydia giggled and agreed to it. ''But it is not likely to come to that. Why, there are postings all over the world. Captain Bernard Hughes will make his mark someday. In the meantime, I simply must stand firm and not give Papa an ounce of encouragement that I shall settle for anyone else but my—''

''—beloved Bernard,'' finished Michele, nodding. ''Yes, I can quite see that might be difficult. You are an attractive young lady and must have scores of suitors.''

''Not scores, actually,'' Lydia said with becoming honesty. ''I am only just coming out, you see. But there is a lord who has approached Papa and asked permission to pay court to me. I do not care for the gentleman in the least. He is cold and haughty—and much older than me, to boot. But Papa is dazzled by the prospect of his only daughter being addressed as 'her ladyship' and he says that I must give his lordship a proper chance to win me over. As though I ever could be won over, when I have Bernard's undying affection.'' She said the last rather scornfully.

''Perhaps once this unwelcome suitor divines the strength of your feelings for Captain Hughes, he will gracefully bow himself out of the running.''

Lydia reflected upon what her cousin had said, but then she shook her head. ''I do not think it likely. That his lordship will divine my feelings, I mean. After all, I do not see how he can overlook my feelings toward *him* unless he is totally insensible. I quake whenever I am in his presence, you see. No, it needs something far more persuasive than my timidity.

to convince his lordship to transfer his intentions elsewhere.''

"If his lordship is as unimpressionable as you say, I can only advise you to be honest with him. Believe me, no honorable gentleman wishes to marry a lady whose heart is bound to another.''

Lydia stared at her in horror. "I? But I could never talk to him in such a way. Why, I would die on the spot from fright.''

"Then there is nothing for it. You shall have to marry him," Michele said cheerfully.

"Oh, now you are teasing me! It is too bad of you! You have such a *look* in your eyes, Michele. I believe that you would tweak the whiskers of the devil himself," Lydia exclaimed. Her eyes suddenly brightened. "I have thought of the very thing. You shall speak to his lordship for me and explain about Bernard and—''

"I shall do no such thing," Michele said firmly. "Quite apart from the distaste I would have for the task, such a course of action would hardly endear me to your father. I thank you, but no. My interference ends with my one small bit of advice.''

"At least while you are here I shall have someone about me who understands," Lydia said, sighing. "I do hope that you will not leave me altogether to the wolf, Michele. Could you not occasionally speak to his lordship so that he is not forever looking at me? When I am around him I feel like a bug must when it is pinned and studied.''

Michele laughed at her cousin's vivid description of social nerves. "Of course I shall. It would be impolite of me to ignore his lordship, would it not?''

"Thank you, Michele! I simply knew that I could rely on you," Lydia said gratefully.

The bedroom door opened and Michele's maid entered, carrying a copper pail of hot water. She paused at sight of Lydia and glanced doubtfully at her mistress.

Lydia at once rose from the bed, shaking the creases from her muslin skirt. "I see that you are getting up a bath. I shall leave you to it, then. We shall meet again at dinner, I expect," she said, going to the door.

"Undoubtedly," Michele said with a smile. Lydia laughed and gave a wave as she left the bedroom.

Michele's relations had already assembled in the drawing room when she went downstairs to join them. She apologized for her tardiness, explaining that her maid had had a little difficulty in making herself understood by the upstairs staff when she had asked for an iron to press her mistress's gown. Michele had been appealed to by both frustrated parties and the domestic crisis had amused her. She was not behind in conveying the ludicrous situation to her audience, setting Mr. Davenport and Lydia off into laughter. But Lady Basinberry merely sniffed. "I assume that we are to dine this evening?" she asked pointedly.

Mr. Davenport hastily offered his arm to his sister and they led the way into the dining room. Lydia made a grimacing face at her aunt's erect back and whispered for Michele's ears only, "Do not pay a particle of heed to Aunt Beatrice's crusty manner. She can be a veritable shrew, but she is really rather softhearted underneath it all."

Michele smiled for reply, keeping private her doubts about her cousin's estimation of Lady Basinberry's character. Lydia was certainly more charitable than she would be herself, she thought.

Dinner was enlivened by Lydia's curious and unending questions about Brussels. Michele answered those about fashion and society, but she drew the line at the most outrageous. "Of course not! I would not dare attend that kind of theater. It is scandalous. But wherever did you hear of it?" she asked.

Lady Basinberry eyed her younger niece. "Pray do enlighten us, my dear Lydia. I am certain we are all consumed with curiosity as to your source," she said cordially.

Lydia had the grace to blush. She had no intention of revealing that it had been Captain Hughes who had made a passing reference about the scandalous entertainment. It would not endear him to her father, she knew. "I am sure that I must have read about it somewhere," she said breezily. Immediately she turned the subject. "Michele, do try the fish. It is quite delicious this evening. Papa, do you not think so?"

Mr. Davenport agreed that the fish was very good, but he smiled knowingly at his daughter. "Aye, you consider yourself a clever puss. I shall allow you to slide away this time, but mind that you are to be more discreet in future. Polite society frowns on a young lady who sports knowledge of those things of which she should not be aware."

"Yes, Papa." Lydia dimpled at him.

"Lydia, did you not say before we came in to dinner that you were in need of a new pair of boots? I have just now recalled the name of an excellent bootier given to me by my friend Mrs. Angleton," Lady Basinberry said.

"Have you indeed, Aunt Beatrice? Pray tell me the direction of the shop, for I shall wish to order a pair as soon as I may," Lydia said.

Under cover of the conversation between Lady Basinberry and his daughter, Mr. Davenport leaned over to address Michele. "You see how it is, Michele. Lydia is but two years younger than you, but she is completely unschooled in how to go on. I have done my best, and so has a string of governesses, but a mother's touch was lacking when it became most needed. However, it has occurred to me that you could prove to be a positive example to my Lydia out in society. She is too timid and naive for her own good, which at times leads her into indiscretion."

Michele smiled faintly. "Whereas I am so staid and worldly?"

Mr. Davenport hastily reassured her that he had not meant to give affront. "I assure you, no such thing. It is just that you do not appear in the least flighty, which Lydia most certainly is. I do hope that I may rely upon you to gently guide my daughter whenever the occasion to do so might arise."

"Of course, uncle." Michele gave a throaty laugh. She did not enlighten her uncle as to the reason for her amusement. She had now been enlisted by both Lydia and her father to look after the best interests of her young cousin. It only needed Lady Basinberry to confide in her, thought Michele.

When dinner was over and the covers removed, Lady Basinberry rose to lead the young ladies from the dining room so that Mr. Davenport could enjoy his port in solitude. But he waved aside the courtesy. "I shall come along with you to the drawing room, dear sister. It would be too lonely for me tonight."

"As you wish, Edwin," Lady Basinberry said with a shrug of her elegant shoulders.

When the company entered the drawing room, Lady Basinberry expressed a desire for music. Lydia offered to play the pianoforte and her aunt bestowed an approving smile upon her. "That will be most enjoyable, Lydia," she said.

Lydia went to the pianoforte and began to play softly. Mr. Davenport settled himself in a wing chair to listen. Lady Basinberry indicated that she wished Michele to sit with her on the settee. When they were seated, she said, "I am happy to have this chance to speak privately with you, Michele. We had such a short visit this afternooon when you arrived. I hope that you have been made to feel comfortable?"

"Indeed, ma'am. The accommodations are quite pleasant. I am grateful for the warm welcome that I have received," Michele said politely, wondering where the conversation was headed. At first meeting she had judged her ladyship to be one who seldom acted without an object in mind, and the past hour and a half in her company had but reinforced that initial impression.

Lady Basinberry smiled slightly. "How could it be otherwise, my dear? You are part of the family. I am only sorry that I have not kept in closer touch with your dear mother. And with my brother-in-law also, of course. I hope that we may become good friends while you are with us."

"And I also, my lady," said Michele with a smile. She had noted that her father was mentioned almost as an afterthought by Lady Basinberry, and it amused her. She had heard her father express himself unenamored of his sister-in-law because she was willful and extremely managing. Apparently Lady Basinberry returned her father's dislike in full measure.

"I wished particularly to speak to you on a subject that

perhaps may cause you some pain,'' Lady Basinberry said.

Michele lifted her brows, somewhat startled. "Indeed, my lady? And what is that?"

"I am aware of your unhappy history. So, too, is your uncle. Our sister confided her concern for you to us. I shall not offer you platitudes, Michele. I myself have but recently come out of mourning and therefore I have every sympathy for the feelings which you have harbored over these last several months. I tell you this so that you may better understand what I shall say next,'' Lady Basinberry said.

She reached out and placed her hand lightly over Michele's loosely clasped fingers. With every appearance of sincerity she said, "My dear, one must put aside one's feelings in the course of doing one's duty. I do not say to forget. That would be insensitive in the extreme. However, your mother wishes for you to again take up the life of a well-bred young woman. Perhaps that shall one day include the usual pattern of marriage and family. That is not my particular concern at this juncture. What I do ask is that you carry out your duty to your uncle and me and in particular to Lydia.''

"And what might that be, my lady?" Michele asked, her dark eyes holding only cool curiosity.

Lady Basinberry sighed and withdrew her hand. "My dear, I ask only that you do not stand in the way of Lydia's happiness. She is impressionable and of a romantic turn of mind. She needs someone other than me, someone nearer her age, to confide in, someone who can show her by example how she should go on. I hope that you will fill that very important role.''

Michele was silent a moment. On the surface, what Lady Basinberry had asked was innocuous enough and no more than what had already been voiced by Mr. Davenport. However, Michele sensed that there was an underlying intent on Lady Basinberry's part, one that she could not quite put her finger on. But at the moment she had little choice but to assure Lady Basinberry of her cooperation, or run the risk of appearing uncivil. "Of course, my lady. I already count myself one of Lydia's friends,'' she said.

Lady Basinberry smiled. There was a look of satisfaction

in her eyes that told Michele that her instincts had been correct.

"I am so glad that we have come to an understanding." Lady Basinberry turned her head to address Lydia. "Thank you so very much, Lydia. That was most entertaining."

Taking the hint, Lydia finished with a flourish and then stood up from the pianoforte stool. She swept a curtsy. "I thank you, ma'am," she said, flashing a pert smile.

Mr. Davenport, who had fallen asleep in his chair, came to himself with a series of snorts. "What? What? Oh, I say, that was marvelous, Lydia," he said.

Lydia ran over to fling her arms about his neck. She laughed at her father. "You know very well that you were snoring away, Papa. You always do when I play."

Mr. Davenport patted her arm. He said with aplomb, "There you are, my dear! I could not pay you a higher compliment. Your lovely music is so soothing that I cannot help myself."

Lydia whooped. "Dear Papa, you are such a Banbury man!"

Michele smiled broadly as Mr. Davenport strenuously denied the allegation and protested his utmost sincerity.

Lady Basinberry shook her head, her own thin lips curving. "Edwin, I must congratulate you on your sense of preservation," she said dryly.

Mr. Davenport got out of his chair, his stays creaking. "It was rather quick-witted of me, I must say," he said agreeably.

"I see by the mantel clock that the hour is well-advanced. I suppose it is time to say good night all around. I fear I am not as indefatigable as I once was."

Lady Basinberry looked at her brother. "I shall take that as a hint, Edwin." Ignoring her brother's bewildered apology, she rose and took affectionate leave of her niece. With a kind word for Michele, she swept out of the drawing room, calling for her carriage.

"I, too, shall wish you all good night. It has been a very tiring day," Michele said. Though she was truly exhausted, she suspected that she would lie awake for some time to reflect upon the household that she would stay with during the months ahead.

Lydia announced that she also intended to seek her bed. The company walked upstairs, leaving the butler to bank the fire in the drawing room and to snuff the candles.

3

The ensuing week saw the gradual settling of the household. Lady Basinberry sent out instructions that her things were to be brought to the Davenport town house and that her own establishment was to be closed for the Season. Her brother eyed with misgivings the mountain of baggage and furniture that descended upon his home, and he questioned the necessity for her moving in.

Lady Basinberry fixed him with a quelling stare. "My dear Edwin, it makes little sense to attempt to bring out two young ladies from a distance. Besides, I cannot justify the expense of keeping open my place when I shall be spending most of my time here."

As Mr. Davenport watched his favorite chair carried out of its usual place and regulated to a back sitting room, he could not find it in himself to agree wholeheartedly with his sister's reasoning. He began to realize that he had opened a Pandora's box by enlisting his sister to act as his hostess and to sponsor Lydia and Michele into society. He would be the loser, since it appeared that his comfortable habits were to be completely overturned.

Mr. Davenport was the only one of the household who viewed a week of wet cold weather as further proof of a gloomy future. Lady Basinberry was in her element, re-arranging the household to her taste and generally earning for herself the reputation of a veritable tyrant.

Lydia and Michele managed to fill the time very well in getting to know each other. Though the cousins were but two years apart in age, Michele was much more mature. Her early life had been as sheltered as had been Lydia's, but Michele had seen more during the last battle of the recently ended war and its aftermath than Lydia was ever likely to experience in her lifetime. Lydia had at once established Michele as her confidante and sounding board. As for Michele, she accepted her sisterly role with a shrug, aware of feeling faintly protective of Lydia's fresh naïveté.

After being immured by the weather for several days, the young ladies began to feel restless. When the sun finally peeked through the gray clouds and the sky looked to be clearing, Lydia begged that they be allowed to go out. Lady Basinberry agreed to a drive about the park that afternoon if the weather continued to improve. The treat was looked forward to by Lydia and Michele with high spirits.

It warmed considerably during the course of the day and the ladies opted to ride with the top of the landau down. However, Lady Basinberry admonished her nieces to make use of their parasols to protect their delicate complexions.

Michele offered to sit with her back to the horses. Flashing her bright smile, she said, "I do not mind in the least seeing where we have been, for the sights are all quite new to me."

"Nonsense, Lydia shall do so," Lady Basinberry said firmly. Lydia agreed at once, and despite Michele's protests, she laid claim to the least-desired seat in the carriage. Michele gave way with good grace, and in answer to Lydia's subsequent query as the landau threaded its way through the London traffic, she admitted that she was glad to be able to see the sights as they approached instead of as they disappeared.

Judging from the number of carriages in the park, the sunshine was a relief to several others besides themselves after a dreary week of rain. Some brave souls even dared the damp grass to promenade the walkways. It was the fashionable hour, between five and six o'clock, to be seen in the park. Lady Basinberry had chosen to yield to her nieces' entreaties, not only on account of the clearing weather, but also because a drive through the park was the quickest way of easing into society. Lady Basinberry bowed to friends and introduced

Lydia and Michele to those who stopped to exchange pleasantries.

A young man on a chestnut cob glanced at the occupants of the passing landau. His head swiveled for a second look; then he swung his mount around and hailed the carriage. Lady Basinberry's driver stopped the landau. The gentleman spared hardly a glance for Lady Basinberry's inquiring expression or for Lydia's wide interest. He stared instead at Michele, and a grin swept over his face. "Michele! By Jove, it *is* you. I could not believe my eyes for a moment," he exclaimed.

Michele smiled, her eyes friendly, and held out her gloved hand to him. "Sir Lionel! It had not occurred to me that I might meet you in London, but of course I should have realized."

Lady Basinberry asked pointedly, "I assume that you are well-acquainted with this gentleman, Michele?"

"Pray forgive me, Lady Basinberry. In the instant of meeting an old friend, I forget my manners," Michele said. "Lady Basinberry, this is Sir Lionel Corbett. Sir Lionel, my aunt. And my cousin, Miss Lydia Davenport."

The gentleman pressed Michele's fingers warmly before letting go her hand. He bowed low in the saddle to the ladies, his carefully disordered locks glinting fiery gold in the sun. "It is indeed a pleasure, my lady. Miss Davenport, your servant! I recall that Madame du Bois spoke with affection of her English family, and upon meeting you this morning, I can readily understand why she should," he said with a wide smile.

Lady Basinberry was not entirely proof against his obvious charm. She unbent enough to bestow the slightest of smiles upon him. "Indeed! So you are acquainted with my sister, sir?"

"Sir Lionel was an officer in the Duke of Wellington's cavalry and was among those who could be counted upon to even up a lopsided dinner party," Michele said with a laugh.

Sir Lionel shot an intent look in her direction. "Quite true! I was but one of your niece's large circle of admirers. But how is it that you come to be in London, Michele? When last I spoke with you, you were quite determined to remain in Brussels. My hopes were quite dashed, if you will recall.''

Michele felt her face warm at his pointed reminder of their last communication. It had been difficult to turn down his passionately phrased proposal of marriage. She was glad to note that her voice was completely steady. ''My dear parents thought it time for me to become acquainted with the English branch of the family, and also with England. And you, Sir Lionel? You are not still in the army?''

''Not I. I resigned my commission the instant I set foot back in jolly old England. I have become an idler, as you see,'' Sir Lionel said cheerfully, gesturing at himself. The scarlet riding coat he wore was of superfine cloth and was accented with bright gilt buttons. Its excellent cut molded tightly to his form and obviously owed nothing to buckram padding of the shoulders. His pantalooned legs were encased in high riding boots with the immaculate white tops that had been introduced by that former leader of gentlemen's fashion, Mr. Brummel. His moderately high starched shirt points rose out of a cravat tied with a *dégagé* style that set the final stamp on a somewhat dandified appearance. Yet there was a sense of alertness about his neat figure that hinted at great physical power even through the mask of indolence he affected.

Michele smiled and shook her head. ''That I do not believe. You will not have given up your sporting. As I recall, you had an ambition to raise the finest jumpers in the isles.''

Sir Lionel smiled and there was a softened light in his eyes. ''I am flattered that you should remember.'' He turned his gaze on Lady Basinberry and Lydia, who had been listening to the exchange with patent interest. ''I shall take my leave for now, but I hope that we shall meet again. If it is not too forward of me, I should like to call on you one day.''

Lady Basinberry gave her hand to him in a friendly fashion. ''Pray do so, Sir Lionel. I am persuaded that we would enjoy your company.'' At Sir Lionel's query, she gave him the direction to the Davenport residence. Sir Lionel bowed once more and sent a familiar grin in Michele's direction before he cantered off.

The landau started forward once more. Lydia could not contain herself. "Michele, he is simply divine. Such elegance and presence. Why ever did you not tell us that you were acquainted with such a fine gentleman?"

"I did not know that I would be meeting Sir Lionel," Michele said, frowning slightly. It had not previously occurred to her, but naturally she would chance upon some of those individuals she had known before in Brussels. The realization brought with it very mixed feelings.

The society on the eve of Waterloo had been glittering and cosmopolitan, with representatives from every nation that had allied itself against Napoleon. The English in particular had been prominent, since not only the army had come, but all of the *ton* as well. In fact, the young English girls who made their come-out in 1815 did so not in London, but in Brussels. Undoubtedly Michele would meet others she had known and who would recall for her other memories that she found bittersweet.

"Sir Lionel strikes me as a pleasant gentleman. I will not be averse to it if he should call." Lady Basinberry noted her niece's drawn brows. "That is, unless you would not care for it, Michele."

"Oh, no, it is a matter of indifference to me, my lady," Michele said with a quick smile. "Sir Lionel once thought of himself as an admirer of mine. I hope that he has remained a friend."

Lady Basinberry regarded her with a worldly expression in her cool blue eyes. "He offered for you, did he? Well, that is something, at least. That touch-me-not air of yours is rather formidable. I was beginning to think of you as hopelessly on the shelf."

"Aunt Beatrice, what a perfectly horrid thing to say!" exclaimed Lydia indignantly.

Michele began to laugh. Her midnight-blue eyes sparkled with the leavening of her somber thoughts. "Indeed it was, Lydia, as I am certain that our aunt is well aware. Am I not right, my lady?"

Lady Basinberry smiled. She gave a pat to her niece's arm. "You'll do, girl. Lydia, do stop gawping. Michele and I understand one another very well. She'll not take hurt from anything that I may say, I promise you."

When the ladies returned home from the park, Lady Basinberry pronounced herself well-satisfied with the consequences of their outing. Her nieces had been introduced to more than a score of acquaintances, some of whom had been kind enough to proffer invitations to the young women to upcoming social functions.

"When we hold our own ball, you may be sure that we shall have full attendance, for it will now get about that I am sponsoring two lovely young misses. Curiosity alone will bring out the gentlemen. I could not be more pleased," Lady Basinberry said, drawing off her lavender kid gloves.

Michele saw the first precipice yawning before her. "My lady, I do not care overmuch for the whirl of society. I would prefer to leave the limelight to my cousin. Indeed, I had quite intended mine to be a quiet visit."

"Oh, no! You cannot mean it," Lydia exclaimed, dismayed. "Why, the Season will not be half so amusing if you mean to sit at home."

"Stuff and nonsense! I shall not hear of it. Why, you are the perfect foil for Lydia, and she for you. Pray try to be reasonable, my girl, if only for Lydia's sake. Her golden head will be wonderfully enhanced next to your striking dark looks. The gentlemen will be drawn like flies to honey. I shall take it very ill indeed if you deprive me of this advantage over the other matrons who are bringing out young misses, Michele."

Michelle surrendered the point with a laugh. "Very well, ma'am. I shall play the proper miss and attend those functions that I must. But I do not promise you that I shall become engaged during the course of the Season."

"I have not asked it of you, my dear." Lady Basinberry threw her niece a slightly mischievous smile. "At least, not yet."

Michele shook her head and laughed again. She knew when she was faced by a formidable opponent, and Lady Basinberry displayed all the signs. That lady had every intention of seeing her tied fast to some unsuspecting gentleman before the Season was out, she thought.

Lydia clapped her hands, delighted by the outcome of the genteel sparring. "What fun we shall have together, Michele! I am so glad that you are here. And I know just the thing to put you into a proper frame of mind. We simply must go shopping. I for one wish to be at the height of fashion."

"How right you are, Lydia," said Lady Basinberry. "I shall accompany you myself in the morning. There are a number of shops in Mayfair that I patronize, in particular a fine modiste. You shall need a dozen new gowns. As for you, Michele, I suspect that you neglected to bring more than the requisite number of dinner gowns, since you obviously expected to dine only at home. I assure you that will not do. As my niece, you must be able to sit down with the Regent himself at a moment's notice. Therefore prepare yourself to be put into the modiste's capable hands."

"Shall we truly dine with his royal highness?" Lydia asked, her eyes round.

Lady Basinberry waved her hand in an arrogant manner. "I have done so a score of times. I do not see why my consequence should not extend to you. I intend to rest an hour before dinner. Pray do not look for me again before the bell," she said.

Lydia persuaded her cousin to go to the upstairs sitting room so that she could show Michele a certain fashion plate of an extravagant evening gown. Michele agreed that it was very pretty. "But I should not care to wear such a fussy ensemble myself, of course," she said. Lydia looked thoughtfully at the fashion plate and decided that she did not really care for it as much as she had before. She solicited her cousin's opinion on another gown, which won Michele's unqualified approval.

The young ladies spent a tolerable hour perusing the latest fashions. Michele decided early on that her cousin had a decided partiality for finery beyond her years. When she diffidently pointed out that a beaded diaphanous gown was certain to prove chilly for the wearer, Lydia immediately agreed. She said brightly, "Oh, I do know it, but it is such fun to pretend to the wickedest extravagances, don't you think?" Michele could not but laugh at Lydia's enthusiasm.

That evening, dinner was a relaxed affair. Michele found herself enjoying Mr. Davenport's anecdotes and Lady Basinberry's acid observations. Lydia was in transports over the next day's shopping expedition and gained laughter from Michele with her professed intention to spend every farthing that Mr. Davenport could be persuaded to part with.

At once alarmed, Mr. Davenport cautioned his enthusiastic daughter on the evils of extravagance. But Lady Basinberry came to Lydia's defense, recommending that her brother not stir into a matter that he knew nothing about, namely, bringing out a properly wardrobed young miss. "I shall tell you to your head, Edwin, that if you mean to cut up stiff over a few paltry bills, I shall wash my hands of the business," she said. Mr. Davenport subsided, muttering under his breath of debtors' prison.

"Never mind, uncle. At least I shall not cost you more than a pence or two, since I shall have my own allowance, which Papa assured me he would arrange to be deposited in the bank," Michele said. She was amused when Mr. Davenport's expression immediately brightened and he was even able to enter into the spirit of the extravagant plans put forth by Lydia. When the small company parted for the night, Michele felt much more at home than she had previously.

4

The following morning Lady Basinberry's confident prediction was seen to be correct. At breakfast a silver tray holding a small number of gilt-edged invitations was brought in for her ladyship's inspection. Lady Basinberry almost purred with satisfaction as she went through the cards. "The Season has begun in fine fashion," she declared.

The butler offered to Michele a small posy in a filigree basket, saying that the flowers had also come that morning. Michele was startled. "For me?" She removed the card attached to the flowers and unfolded it.

Lydia could not contain her curiosity. She craned her neck to see the script on the card, but she was unable to read it. "Who is it from, Michele? How exciting it all is! Why, you have not been in London above a fortnight, and already you are receiving tokens."

Michele read the card's message, and a frown entered her dark blue eyes.

"Cousin, who sent it?" Lydia demanded impatiently.

"The flowers are from Sir Lionel Corbett. He sends the posy as a token of his everlasting admiration," Michele said slowly. She was not at all certain that she liked the wording of the message. But surely Sir Lionel, having once been assured of her friendship, if not her heart's regard, would be more circumspect than to set up a flirtation with her.

"A vastly pretty sentiment," Lady Basinberry said approvingly. "The invitations to our little ball have already gone out, but I think that I shall have one sent around to Sir

Lionel as well. One cannot have too many gentlemen languishing about one's feet. With each gentleman, one's credit is that much more enhanced."

Lydia giggled. "How very outrageous you are, Aunt Beatrice. Do you not agree, Michele?"

Michele set aside her perturbation over Sir Lionel's communication and joined in the general air of gaiety. "Indeed! If Lady Basinberry has her way, we shall find ourselves up to our necks in admirers and unable to choose from among scores of offers."

"I did not give you credit for so romantic an imagination, Michele. You have quite raised my hopes for you," Lady Basinberry said. "I must do my utmost in securing these vast numbers of admirers, if for no other reason than to witness the resulting circus."

"I protest, ma'am. I am not in the least romantic, but I shall plead claustrophobia," retorted Michele.

Lady Basinberry laughed. She eyed her niece with more warmth than she had before. The girl was really quite witty when she put herself to it, she thought. It was an attribute that would shine to advantage during the Season. With her thoughts once more brought to consideration of the social round soon to begin, Lady Basinberry reaffirmed her former declaration that her nieces must be properly outfitted for the Season.

Soon after breakfast the three ladies set forth in Lady Basinberry's landau, London's innumerable shops as their destination.

Several merchants were visited, including a bootier, two milliners, a glover, and a modiste. Lydia was measured for the boots that she had desired. Soft slippers and walking shoes were also ordered. Michele purchased for herself an extravagant chip-straw bonnet that won envious accolades from Lydia and a noncommittal shake of the head from Lady Basinberry. Six pairs of soft kid gloves were purchased, as well as several chemises and camisoles and a dozen pairs each of silk stockings for Lydia and Michele. Lady Basinberry found a parasol and decided that a bunch of small black egret feathers would do marvels for one of her turbans. An evening reticule of knotted silver thread, half a dozen dainty lace handkerchiefs, and several lengths of satin and velvet ribbons for trimming a bonnet and a gown were pronounced absolutely necessary by Lydia.

The hours sped by and it was not until the morning was flown that Lady Basinberry pronounced herself satisfied with the results of the outing and ordered the landau directed toward home. The packages were so numerous and unwieldy that two footmen were required to unload the landau and carry the packages upstairs.

The lengthy shopping expedition had exhausted Lady Basinberry's reserves of energy. She indicated to the butler that she would take tea in her rooms so that she could recuperate in private.

Mr. Davenport was out at his club, as was his usual custom in the middle of the day, and so Michele and Lydia were left to their own devices. After they had consumed their tea and biscuits, Michele acquiesced to Lydia's suggestion that they go upstairs and look over their purchases.

The young ladies were inspecting their new acquisitions with a great deal of merriment when there came a knock on the bedroom door. At permission to enter, a maid brought in word that a certain gentleman had called for Miss Davenport.

In obvious dread of the answer, Lydia asked, "Is it . . . ?" At the maid's sympathetic nod, her face drained. "No, no! I do not wish to see him," Lydia exclaimed, clasping and unclasping her slender hands.

Michele was astonished by her cousin's whitened face and agitated manner. "Lydia! What is wrong? Why do you behave this way?"

Lydia turned to her. "It is him! The gentleman that I told you about. Oh, Michele, pray come with me. I dare not meet with him alone."

"But surely Lady Basinberry would not allow you to receive a gentleman alone. She will also be notified of his lordship's arrival and will naturally come down to chaperon you," Michele said, surprised.

"Of course Aunt Beatrice will come down. But it is as

good as being alone, for she favors him too. Michele, he
is so cold and . . . and aloof. He puts me out of all
countenance. I . . . I never know what to say. I beseech you,
pray come with me. Just knowing that you are there shall
be a support to me,'' Lydia said, a pleading expression in
her large eyes.

Michele could not withstand her. ''Of course I shall
accompany you. But I wish you to know that I find you very
silly.''

''Yes, I know that I am. You are truly the best of cousins,''
said Lydia, at once relieved and smiling.

As the cousins made their way downstairs, Michele had
difficulty believing that Lydia was as fearful of her suitor
as she made out, for she chattered away as though she had
not a care in the world. But as they reached the drawing-
room door, Lydia's chatter died away and the anxious look
reappeared in her eyes. She reached out for Michele's hand.
Michele gave her fingers a reassuring squeeze and then
motioned for Lydia to go ahead of her.

Lydia squared her shoulders and entered the drawing room.
She walked gracefully over to the gentleman who stood at
the mantel contemplating the fire in the grate. ''My lord,
it is good to see you,'' she said steadily.

The gentleman raised his head. He stepped forward to take
her hand, and with an awkward movement of his right arm
he carried her fingers to his lips. ''Miss Davenport, you
appear in looks this afternoon.''

Lydia bestowed a constrained smile on him and drew
forward her companion, who had unaccountably stopped a
small distance away. Lydia wondered at her cousin's queer
expression. ''Lord Randol, I would like you to meet my
cousin. She has recently come to England from Brussels and
shall be staying with us during the Season.''

Lord Randol turned his head. A livid scar ran down the
entire right side of his face, lending him a fascinating sinister
appearance. But it was not this that had caused Michele's
face to drain of color. Her eyes bore an expression of
profound shock as Lord Randol's gray eyes met hers. The

polite smile on his lips froze. "Mademoiselle." His voice was utterly cold.

There was a rushing in Michele's ears and she feared she might faint. Certain that she must be seeing a ghost, she stared at the viscount. "My lord," she whispered.

Lydia looked from one to the other, astonished. It was obvious that her cousin was somehow acquainted with Lord Randol. She was about to inquire about the circumstances when the butler announced a second visitor.

Lydia whirled about, all other thoughts flying out of her head. With a glad face she went quickly across the drawing room, her hands outstretched to the military gentleman who had entered.

He caught one of her hands and bowed over her fingers. "Miss Davenport, I was just inquiring about you of Lady Basinberry," he said lightly.

Lydia's eyes flew to her aunt, who stood just beyond the gentleman's shoulder. "Captain Hughes, how kind of you," she said primly.

Lady Basinberry was not fooled by her niece's polite formality, but she allowed a tiny smile to play over her mouth. The chit at least made an attempt at discretion, she thought. Her gaze went to the other couple in the room and she was struck by their stiff attitude. At once she concluded that her elder niece was awkward in social situations, and she sighed. If that were true, it was going to prove difficult to establish the young woman.

Michele was unable to take her eyes off Lord Randol. "I thought you dead," she said faintly.

Lord Randol gave a harsh laugh. His eyes were hard and mocking. "Did you, indeed? I am sorry to disappoint you, mademoiselle."

The color was returning to Michele's face. She put out her hand in an unconscious gesture. "Anthony—"

Whatever she meant to say died before the blaze of contempt in his eyes. "I have no desire to hear anything you might have to say, mademoiselle," he said cuttingly. Abruptly he left her, without the courtesy of a bow, to greet

Lady Basinberry. "My dear Lady Basinberry, this is an unlooked-for pleasure. I have not seen you in some time. I trust that you are as well as always."

Lady Basineberry gave her hand to him. "Indeed, I go on quite well. I have put away black gloves, as you see, and I am returned to London for the Season. I am sponsoring my niece Lydia and her cousin, Mademoiselle du Bois. You have met my elder niece, my lord?"

"Indeed," said Lord Randol. His voice held the slightest edge to it. He summoned up a smile of incredible charm. "The Season will prove a challenge, surely."

Lady Basinberry laughed. "But one that I am well-prepared to meet, my lord. One does not launch three daughters creditably without learning a trick or two."

Left standing alone, Michele stared at his lordship's broad back. The tears burned in her throat. She was horribly hurt and humiliated by his cruel snub. Even so, her gaze hungrily traveled over his athletic figure, set off to perfection by his superbly cut dark green coat and the close-fitting pantaloons that were smoothed into high boots of soft glossy leather. Except for the wicked scar on his face and the coldness of his manner, he appeared to be the same gentleman to whom she had once promised her heart.

But when she saw the awkward way in which Lord Randol raised Lady Basinberry's hand in greeting, Michele realized that he was marked by more than the facial scar. There was a stiffness in his movement that had nothing to do with lack of grace and Michele realized that he had suffered horrible wounds. She had seen enough of the damage that flying shrapnel could do to a man's flesh to be able to vividly imagine what had happened to the right side of Lord Randol's body. It made her sick to her stomach, and all at once she again seemed to smell the dirt and blood and to hear the pathetic cries of the wounded begging for aid and for water.

Michele gaqve a quick shake of her head. Those were memories only, memories that many carried. Her experiences of tending the wounded on the streets of Brussels were not unique. Many of the ladies had done so. And like many others, she had hoped and yet feared to find the one beloved face among all those others. She had never found him. She had subsequently been told by a mutual acquaintance that he had died of ghastly wounds in a military hospital tent before he could be gotten back to Brussels from the battleground.

Michele's thoughts whirled in deepest agitation. She put one cold hand against her cheek, thinking confusedly that Lord Randol had not died. He had survived his wounds. He was here in London. And he despised her. She had seen it plainly in his arctic gray eyes. She wanted to burst into tears on the spot, but knew that she could not, and it was that thought that finally steadied her.

Michele raised her chin as she gathered her pride like a tattered cloak of protection about herself. It was ingrained in her that only the ill-bred indulged in public scenes. Despite the shock that numbed her, she must behave as though nothing was amiss. But she felt sick to her stomach at how horribly wrong had been his lordship's greeting. In her wildest, most improbable dreams of finding him alive, she had never imagined that she would be treated with such brutality. Michele swallowed against the sudden closing of her throat, and deliberately she turned her thoughts away from the hurt she felt. There was no reason that he should despise her. She had done nothing to incur his enmity. A flicker of righteous indignation warmed her numbed misery, and she latched on to it gratefully. She fed her building anger until the threat of imminent tears was gone. She would not accept such callous treatment tamely.

Her eyes darkened nearly to black with anger, Michele sailed over to the small group and inserted herself at Lydia's side. Ignoring Lord Randol, she smiled at the other gentleman and said in her throaty voice, "Pray introduce me, cousin."

Lydia's eyes were shining and her face held a soft bloom of color. "I shall be delighted to, Michele! This gentleman is Captain Bernard Hughes, who has become a close friend. Captain, may I present my cousin, Mademoiselle Michele du Bois."

As Captain Hughes and Michele exchanged pleasantries,

Lydia slid a speculative glance in Lord Randol's direction. His expression was more forbidding than usual and his eyes dwelt on Michele's animated face with uncommon intentness. Lydia smelled the unmiskable scent of a mystery. She said, "You have already met Lord Randol, of course."

Still smarting from the viscount's shocking rebuff, Michele spared a scant glance for his lordship. "We have met, yes," she acknowledged coolly. She had the satisfaction of seeing a flicker of temper in his hard eyes. She turned her gaze once more on Lydia's military gentleman. "I believe that you indicated you were in the 33rd, Captain. I met a few of the company before Waterloo. Pray do sit with me a few moments and tell me whatever became of them." Michele drew the captain away, catching Lydia by the arm so that her cousin was made to accompany them to the settee. Lord Randol was effectively left to Lady Basinberry's attentions.

That lady was astonished by Michele's odd manners, but she marked it down to the influence of foreign society. She turned to Lord Randol and launched what she thought an unexceptionable conversational gambit. "My brother has confided to me that he favors your suit for his daughter. I am quite pleased, my lord. Lydia is a fine young woman, and for all her youth, she will be worthy of the position that you have chosen to bestow upon her."

Lord Randol seemed disinclined to engage in polite conversation. Indeed, he seemed irritated by Lady Basinberry's remark. "So I should hope, ma'am. Miss Davenport's antecedents give me no cause for concern that it could be otherwise," he said shortly.

Lady Basinberry was disconcerted. "Quite." A short silence fell as she recovered from Lord Randol's rude retort. She considered that his lordship was behaving rather haughtily, considering that the Davenport bloodline was an honorable one that stretched back hundreds of years. Indeed, when it came down to it, the Davenports could boast a few generations more than did his lordship's own line, she thought with rising indignation.

With an effort, Lady Basinberry swallowed back a sharp set-down. Lord Randol was undoubtedly a good match for

Lydia; moreover, one who had been given her brother Edwin's stamp of approval, and must therefore be allowed more slack. She set herself to engage the dour gentleman's interest, but it proved a task beyond even her formidable powers. At every outbreak of merriment among the trio opposite, Lord Randol's oddly angry gaze shot again in their direction. His attention was obviously not on Lady Basinberry's increasingly labored conversation.

At some point Lord Randol actually broke across one of Lady Basinberry's anecdotes to throw a question to Captain Hughes. "In the 33rd, I believe you said? I knew a chap by name of Weatherford whose brother was in the same company. Perhaps you knew of him?"

"Aye, a capital fellow," Captain Hughes said. He began to share a reminiscence with Lord Randol, and his lordship maneuvered himself out of Lady Basinberry's immediate sphere.

Lady Basinberry purpled with affront. Michele and Lydia, who, though they listened to the gentlemen, were not actually included in the conversation, heard their aunt's muttered exclamation. "Well! I have rarely been more ill-used in my life. But we shall see who snubs whom." Lady Basinberry raised her voice. "I think the gentlemen have bored one another long enough. Lydia, present your military suitor to me in proper form," she said, irritation snapping in her eyes.

Lydia flushed. "Aunt Beatrice! I have never said—"

"But your father has, and therefore I wish to grill the good captain on his expectations." Lady Basinberry inexorably carried Lydia away and a moment later had quite adroitly cut Lord Randol from the conversation.

Lord Randol found himself standing beside Mademoiselle du Bois once more. He did not seem to be affected by her lovely face, or by the fact that the soft green day dress she wore showed to advantage her curvaceous figure. Instead he regarded her with a chilling gaze. "It occurs to me that your presence here puts me in an awkward position," he said.

"Indeed, my lord? I cannot imagine why. However, I must be candid and say that your own appearance has dealt me a grave shock," Michele said quietly. She did not understand the palpable hostility that radiated from him. However, that in itself was far less important than the puzzle of why he had never attempted to get word to her. Surely he had known that she would have welcomed the news that he lived.

"That fact alone must give me cause for satisfaction. The question remains, however: what should I do next?" he said.

"I do not understand."

His eyes glistened. "I have requested permission to address Miss Davenport, as you have undoubtedly been informed. However, her antecedents are not as spotless as I had assumed, since I discover that she is related to one whom I hold in acute antipathy. I must consider the wisdom of continuing my suit for her hand."

Michele gasped, reeling anew at his heavy insult. Before she could gather her wits, his lordship bowed and walked away, ostensibly to take his leave of Lady Basinberry.

Lydia, freed at last of her aunt's firm grip, seized the chance to speak to Michele. She had never before seen her cousin livid with anger, but Michele's high color and the flash in the depths of her eyes impressed her. "Michele! Whatever did he say?"

Michele turned her angry eyes on her cousin. "Nothing of importance, *ma petite*. I shall say one thing only, and that is that his lordship is hard and arrogant and despicable. I do not know in the least what I found to like in him!"

5

Lydia's mouth fell open. She recovered quickly, all the more determined to discover the history that obviously lay between her cousin and the obnoxious Lord Randol. But before she could further tax Michele about it, Lady Basinberry claimed her attention.

"Lydia, here is Captain Hughes preparing to wish us good day. Michele, I know that you will want to say good-bye as well, since you found so much in common with the gentleman," Lady Basinberry said.

"Quite," said Michele, pinning a smile to her lips and giving her hand to Captain Hughes. "It was enjoyable to talk of old friends, Captain. I hope that we shall soon meet again."

He bowed, expressing himself honored by her regard. He took a more lingering leave of Lydia, and though nothing but polite pleasantries were exchanged, their gazes communicated much more to one another.

The gentlemen had not actually tarried long, but Lady Basinberry said that she hoped there would not be another caller that day. She professed herself put out of all patience after attempting to entertain the glowering Lord Randol. "I mean to retire to my sitting room and swallow a headache powder," she said.

Lydia waited impatiently until Lady Basinberry had exited the drawing room, and turned instantly to her cousin. "Michele, I simply must know where you became acquainted

45

with Lord Randol. Why, I have never seen such a look of astonishment on his face as when he saw you.''

''I do not know what you mean. His lordship did not seem at all put out of countenance,'' Michele said evasively. She moved to the table and picked up a porcelain statuette, only to set it down again.

''Cousin! Pray do not tease me,'' begged Lydia. ''I perceived instantly that you had met him somewhere, and you have admitted to it yourself. Pray tell me, for I shall die of curiosity otherwise. Was it in Brussels?''

Michele debated a moment before she gave a reluctant nod. ''*Oui*, it was in Brussels that I met Lord Randol. He was an officer and I had just come out into society.''

Lydia clasped her hands in front of her modest bosom. ''Oh, how exciting it all is! I saw at once how it was, of course. You were in love with him and something happened. That is why you exchanged such a *look* with his lordship. He was the cruelest of monsters and broke your heart,'' Lydia said, thoroughly charmed by her imaginings.

''What foolishness you talk!'' Michele said sharply. She was already deeply upset by the encounter with Lord Randol, and her cousin's blithe words had an odd effect on her. She took a quick turn about the drawing room. ''It was not at all like that. It was an enchanted time of balls and frantic excitement. One was swept up in the magic. The rumblings of war seemed unreal, but poised like a deadly sword above our heads. The sword struck, sharp and swift, and the magic was gone.'' She paused at the window, drawing back the drapery with one fine-boned hand, but she did not see the stream of carriages that passed on the street below. She was recalling a different time, one of intense and sweeping emotion.

Lydia realized that her cousin was caught up in her remembrances, and she asked tentatively, ''What happened then, Michele?''

''What?'' Michele looked around, startled. ''Oh, the soldiers and officers marched away. It was odd, really. Many were still in evening clothes.''

''Lord Randol was horridly wounded at Waterloo. Bernard

. . . Captain Hughes once confided to me that it was a miracle that his lordship survived at all,'' Lydia said. "Did you . . . did you see him then?''

"I could not find him. I was told that he had died,'' Michele said shortly.

"Oh, Michele!'' Lydia ran to throw her arms about her cousin. Her eyes brimmed with sympathetic tears. "I can but imagine what it would be like to be told that my beloved Bernard was dead. You must have gone through unspeakable torment, for though you have not said it, I know you cared for Lord Randol.''

Michele remembered the hatred in his lordship's hard eyes, and was possessed of a wild desire to laugh. "Cared for him? *Oui*, I cared for him. We were to be married.''

Lydia fell back in speechless astonishment. She regarded her cousin for several horrified seconds. "Married? You were engaged to Lord Randol? But I cannot believe it is true. His is such a cold, unfeeling nature that I am persuaded no lady in her proper mind could love him. Indeed, when I think that Papa wishes me to accept his lordship's suit, I am over-come with terror. Michele, how could you have loved him?''

Not trusting her voice, Michele waited to gather her equilibrium before she answered. "The officer that I knew was of an engaging personality, charming and devilish by turns. Lord Randol poked fun at the ironies of life, and his eyes invited one to share in his amusement. I was . . . very impressionable.'' Michele looked into the distance for a moment, before she shook herself free of her memories. She shrugged, her hands turned palms-up, and smiled faintly at her cousin's appalled expression. "It was all a very long time ago. And the gentleman that I once loved is gone.''

"But he isn't. He stood in this very room not more than a half-hour ago,'' Lydia said, again shaken. "Oh, Michele, surely you do not mean to let him pass out of your life yet again!''

Michele shook her head and raised her hand in a quick negative gesture. "Lydia, you do not understand. I saw the proof in Lord Randol's eyes. What I was told is true: my fiancé died at Waterloo.'' She saw that her cousin was prepared to argue the point, and she forestalled her. "Not another word, cousin, or I shall instantly inform my uncle what I have related to you. Since he might fear that my prior acquaintance with Lord Randol is a threat to your own interests, he would very likely pack me off back to Brussels. And I would very much dislike cutting my visit so short."

"I have already sworn that I do not wish to accept Lord Randol's suit, so that is utter nonsense," Lydia said, tossing her head. Despite her scoffing tone, however, she felt that her cousin had raised a valid point, and it gave her pause to think. Her father was not always the most sensible of gentlemen, as witness his extraordinary ambition to see her wed Lord Randol instead of her own choice, Captain Bernard Hughes. Certainly her father would react badly if he learned of Michele's previous engagement to Lord Randol, and because she had taken an instant liking to her cousin, she did not want to see her leave before the end of the Season. She would say nothing to her father, Lydia decided. Quite apart from the consideration of her father's reaction, Michele's confidences had given her the glimmer of an idea that appealed to the depths of her romantic soul.

She said suddenly, "Very well, I shall say nothing to Papa. But I must say it is a good deal too bad that his lordship is not still pining after you. I would not miss him in the least as a suitor. He is far too grim to suit my taste."

Michele thought about how hard and bitter Lord Randol had seemed. "I must agree that his lordship does not seem a likely husband for you, Lydia," she said reflectively.

Lydia spread her hands. "Now you understand what I feel. Michele, promise me that you will help me to depress Lord Randol's unwelcome attentions. After your extraordinary revelation, I have an even stronger desire to discourage his suit. I could never bear to watch my Bernard walk out of my life."

Michele looked sharply at her cousin, sensitive to an implied criticism. But Lydia's expression was innocent of any hurtful insinuations. "Lydia, I do not think that—"

Lydia interrupted her. "Oh, do you not see, Michele? Quite apart from my love for Bernard, how could I possibly form any attachment for Lord Randol, knowing that he once loved you? I would always feel as though I was betraying you, my dearest of cousins. Pray say that you will help me, do say you will?''

Michele smiled even as she sighed. ''Oh, very well. I shall attach myself to you like a shadow, and frown away the unwanted gentleman. But I hope you realize what it is you ask of me.''

Lydia threw her arms about her. ''Oh, I do! Believe me, I truly do. And I shall make it up to you, that I promise. You shall be my maid of honor when I wed my wonderful Bernard.''

''Certainly that is sufficient reward,'' Michele said wryly.

Lydia laughed at her, recognizing the irony in her cousin's statement. ''Of course it is! Why, what more could one wish?''

Much later, Michele was to wonder how she could have bound herself by such an easy promise, when its consequences were to create circumstances so uncomfortable for herself.

The drawing-room door opened and Mr. Davenport entered. ''Here you are! But where is your company? I was informed that two gentlemen had called. I did not think that your visitors would be gone so soon, particularly Lord Randol. How did you find his lordship, Lydia?'' he asked.

Lydia threw a speaking look at Michele before she answered her father. ''He is the same, Papa, quite unapproachable and perfectly terrifying.''

''I hope that you made an effort to conquer your nervousness, Lydia,'' Mr. Davenport said, perturbed.

''I was more comfortable during this last visit,'' said Lydia with perfect truth, thinking of Captain Hughes's welcome appearance. She smiled at her cousin. ''Of course, Michele has been of encouragement to me.''

Mr. Davenport beamed. ''Good, good! I am happy to hear it. Michele, I am glad I have found you. I have been wanting to discuss a financial matter with you. Pray, won't you join me in my study?''

''Of course, uncle.'' Michele accompanied Mr. Davenport

to the study, and after he ushered her inside, he closed the door. He gestured for her to take a seat beside his desk, and himself dropped into the well-worn chair behind the massive mahogany piece. "Is there some problem that I should be aware of?" Michele asked.

"Not at all. I simply wished to be certain that you are aware of your father's arrangements for you while you are in England," Mr. Davenport said. "He has written to me that he has caused to be deposited in the Bank of England an account for which you are to have complete access. It is irregular that François did not designate someone to be your banker, as it were, but I am certain that you are completely deserving of his trust." There was a faintly quizzical note in his voice and he stared at Michele with a contemplative expression in his eyes.

She smiled at his obvious uncertainty at the wisdom of the arrangement. "I am quite used to managing my own allowance, uncle. You need not be concerned that I shall suddenly pauper myself in a whirl of expenditures."

Mr. Davenport coughed. "Of course not. I never thought it for a moment. But I did wish you to be informed that any funds that you might need are readily available to you."

"I appreciate your meticulous attention to duty, sir," Michele stood up. "If that is all—"

Mr. Davenport held up his hand. "Actually, it is not. Something has been tickling at my mind these several days, and I have reread some of your mother's old letters. Michele, I have learned that you were once engaged to Lord Randol. It is with some degree of dismay that I broach this matter to you, but in the interests of our family, I feel that I must. You see, the viscount has requested permission to press his suit with Lydia, and I fear that your presence here will—"

"My former association with Lord Randol need not concern you, uncle. It was long ago dissolved through circumstances that I shall not go into. His lordship is completely free to bestow his suit where he pleases." Michele felt the stiffness of her own smile and she hoped that her uncle would not perceive it.

Mr. Davenport preferred not to look beyond the surface

of what he was offered, and his expression showed immense relief. "Thank you, my dear. I am greatly eased by your reassurance, and in light of it, I can think of nothing better than to have you staying with us. I only regret that you find yourself in the awkward position of consorting with his lordship, as assuredly you must in the circumstances."

"Pray do not trouble yourself, uncle. I am quite capable of handling any awkwardness that might possibly arise. Do, pray, excuse me. I wish to pen a letter before dressing for dinner," Michele said, hiding her anger.

"Of course, of course!" Mr. Davenport opened the door for her. He stayed her for a moment longer. "Your graciousness is most appreciated, for I doubt that I need tell you that I have high hopes for Lydia's finally coming around to his lordship's suit."

Michele inclined her head in a gesture of understanding, but she left the study with oddly turbulent emotions. Prominent among them was her conviction that she would find it very difficult indeed to sit by quietly while Lydia became engaged to Lord Randol. "In that instance, I suspect that I must play the coward who crept softly away before the end of the skirmish," she said aloud, greatly startling the footman whom she passed at that moment.

6

Miss Lydia Davenport and Mademoiselle du Bois were launched into London society a few weeks later. Lady Basinberry had spared no effort or expense on her nieces' behalf, especially since Mr. Davenport had unwittingly given her carte blanche to do as she wished by saying that he did not want to be bothered with the nonsense except to be sent the bills. Lady Basinberry therefore took full advantage of her brother's generosity. A full string orchestra was engaged, the ballroom was hung with new sarcenet-lined draperies, the cook was consulted with, and a lavish selection of refreshments was decided upon for the refreshment table. The afternoon before the ball, very nearly an entire hothouse was transferred to the Davenport ballroom. It was the overwhelming sight of the riotous blooms that finally caused Mr. Davenport's face to blanch, and he tottered away to his study, ordering the butler to bring him a bottle of cognac. "I am utterly undone," he was heard to mutter.

Two weeks before, Lady Basinberry had inspected Michele's wardrobe and pronounced all of her gowns too dowdy for an opening ball. She had taken Michele firmly to task, declaring that she would not have a niece of hers appear in rags.

"Come, ma'am! It is not as bad as all that!" Michele protested, laughing.

"You might as well give over, Michele. Our aunt is not likely to cease her bullying unless you do," Lydia said, greatly entertained. She herself had no difficulty in accepting

53

Lady Basinberry's declaration that she required a new gown, and she could not really find it in her heart to sympathize with her cousin's odd reluctance to do the same.

"Lydia speaks the unvarnished truth, my dear. I am known to be quite obstinate when I wish something to be done," Lady Basinberry said.

"I suspect that to be an understatement, my lady," retorted Michele. But she did at last give in to Lady Basinberry's insistence, and quickly found herself in a whirl of fabrics and at the mercy of a voluble French modiste. The consultation and choosing of fabrics, the measuring and the countless fittings, left Michele feeling very much like a pincushion.

The finished gown was delivered at the town house just hours before the ball. Upon seeing herself in the gown, even Michele was forced to concede that the effort had been worthwhile. The gown was an intriguing liquid blue that shimmered to shades of gray when she moved. The high waistline emphasized her high full bosom and the skirts fell away to cling to the curve of hip and thigh. Pearls adorned her ears and were twisted about her slender neck. Her soft black hair was held in place with a pearl comb.

Before going downstairs, Michele inspected herself in the cheval glass. The maid put the finishing touch to Michele's toilette by pinning to her low bodice a nosegay of white roses and delicate gypsophila. The corsage had been sent up by her uncle, and she had received it gratefully. A spray of carnations had been delivered for her from Sir Lionel, and she had frowned when she read the attached note, because it expressed warmer sentiments than she was prepared to encourage in any gentleman, and particularly in one whom she had once deeply hurt with her rejection.

"*Magnifique*, mademoiselle," the maid murmured.

Michele surveyed her reflection critically, not really seeing the raven-haired, blue-eyed beauty who returned her stare. She did not particularly anticipate the evening's entertainment, but she had agreed to participate in the offerings of the Season. She had long since come to realize that that was the subtle substance of her promise to Lady Basinberry. It both annoyed and amused her that she had allowed herself to be so neatly handled by her ladyship. There was no denying that Lady Basinberry was experienced in gaining her own way.

Following a knock on the door, Lady Basinberry herself swept into the bedroom. She was attired in a purple satin gown that lent elegance to her spare frame. Adorned by a single curling black feather, a turban of the same satin covered her head. Upon seeing Michele in her finery, she gave an approving nod. "Michele, you look lovely. I have just come from Lydia's bedroom. She sends her regards and an adamant request that you wait upon her before we descend."

"Thank you, my lady. I am ready now, so I shall go at once to Lydia." Michele flashed a smile for the elder lady. "I hope that your expectations for the evening are realized, my lady." She knew how much time Lady Basinberry had put into the planning of the ball, and even though she could not be wholly enthusiastic about the upcoming evening, she could yet hope that Lady Basinberry's efforts were rewarded.

Lady Basinberry smiled and her eyes lit with amusement. She was quite aware that this niece of hers had ambivalent feelings about her presentation into English society. "I believe that it will go off very well. I anticipate that both my lovely nieces will be a complete success tonight, even though one prefers to hope otherwise."

Michele laughed, shaking her head. "How do you know my thoughts so well?"

"You forget that I am an old woman grown wise to the ways of the world and the hearts of men. Pray go and discover what is of such importance to Lydia, but do not tarry long. I shall await you both downstairs. Our guests should begin to arrive quite soon."

Michele went along the hall and knocked on Lydia's door. It was opened immediately by her cousin's maid. From inside came Lydia's urgent query: "Michele, is that you?"

"Yes, it is I," Michele said, stepping inside.

Her cousin was standing before her cheval glass. She was dressed for the evening and looked ethereally lovely with her blond hair haloing her even features. Unlike Michele, Lydia had never been presented before to society and so she wore the traditional pale color deemed appropriate for a young lady. Her gown was pale pink satin, and tiny beads had been embroidered over the bodice. Lydia's appearance was perfect, down to the tiny matching pink satin slippers that peeped from beneath her hem, but she wore a look of distress.

"Lydia, whatever is the matter?" Michele asked, going to her cousin's side.

Lydia motioned dramatically at a trio of posies that lay on the dresser. "Do but look! What am I to do, Michele? One is from dear, dear Papa, and this—such sweet rosebuds!—from my beloved Bernard. *That* is from Lord Randol." Her shaking finger pointed to a lovely arrangement of white carnations. She looked up in despair. "I so wish to wear Bernard's flowers, but Papa would be furious. He was present when I received the ones from Lord Randol, you see, and he said quite archly that he would not be at all offended if I should choose another's offering over his own. Michele, you simply must help me."

Michele thought for a moment while Lydia regarded her with anxious eyes. "The most diplomatic route would be to wear the gift from your father. However, in order to please him, you must wear the one from Lord Randol."

Lydia's face fell. "Oh, I had so hoped that . . . well, it is of little consequence. I shall do as you suggest." Listlessly she picked up Lord Randol's carnations and gave them to her maid so that they could be pinned to her gown.

Michele laughed at her cousin's forlorn expression. "Come, Lydia! It but takes a little imagination to turn this fine dilemma to advantage. Do you not think that a few pink rosebuds twisted into your hair fillet would prove charming?"

Comprehension dawned in Lydia's eyes. She threw her arms around Michele and gave a delighted giggle. "I do thank you! What a splendid, splendid notion!" She whirled away to address her maid, who had anticipated her and was already carefully taking apart the posy from Captain Hughes.

Michele remained with Lydia until the transformed fillet was pronounced to be perfect. Then she and Lydia left the bedroom and went downstairs.

The first guests had begun to arrive and the young ladies joined Lady Basinberry and Mr. Davenport in forming a receiving line. As each guest was announced and greeted, Lady Basinberry introduced her nieces. Michele smiled and extended her hand innumerable times. Some of the faces were familiar to her, and then she was able to exchange more than the barest pleasantries. One such personage was the Countess of Kenmare.

Lady Kenmare clasped Michele's hand in both of her own. Her pleasant expression was warmed by genuine friendliness. ''My dear Michele, how happy I am to see you again. We quite lost touch with your family once we returned to England, which I have always regretted. You and Abigail were such good friends,'' she said.

''Yes, and I would like to see her again while I am in London. Is she with you this evening, my lady?''

Lady Kenmare shook her head. ''I wish that she were. But she is at home in Scotland, preparing to make me a grand-mother.'' She laughed and her wide gray eyes twinkled. ''I do not feel at all old enough to don such a role, but some-times these things are thrust upon one.'' She said a few more kind words and promised to call on Michele in the near future before she moved on.

''My dear, I did not know that you were acquainted with the Countess of Kenmare,'' Lady Basinberry said, regarding her niece with astonishment.

''Nor did I,'' Michele said, laughing. ''When I saw her ladyship in Brussels, she was a mere widow. Her daughter and I were brought out in the same year. It is quite astonishing to hear that Abigail is a matron and a mother-to-be.''

Lady Basinberry was on the point of remarking that Michele should have been in the same position, when her attention was distracted. She stared hard at the young gentleman who was bowing low to Lydia. ''Captain Hughes, I believe,'' she said, inserting herself beside Lydia.

Captain Hughes smiled and made his obeisance to her lady-

ship. He was not at all put out of countenance by Lady Basinberry's cool tone. "Kind of you to remember me, my lady.
I hope to visit more with you and your delightful nieces later
in the evening," he said jauntily, sliding a glance at Lydia
before he moved on to exchange a friendly word with
Michele.

Mr. Davenport had noted what appeared to him to be an
outrageously flirtatious wink at his daughter. He nudged his
sister and said in a low voice, "The boy is tenacious,
Beatrice. You shall have to be a veritable watchdog to see
that he does not monopolize Lydia. I do not wish her other
suitors, and one in particular, to be put off."

Lady Basinberry snorted and said with some asperity,
"Pray do not aspire to lecture me upon my duty, Edwin.
After creditably marrying off three daughters, I think that
I know better than you how to arrange these matters."

"Of course, Beatrice. I bow to your wide experience,"
said Mr. Davenport, not at all insulted. In fact he was immensely pleased that he could allow the responsibility for
his daughter's future to rest squarely in his sister's capable
hands.

Michele's pleasant interchange with Captain Hughes was
brought to an abrupt end when she glanced around to meet
Lord Anthony Randol's unfriendly gaze. She felt her heart
jump into her throat. Her expression altered and Captain
Hughes turned his head quickly to look at his lordship in some
surprise. He said a few more gracious words that Michele
replied to in a disjointed fashion, and she hardly noticed when
Captain Hughes withdrew. All her attention was riveted on
Lord Randol.

Despite the jagged scar that began above his right brow
and narrowed down nearly to the jaw, his lean face was
disturbingly attractive. The proud lift of his dark head, the
breadth of his shoulders, his straight stature, were all as she
remembered. But the cold expression in his gray eyes
reminded Michele that he was not the same man she had once
loved. She took a steadying breath and inclined her head.
"Lord Randol."

He smiled, though there was little amusement in the curl

of his lips. He took her gloved hand and with the stiffness characteristic of any movement of his right arm, he lifted her fingers to his lips for the briefest of seconds. "Mademoiselle du Bois. You are perhaps lovelier than when we first met. We all change, though not necessarily for the better." He made a slight gesture toward his disfigured face. The expression in his eyes was sardonic as he awaited her reaction.

Michele nodded in a matter-of-fact fashion. She knew better than to allow herself to exhibit any emotion over his scarred countenance. She had seen too often, with others who had been maimed, how the least measure of pity either encouraged self-pity or induced bitter rage. "That is true, my lord. The war, and in particular Waterloo, changed many things. This is my first Season in London. Undoubtedly I shall meet many old acquaintances," she said, managing a credible smile. It was difficult to remain coolly impersonal when what she really wished to do was to ask what had so embittered him toward her.

Lord Randol stared at her for a moment, a sudden frown forming between his brows. He had expected something quite different from the lady's prosaic attitude, and he was unaccountably infuriated that she had not reacted as he had assumed she would. Abruptly he bowed. "Mademoiselle." He walked away to mingle on the crowded ballroom floor.

Michele looked after his lordship, not knowing what to think. There had been almost a look of surprise in his eyes. The next instant a shutter had seemed to come down over his expression and he had turned on his heel.

Michele jumped at a touch on her elbow. "How you startled me, Lydia!"

"Did I? I am sorry. Michele, our aunt says that we have done our duty for the evening. She has given permission for us to leave the receiving line."

There was such a note of relief in her voice that Michele laughed at her. "Let's not tarry, then. Her ladyship may reconsider her magnanimity at any moment."

Lydia laughed as they entered the ballroom together. It was a colonnaded chamber of graceful proportions, its length

evenly marked by tall velvet-draped windows. Countless
arrangements of cut flowers scented the air, and bunches of
burning candles threw a bright glow. A respectable crowd
laughed and talked, some twirling about the marble floor to
the musicians' strains, while others were content to stand
about or sit in the chairs grouped around the room.

Michele and Lydia were immediately claimed by gentlemen desiring to squire them around the dance floor. They
never suffered the humiliation of standing out of a set for
the lack of a partner, and the evening went quickly with the
dancing. At one point Michele found herself in the same
quadrille as Lord Randol. As they came together in the movement of the country dance, he said, "How serene you appear,
mademoiselle. I am surprised."

"I do not understand you, my lord," she said, not quite
steadily. She felt his antagonism in the hard grip of his fingers
on hers.

He laughed and his flinty gray eyes mocked her. "Do you
not, mademoiselle? You were not used to be one so bereft
of wit. Perhaps I may enlighten you one day."

Michele looked full into his face. Deliberately she threw
down the gauntlet to him. "I would welcome such enlightenment, my lord!"

Lord Randol stared down at her. His lips twisted in the
semblance of a smile. "Would you, indeed?"

The dance separated them then, and when they came
together again, Michele declined to meet Lord Randol's
occasional glance, preferring to maintain a cool and detached
demeanor. He did not address her again, for which she was
thankful. When the set was ended, Michele was claimed by
her original partner and walked away from Lord Randol with
only a polite nod.

Though several times afterward she became aware of Lord
Randol's scrutiny, he apparently did not intend to approach
her for the remainder of the evening. What she did not know
was that he started toward her once, before stopping abruptly,
his fists clenching and unclenching. He had then turned on
his heel and swung away, his visage cold and forbidding.

7

Michele was not surprised when Sir Lionel Corbett made an appearance at the ball. After receiving the flowers and his note, she had prepared herself to treat him with nothing more than cool friendliness. She gave her hand to him. "Sir Lionel, this is well-met indeed," she said.

He raised her hand to his lips and ardently kissed the tips of her fingers. "You have no notion what thoughts ran through my head when I first caught sight of you in the park," he said in a lowered voice.

Michele gently drew her hand from his warm clasp. She kept her tone light. "I know that I was startled on my first outing to discover a personage known to me. However, I suppose that it is only to be expected. I have greeted a few others who were once acquaintances, among them the Countess of Kenmare. Her daughter was one of my dearest friends. Surely you will recall her, Miss Abigail Spence."

"Yes, of course. I believe I heard that she married some Scotsman or other," Sir Lionel said. He glanced at the flowers pinned to her gown. When he saw that they were not his offering, his lips tightened. But almost instantly his expression altered to one of pleasantness. "I hope that you will save me a turn about the floor, mademoiselle. As I recall, we were paired rather well, in dance as well as in other ways."

Michele smiled to hide her irritation at his rather obvious attempt to reestablish a familiarity that she was plainly unwilling to allow. "Perhaps a country set, Sir Lionel."

He realized that he had erred. He raised her hand once more, this time merely brushing his lips across the back. "I shall look forward to the moment, Mademoiselle du Bois," he said formally. There was a quirky set to his lips, however, that let Michele know that he had deliberately taken his cue from her own sudden formality. She shook her head, reluctantly laughing, as Sir Lionel sauntered away.

Michele's next partner claimed her then, and she forgot Sir Lionel in the pleasant business of dancing and amiable conversation. Some minutes later, when she chanced to meet her cousin during a lull in the dancing, she was amused by the high excitement in Lydia's eyes. "Why, Lydia, one would think to look at you that you were thoroughly enjoying yourself," Michele said teasingly.

Lydia giggled. "I am, so very much! I never knew how much I would enjoy a ball. Everyone has been vastly kind to me. And what do you think? I have danced twice with Bernard, and nary a word from Aunt Beatrice or Papa."

"Have you also danced with Lord Randol?"

Lydia made a face. "Yes, I have executed my duty most conscientiously and given him two sets as well. I have also danced with a score of others, so that no one may point a finger at how I have *favored* any particular gentleman over another."

"That was well-thought-of," Michele said, amused.

"I thought so too," Lydia said, nodding. "I am not nearly so flighty as Papa and Aunt Beatrice like to think me. I shall have Bernard. And with you to support my spirits, I shall never lag for lack of confidence."

Michele laughed and shook her head. "You are such a positive soul, Lydia. I almost fear for your Captain Hughes. He will need the strength of a saint to see you safely through the hardships of life."

"You need not fear for Bernard. I may always rely upon him." Lydia had glanced about as she spoke, and suddenly she gripped Michele's arm. "It is Lord Randol, coming toward us this moment. I have already danced with him twice. Another set, and everyone will think that we have come to an understanding. What am I to do?"

"Why do we not wait to see what his lordship wants before you become hysterical, cousin," Michele suggested quietly.

Lord Randol bowed impartially to the ladies, but he reserved a flicker of a smile for Lydia alone. "Miss Davenport, I see that you do not dance. Perhaps you would honor me once more."

Lydia identified the strains of music that were starting up. With relief she said, "I am sorry, my lord, but as it is my come-out, I am not permitted to waltz. However, my cousin is already out, and she waltzes divinely."

Michele stared at Lydia, appalled. She swiftly glanced at Lord Randol, who had registered an expression similar to what she was feeling.

In an instant, however, his lordship's face smoothed to polite indifference. He bowed with seeming alacrity. "Mademoiselle, I would be delighted."

Michele curtsied before placing her hand in his. With an unreal feeling she allowed him to lead her onto the floor and to take her into his arms. His left hand formed a loose circle about her fingers and his other hand pressed lightly against her slender back. Michele could feel the warmth of his arm where it encircled her. She closed her eyes for the smallest second. It all rushed back to her with such force that she felt giddy.

"So you feel it too," Lord Randol said. His harsh voice caused her to stiffen. She stared up at him, a questioning look in the depths of her deep blue eyes. "Pray do not go all wooden on me, mademoiselle. It is most difficult to guide a mannequin about the floor."

Michele flushed and her lashes swept down to hide her vulnerability. "I apologize, Monsieur," she said in a low voice.

Lord Randol smiled, a devilish light in his eyes. "Your tongue betrays you, mademoiselle. I have not forgotten that you had a habit of lapsing into French whenever you felt most burdened." The observation appeared to give him satisfaction.

Michele looked up at that, a spark of anger in her eyes. "Is it any wonder that I should feel burdened, my lord? The circumstances that I find myself in are bizarre in the extreme,'' she retorted.

''I am only too aware of how that might be, mademoiselle. I have appeared as a ghost from the past, and not a particularly welcome one at that.'' As Lord Randol stared down into her face, his expression slowly altered.

Michele felt the instant that his hand tightened about her fingers and his arm drew her nearer to him. Quite suddenly and horribly she knew what he meant to do. And it would taint her most cherished memories. ''No, do not!'' she said urgently.

He glanced down at her. There was an implacable look about his mouth. ''For a moment only we shall pretend the magic remains, mademoiselle,'' he said softly.

The next instant he swept her into an unbroken series of turns. They circled the ballroom once, twice, their passage graceful and extravagant in style. The murmurs of several individuals quickly brought the swiftly gliding couple to the attention of others.

Lady Basinberry looked on the entrancing spectacle in astonishment. ''My word! Michele and his lordship appear as though they have danced together scores of times!'' she exclaimed. Beside her, Lydia jumped, then cast a swift glance at her aunt. But Lady Basinberry did not appear to notice her younger niece's guilty start.

Michele was caught up in the exhilarating rush of air, the sense of weightlessness, the breathtaking intimacy of the waltz. But tonight it had all become twisted and ugly. She knew that she would never again recall those long-ago happy times without remembering also this last waltz, a waltz that had been forced upon her with spiteful spirit.

When the waltz at last came to an end, Michele tore herself free of Lord Randol's slackening embrace. Her eyes sparkled through unshed tears. ''You are cruel and unfeeling. I despise what you have become, my lord!'' she said in a low voice.

''What I have become is solely owing to your gracious influence, mademoiselle. If you come to despise me even half as deeply as I hold you in contempt, then I shall be well content,'' Lord Randol said harshly.

Michele turned from him and stumbled blindly away. Her control was very nearly shattered to pieces. It hurt to breathe as she forced back the uneven sobs that threatened to escape her. She blundered into someone and rocked from the impact. ''*Pardon*!''

Hands steadied her. ''Mademoiselle du Bois! Are you quite all right?''

Michele focused on the concerned countenance before her. She made an attempt to smile. ''Of a certainty, Captain Hughes. I . . . I was overcome for a moment by the heat, I think.''

Captain Hughes shrewdly regarded her, then cast a glance after the retreating figure of the viscount. ''What you are in need of is an ice, mademoiselle. Allow me to find you a chair, and I shall procure one for you.'' Waving aside Michele's incoherent protest, he firmly guided her to an empty chair at the edge of the dance floor. ''I shall be back in a trice,'' he said, leaving her with a smile of reassurance. He was as good as his word, and quickly returned, an ice in either hand. Michele accepted one in a rather subdued manner. Captain Hughes sat down on the chair beside her. He was apparently content simply to watch the whirling company on the dance floor without feeling it incumbent on him to converse.

Michele was grateful for the gentleman's discreet handling of what could have disintegrated into an embarrassing scene. Within a few minutes she was able to collect herself, and she touched Captain Hughes on the sleeve. He turned an inquiring gaze on her. ''Thank you, sir,'' she said.

He nodded. ''Happy to oblige. If you wish it, I will escort you over to Lady Basinberry.''

Michele shook her head. ''I would much rather sit quietly with you a few moments longer, Captain,'' she said.

''Of course. I am completely at your service, mademoiselle,'' said Captain Hughes promptly. He settled himself in his chair with every evidence of ease. He made an inquiry about Brussels, and for the next ten minutes he and Michele enjoyed an easy conversation.

By the time Captain Hughes escorted her to Lady Basinberry's side, Michele felt that she knew a good deal more about him. He had shown himself to be a kind, thoughtful gentleman of warmth and good sense. She thought that Lydia was fortunate indeed in her choice. Captain Hughes bowed and tactfully slipped away after exchanging a few words with Lady Basinberry and her friends.

Michele disengaged herself from the conversation to claim a nearby chair. Sir Lionel appeared almost instantly before her and he gestured toward the dance floor. "I believe it is the country set that I was promised, mademoiselle," he said.

Michele's heart sank. She really did not feel at all in the mood for another dance. And especially not with Sir Lionel, who had already proved himself so importunate. "As an old acquaintance, I know that you will not take it amiss when I confide that I prefer to sit out this set," she said with a smile.

He shook his head. "Come, Michele. You must honor your promises, you know," Sir Lionel said, his voice teasing. He waited, his hand out to her.

Michele shrugged gracefully and stood up, placing her hand in his outstretched palm. "Very well, sir. But I warn you that I am not very good company at the moment."

Sir Lionel piloted her into a forming set. When he replied, his voice had lost some of its warmth. "You have no need to explain. As everyone else, I saw that waltz with his lordship. But perhaps I alone was able to divine something of your feelings." He went on with suppressed violence, "Ah, Michele, how I wish you had not met him again!"

Michele's eyes flew to his face, but the beginning movement of the dance prohibited easy speech. When they came together, Sir Lionel said, "Forgive me. My only excuse must be my high regard for you. Lord Randol is—"

She said swiftly, "Sir Lionel, I have no wish to discuss his lordship with you or anyone else. I hope that is clear, sir."

With an understanding glance, Sir Lionel nodded. He commented on the weather, giving reassurance to Michele that he would abide by her wishes and making it possible for her to relax and enjoy the lively country set.

Lord Randol left the Davenport ball immediately after his unsatisfactory waltz with Mademoiselle du Bois. He had expected to derive a certain pleasure from the mademoiselle's distress. Instead, the manner in which she had turned from him, and the glimpse he had had of tears beginning to fall, had left him unaccountably disturbed. He was infuriated by his weakness, and on the instant had sought out Lady Basinberry to take his leave.

He had intended to drop in at another engagement, but his restlessness of spirit led him instead to his club. He was not displeased by his unconscious choice, and he called for a bottle of brandy. Ensconcing himself at a solitary table at the farthest end of the game room, Lord Randol settled himself for a serious bout of drinking. More than one acquaintance, upon recognizing his lordship, had started toward him, only to hesitate at his black expression and then quietly withdraw without bringing himself to the viscount's attention.

Hours later the waiters who stood unobtrusively at the far end of the room gazed over at the lone gentleman who sprawled carelessly in his chair. A bottle stood at his elbow and a glass was held firmly in his left hand. As his audience watched, Lord Randol tossed back the contents of the glass. He reached again for the bottle.

"How is his lordship?" a waiter asked one of his fellows.

The other shook his head. "I just took over a fresh bottle to him. I've never known his lordship so black, nor so determined to drink himself senseless."

"Likely we'll end by helping his lordship to a cab," observed the first, and his companion agreed.

Unaware that he was the topic of such concern, Lord Randol broodingly regarded the gaming room of White's. Even at that late hour there were several gentlemen at the green baize tables, flushed and the worse for wine. Their cravats were loosened and their careful pomades disturbed. Their eyes glittered feverishly or appeared bored, according to their degree of desperation or their dispositions, as they concentrated on the turn of the cards or the clicking roll of the dice.

But Lord Randol's thoughts were not on the gamesters. He fumbled in his pocket for his timepiece and focused on it with difficulty. "Three in the morning, by God," he said aloud. He had been drinking steadily for three hours in an effort to expunge from his thoughts a certain lady's midnight-blue eyes and lovely face. He had not been successful.

Instead, he was haunted by snatches of memory. Brussels in the sweet-scented spring and early summer. A moon-washed kiss. The sweeping magic of a waltz with the lady he loved held close in his arms.

Lord Randol gave a short bark of laughter and lifted his glass in a sardonic toast to those lost moments. The battle of Waterloo had crushed everything worth living for, but still he survived.

The waltz earlier that evening had been much like those others. The woman he had loved was still breathtaking to his senses. But he had learned a most painful lesson, one that he would never forget. His lady's beauty cloaked a nature that was shallow, cruel, and weak.

Mademoiselle Michele du Bois had abandoned him when he most needed her. Her professed love had been the mouthings of a selfish creature, a creature who could not bring herself to comfort one who suffered the agonies of terrible wounds.

He had lain for weeks between life and death, hoping that she would come, despairing that she did not. His fevered dreams had been fretted by visions of her laughing eyes and her incredible throaty chuckle. He had even believed that he could feel her warm pliant lips on his.

But she had not come. She had not visited the bedside of the man who had pledged his heart and his very soul to her. She had denied the love of the man whose body was scarred and made too ugly for her to bear.

Lord Randol set down his glass with violence. Dear God, how he loathed her. He hated her for what she had done. But most of all he despised himself for being drawn to her still. Her glance, her every gesture, was a siren song to him.

He had never been able to forget her. His sole comfort had been that he was not tortured by the sight of her. But now she was in London. And he was incapable of ignoring her existence. He wanted to hurt and humiliate her. He wanted to punish her for her betrayal. The fumes of the brandy parted in his mind to reveal a startling vision of himself making passionate love to a beautiful woman whose face was Michele's.

Lord Randol abruptly stood up. He swayed slightly. With stiff and careful steps he walked toward the club entrance. One of the waiters offered to hail a hackney, but his lordship indicated tersely that he intended to walk home.

8

The ball ended in the small hours, and not surprisingly, the Davenport household rose late the following day. Michele wakened only when her maid pulled back the curtains and sunlight spilled into the bedroom. "What hour is it?" she asked, cracking a yawn and stretching. When the maid informed her it was nearly noon and that Lady Basinberry awaited her in the breakfast room, Michele scrambled out of bed.

Less than an hour later she had finished her toilette and descended to the breakfast room. "Good morning, my lady," she said cheerfully, going in to seat herself at the table. Lady Basinberry was sipping her tea and nodded a greeting. A footman asked Michele quietly what she would like served to her from the sideboard, and she requested biscuits and eggs.

Lady Basinberry set down her cup. "Lydia will be down shortly. I wished to have us all together so that we can discuss the invitations."

"Invitations? Have some arrived, then?" For answer, Lady Basinberry swept a hand in the direction of a silver tray overflowing with cards. Michele was astonished. She picked up one to glance at the ornate script. "All of these have come this morning?"

"The butler informed me that a positive stream of them commenced at first light. Our little ball was a complete success," Lady Basinberry said complacently. At that moment she saw her younger niece in the doorway. "There

71

you are, Lydia! Come see the invitations that you and
Michele have garnered.''

Lydia sat down at the table and declined anything but toast
and chocolate. She eyed the immense stack of cards.
''Heavens! We shall be running all Season. How ever will
we be able to attend all of these functions?''

''We shan't, Lydia. We shall decline a share of them,''
said Lady Basinberry as she perused a card. ''I believe this
is one that we shall decline. I have never liked Emma Wain,
and fortunately her musical evening is the same date as the
Countess of Kenmare's dinner party, which we most certainly shall attend. Michele, the countess enclosed a personal
word for you.''

Michele took the card to read the short note. She smiled.
''The countess is very kind. I am flattered that she thinks
so well of me.''

''I understand from those who are best acquainted with
her that the countess is exceptionally warmhearted. It is
wonderful indeed that you are known to her, for her influence
will go far in introducing you into the *ton*.'' Lady Basinberry
smiled and there was a frosty twinkle in her faded eyes. ''And
Lydia will certainly not suffer by the association.''

''Aunt! You are making Michele's friendship with Lady
Kenmare sound dreadfully mercenary,'' Lydia said.

''My dear girl, you will find as you become older that it
is whom one knows that will open the greatest number, and
the most stubborn, of doors,'' Lady Basinberry said cynically.
She moved on to other invitations, choosing several for a
careful stacking and dispatching others with a flick of her
wrist and a pithy remark. Michele and Lydia discussed those
that Lady Basinberry thought desirable, and Michele was
surprised that she was nearly as enthusiastic as Lydia at the
prospect of attending the functions. Perhaps coming to
London had changed her in some way, she thought, and she
tried hard not to dwell on a certain gentleman's face.

The ladies lingered long over breakfast, and when at last
they rose from the table it was to the footman's announcement that a caller had arrived. The visitor proved to be only
the first in a stream of morning callers, among whom was

Lord Melbourne's sister, the beautiful Lady Cowper. She greeted Michele with extreme friendliness. "My dear Michele, I feel that I already know you. I am so happy to actually make your acquaintance. Your dear mother and I were once close friends. When I received her letter informing me of your direction, I simply had to call upon you."

Michele was surprised by the lady's familiarity. "Thank you, my lady. I am aware of the honor you show me."

Lady Cowper smiled and chatted at some length on various topics before she turned to Lady Basinberry and said, "I shall myself sponsor Mademoiselle du Bois to Almack's. It is the least I can do for my dear friend Helen's daughter."

Lady Basinberry did not bother to disguise her delight. "That is most handsome of you, my lady."

"Indeed, I am most grateful," said Michele, aware from her aunt's complacency and a suppressed squeak from Lydia that a deep honor had been bestowed upon her.

Lady Cowper smiled in a kind way at Lydia. "I know that Miss Davenport has already been taken under kind Lady Sefton's wing, or otherwise I should extend my patronage to her as well. What I can do is make certain that both young ladies are never without proper partners."

"Your kindness is most appreciated," Lady Basinberry said, almost purring in satisfaction.

Lady Cowper stood up and began drawing on her gloves. "I must be going now. But I shall not forget the voucher, I promise you."

When Lady Cowper had finished with her good-byes and had been seen to the door, Lady Basinberry turned a satisfied glance on Michele. "I am extremely pleased, my dear. Lady Cowper is the most popular patroness of Almack's and she has just extended entrance to the most exclusive assembly in London. Your position in society is assured."

"I had feared that it was," Michele said with a mock sigh. "I shall not be allowed to enjoy a quiet Season after all."

"Is it not exciting? Why, Michele may go with us next Thursday evening, Aunt Beatrice," Lydia said.

"Truly, a momentous evening is in store," Lady Basinberry said dryly. "But do be prepared, Michele. Almack's is not known for its refreshment table. The company shall be served only lemonade, tea, bread and butter, and stale cake.''

Michele made a face. "If that is so, why does anyone attend the assembly rooms at all?''

"To be seen, of course. And also to eye the best of eligible *partis*," Lady Basinberry said. "I have high hopes for you both when once you stand up at Almack's.''

Lydia groaned. "Pray do not scheme for us, Aunt Beatrice. It will be so much nicer if we may simply stand up with whoever signs our dance cards.''

"My dear Lydia, I never scheme. I merely influence," Lady Basinberry said mendaciously.

"As perhaps we have already seen. I wonder who reminded Lady Cowper of her friendship with my mother?'' Michele asked. She smiled at the sharp glance Lady Basinberry shot at her.

The week sped past in a flurry of engagements. Each evening the ladies attended at least two social functions, and they rarely returned home before the small hours of the morning. They scarcely saw Mr. Davenport, who preferred to pursue his own quiet amusements, unless they chanced to dine at the town house before going out. But he did not appear to feel neglected, and he told Michele and Lydia that he was happy to see that they were enjoying themselves so well.

Michele met several people, both ladies and gentlemen, whom she had been acquainted with in Brussels, and she felt increasingly at home in English society as a consequence. It was an odd feeling, as though part of her had been left behind in a different time, and the only sour note was the cold hauteur with which Lord Randol treated her whenever they chanced to meet.

On Thursday, the ladies set off for Almack's. The assembly rooms were small for the large company that had gathered. Lady Basinberry observed that it did not seem as stuffy as usual. Michele glanced at her ladyship but made no comment. She could not understand why Almack's should be such an exclusive place. The musicians were uninspired and rarely played anything more daring than a country dance. The refreshments were all that Lady Basinberry had described, being stale and scant. Yet *entreé* to this most exclusive company was avidly sought by every personage who aspired to rub shoulders with the *haut ton*. Once denied entrance by one of the patronesses of Almack's, an individual's social standing was irrevocably sealed into a lesser circle.

Michele glanced about the company and took note of a disproportionate number of young misses. "It appears to me that the gentlemen do not care to attend Almack's so much as the ladies," she said.

Lady Basinberry smiled. Her eyes gleamed. "You've noticed that, have you? Almack's is sometimes referred to as the Marriage Mart. Hopeful mothers bring their unmarried daughters to this most august place in order to catch the eye of some eligible gentleman, just as I have done with you and Lydia this evening."

Michele wrinkled her nose. "Assuredly I must thank you for your diligent dispatch of duty, my lady!"

Lady Basinberry laughed. "Pray do not worry your head over it, Michele. Lydia does not. See, she is making sheep's eyes at that gentleman who is partnering her down the set, even though she vows that her heart is given over to that soldier of hers."

"You advise me to flirt, *en effet*?" Michele asked, raising her heavy brows.

"Of course, my dear. How else am I to marry you off?" Before her niece could form an appropriate reply to this outrageous statement, Lady Basinberry nodded at an approaching gentleman. "Perhaps this will be the gentleman I shall snare for you."

Michele looked around quickly, to meet Sir Lionel Corbett's gaze. He smiled at her and there were both pleasure and admiration in his glance. "Michele. I knew that if I haunted this place long enough, you would sooner or later make an appearance."

"Sir Lionel." Michele acknowledged his greeting with a friendly smile, neither encouraging nor discouraging. "I know that you must remember my aunt, Lady Basinberry."

Sir Lionel made a deep bow. "I could not be so ungallant as to forget. My lady, I hope that I see you well?"

"I am invariably well, Sir Lionel," said Lady Basinberry. "I was just remarking to Michele that she should enjoy herself this evening. Perhaps you will add your persuasions to mine, sir."

"With pleasure, my lady. If the mademoiselle will accompany me, I shall procure for her a lemonade and endeavor to bend her ear with an amusing tale or two."

Michele glanced at Lady Basinberry's satisfied expression as she placed her hand on Sir Lionel's arm. "A lemonade, I believe you said? I should like something a bit tart about now," she said. As Sir Lionel bore her away, Lady Basinberry looked startled, then amused.

"Sir Lionel, there is a question that I must ask you," said Michele. Almost from the moment of discovering that Lord Randol was very much alive, she had wanted to inquire of Sir Lionel why he had not notified her of his lordship's continued existence. Better than nearly anyone else, Sir Lionel Corbett had known the depth of her feelings for Lord Randol. She had not felt equal to the task during Lady Basinberry's ball, especially after the disastrous waltz with Lord Randol, but she had had several days to reflect, and her curiosity had become stronger than her diffidence.

Sir Lionel glanced down at her quickly, hearing the determination in her tone. He looked discomfited. "It is about Lord Randol, of course. Believe me, I realize that I owe you an apology. It gave me a queer start when I chanced to meet him at Brooks's, I can tell you. I never thought to see him again in this life. I should have written to you at once. I see that now."

Michele shook her head. His half-apologetic explanation had satisfied her. "Pray do not take yourself to task, Sir Lionel. It was his lordship's place to write to me, not yours. I only wish that I had been forewarned before coming face-to-face with him."

Sir Lionel grimaced. "That I can well understand. I was in a bit of a quandary after I discovered that you were in London. I did not want to stir things up, as it were. And too, his lordship is not often found at social functions. It is just recently that he has been seen about. I have since heard that he spends most of his time in the country or with his cronies of the Four-Horse Club. He is still considered a notable whip, despite the partial incapacitation of his right arm, apparently. But I imagine that it is his face that works mainly to keep him out of society. It must be dashed awkward. Any lady must shrink from that scar, especially yourself. He would do better to remain secluded on his own estates, I've often thought.''

Michele was stunned by Sir Lionel's callousness. She had never thought of Lord Randol's scarred face as a hindrance to his social life. Actually, if the truth be known, she rather thought the scar gave him a certain dangerous appeal. Before she could disabuse Sir Lionel of his erroneous impression, an acquaintance hailed the gentleman and the moment was lost.

Sir Lionel introduced his friend. "Michele, allow me to present to you Robert Nathan, Esquire. Robert, this lady is Mademoiselle du Bois.''

Mr. Nathan, who had taken Michele's hand and was preparing to make his bow, instead stared hard at her face. She lifted her brows at his rude manners, and he flushed. "Mademoiselle, forgive me. But you must realize that I am meeting a legend. Sir Lionel has mentioned your name on several occasions, always in the most flattering of accolades.''

Michele smiled. "No, I cannot be insulted after such a pretty speech, Mr. Nathan. But surely you mistake the matter. Sir Lionel and I are such old friends that he knows all my faults, and I his.''

"Robert, my friend, we are making our way to the refreshments. I hope that you will excuse us, for Mademoiselle du Bois has professed herself expiring from thirst,'' Sir Lionel said.

Mr. Nathan shot him a startled glance. Then a smile of understanding spread over his genial face. "Of course. I shall not delay you a moment longer. Mademoiselle, it has been a pleasure.'' He bowed and moved away.

Sir Lionel eased Michele onward. He glanced down at her. "I trust that you are not put out at my subterfuge. But I could see that Nathan's indiscreet tongue was making things deuced awkward."

"I think perhaps it was more awkward for you than for me," Michele said with a too-bright smile. It annoyed her that Sir Lionel had apparently talked her up with all his acquaintances. She had become familiar in the past with the fact that gentlemen bandied casual descriptions of the women of their acquaintance, and she was not amused to learn that she had become one of such company. That she had was certainly attested to by the manner in which Sir Lionel had hustled her away before she could hear more from Mr. Nathan.

They had reached the refreshment table. Sir Lionel offered a lemonade to her, but Michele spurned it. They stood there a moment, a lovely lady and her handsome escort. Sir Lionel's blond hair seemed to shine in the candlelight and he appeared very elegant in his formal attire. He was smiling with a faintly quizzical look in his eyes. "You are displeased with me. I am sorry for it. But I cannot change what has gone before. Only believe that if I spoke of you to anyone, it was with the utmost respect."

Michele shrugged and allowed a smile to cross her face. "It is of no consequence, I suppose. I shall not be staying overlong in London, and so I do not think that my reputation shall suffer too much from whatever revelations Mr. Nathan may summon up." She pretended not to see the expression of acute disappointment that entered Sir Lionel's eyes. She had never wished to arouse any hopes in his breast, and perhaps her frankness now would serve to convince him of it. "There is Lady Cowper. I must go to pay my respects, for it was she who bestowed a voucher upon me."

"Of course." Sir Lionel escorted her over to greet Lady Cowper, but he was soon edged out of the conversation when her ladyship took Michele off to meet someone.

It was midnight when Michele and the Davenport ladies left Almack's. Lady Basinberry said that she was very satisfied with the way the evening had gone. "I was happy to see that you were both so circumspect as to stand up no more than twice with any one gentleman,'' she said. She glanced at her elder niece. "Though I could not but notice that you and Sir Lionel had rather a long *tête-à-tête*, my dear. I hope that it proved interesting?"

Michele smiled at her aunt's inquisitiveness. "Quite unexceptional, I assure you, my lady. Sir Lionel and I merely traded observations on some of the company."

"What a pity," Lady Basinberry said, not believing a word of it. She had thought at one point to have seen a spark of anger in her niece's dark eyes while she was in Sir Lionel's company. But if Michele chose to keep her own counsel, she was certainly not one to beg for enlightenment. It would be interesting to see how that relationship developed, she thought.

The carrriage pulled up to the town house and the ladies went inside. Michele said good night to her aunt and her cousin and entered her bedroom. It was not until the maid had undressed her and she was in bed that she recalled Sir Lionel's observation concerning Lord Randol's scar.

She thought it over, and in her mind's eye she could see Lord Randol's expression when he had presented himself to her in the receiving line at Lady Basinberry's ball. He had deliberately directed her attention to his face, and had appeared almost surprised by her lack of reaction. It was almost as though he had anticipated a shrinking or a look of revulsion from her, Michele thought. Her breath caught at the sudden thought. Was it possible that he felt his scarred face had so totally marred him that he had been afraid to let her know that he lived?

Michele could scarcely believe that such a thing might be true, but certainly it went far in explaining Lord Randol's bitterness and his cold hauteur toward her. Michele punched her pillow in a futile attempt to make it comfortable. She said angrily, "Anthony, how could you be such a fool?" She felt that she had to discover if what she had guessed was the truth. Otherwise she would wonder all her life whether his lordship could come to love her again.

9

Michele buttonholed her uncle before he could leave for his club. The night before, she had come up with a strategy that she hoped would kindle more in Lord Randol than his contempt. In Brussels she had shared with him a keen interest in driving and horses. It was possible that their mutual sporting tastes could prove to be a bridge between her and her lordship. "Uncle Edwin, I have a favor to ask of you," she said.

Mr. Davenport eyed his niece's determined expression with foreboding. "Of course, my dear. Whatever it is in my power to do, I shall naturally do for you."

Michele smiled pleasantly. "I appreciate your willingness, sir. It is a small matter, really. I wish to know where I might hire a carriage-and-four."

Mr. Davenport blinked, completely bowled over. "A carriage-and-four! Why, whatever for?"

"Actually, it had ought to be a phaeton. I want good cattle, not a team of slugs. Oh, and I wish the rig within the fortnight," said Michele, hardly heeding the growing consternation on her uncle's face.

Mr. Davenport took hold of her arm and steered her into his study. "See here, Michele. This is quite an expense that you are speaking of. I hardly think that your father would approve of your allowance, as substantial as it is, to be squandered so outrageously."

Michele acknowledged the truth of his observation. "Indeed, you are correct, sir. Hiring a rig would be terribly uneconomical. Papa would never have countenanced it. I shall buy a phaeton and a team instead. Where does one go to arrange for that sort of thing?''

Mr. Davenport stared at her. Then he said heavily, ''A lady does not go to arrange the procurement of a carriage.''

''I understand, of course. Then I must request the services of a gentleman to do so for me,'' she said. When her uncle did not immediately offer to take on the service for her, she put up her brows to express well-bred surprise.

Mr. Davenport accurately read her expression. ''I am sorry to have to disappoint you, Michele, but I shall not be that gentleman. I cannot condone such an unnecessary expenditure. Indeed, I do not think that your father would thank me if I took it upon myself to pauper you by acceding to this whim of yours.''

Michele looked at him. There was a distinct coolness in her midnight-blue eyes. ''You mistake the matter, sir. It is not for you to render or withhold your permission. However, that is neither here nor there. You have given me all the information that I shall require of you.'' She swept out of the study, leaving her uncle prey to conflicting emotions, primary among them the strong wish that he had never agreed to have his niece visit for the Season. She reminded him on occasion too strongly of a younger version of Lady Basinberry.

Michele was angered by her uncle's refusal to aid her, but she was not entirely without recourse. She recalled that Lord Randol had spoken of a certain Captain Becher with admiration. His lordship had described the racing that some of the officers got up across the Spanish plains between engagements with the enemy, races that were dangerous for both horses and riders because of the numerous rabbit holes. Captain Becher had been a talented and intrepid rider with a keen eye for horseflesh.

Michele thought since she had been in London she had seen Captain Becher's name more than once in the newspaper. She went to the library to scan the racing news, and it was not long before she found the reference to Captain Becher.

She smiled to herself. She would have her carriage yet. Michele penned a quick note to Captain Becher, requesting that he wait upon her at his convenience.

Late that afternoon she was gratified to be informed that a Captain Becher had called. Michele agreed to see the gentleman, and the butler withdrew to inform the visitor.

"Captain Becher? Who is that, Michele?" Lydia asked, curious.

Michele shook her head warningly, aware that her guest was close by. The gentleman entered the drawing room and Michele greeted him with an outstretched hand. "Captain Becher, how good of you to honor me with a visit."

He bowed, slanting an amused glance at his hostess. "I could hardly ignore such an intriguing request, mademoiselle," he said.

Michele introduced Lydia, who frankly stared at the gentleman. He was a well-knit man, not above average height, his countenance dominated by a long nose and firmly held lips. His whiskers were dark and extremely heavy, growing far down his jawline to his chin. Lydia thought she had rarely met a gentleman who exuded such an air of nervous energy.

Michele gestured for Captain Becher to be seated and offered him refreshment before she began to tell him why she had approached him. Briefly she explained what she had been told by Lord Randol. "And as I do not know any gentlemen in London who might be depended upon for their good sense in choosing decent horseflesh, I have been so bold as to call upon you, sir. I hope that I may persuade you to act as my agent in purchasing a phaeton and a team of four, since I have been told it is not usual for a lady to do so for herself," Michele said.

Captain Becher reflected a moment. "I have no objection to doing so. However, may I be permitted to ask a question?" Upon Michele's nod, he said, "I have seen Lord Randol at some of the races, as well as heard that he has taken up his old position with the Four-Horse Club. He was always a deft one with his left hand, and his wound has hardly affected the excellence of his driving, I am told. The point is this, mademoiselle. Surely his lordship, who is well-known to you, would be more properly the personage to approach for this commission than a stranger such as myself.''

''His lordship and I are no longer as close friends as we once were,'' Michele said quietly.

Captain Becher was intelligent enough to allow the matter to drop. ''Then I shall be most happy to act as your agent, mademoiselle. Only give me your instructions and I shall endeavor to have a worthy rig for you in the shortest possible time.''

''Thank you, Captain.'' Michele told him exactly what sort of carriage and team she required, as well as the amount that she was prepared to pay. She mentioned a commission for the captain's services that he accepted with every sign of gratification. Shortly thereafter Captain Becher took his leave, promising that he would communicate with her again very soon. He bowed to Michele and Lydia and left the drawing room.

Lydia leaned back against the settee and regarded her cousin with astonished admiration. She had listened to the transaction with growing wonder, and now she shook her head. ''Michele, I am utterly awed. I would never have thought of engaging the services of a professional rider to set me up with a phaeton-and-four. Indeed, I would never have thought of getting a carriage at all. I have driven only the veriest bit, and I was quite unbelievably clumsy at it.''

''I am used to driving myself about. It is an activity that I took much pleasure in at home,'' Michele said.

Lydia eyed her contemplatively. ''Is what Captain Becher said true? Is Lord Randol an excellent driver?''

''His lordship was always something of a whip.''

''How strange that I was not aware of it. But then, Lord Randol rarely speaks of himself and he has never offered to take me up for a drive,'' Lydia said. She asked in an offhand manner, ''Did you often drive with his lordship?''

''Yes,'' Michele said shortly. She was reluctant to have Lydia probe further into her past and she was therefore glad when Lady Basinberry entered the drawing room. Her relief was short-lived, however, as Lydia immediately informed her ladyship of Michele's startling decision to possess a carriage.

"Indeed! How very suitable. It is becoming the fashion for young ladies to tool themselves sedately about the park. I do trust that you are a handy whipster, Michele, and shall not discredit yourself," Lady Basinberry said.

Michele smiled. "I am accounted a fair whip, ma'am." She had been schooled in driving by a gentleman well-versed in the activity, and as she recalled the leisurely and memorable instruction that Lord Randol had shown her, she could not keep from hoping that their shared passion for driving could somehow bridge the yawning gap that presently lay between them. She assured herself that she did not want to cut Lydia out with the viscount, but only to discover what had happened that had so changed his feelings toward herself.

Lady Basinberry nodded, satisfied. "Good, I am happy to hear it. You shall do me credit, despite yourself, dear niece." She smiled at Michele and then glanced at Lydia. "Lydia, the reason I have come in is that I recalled that you had purchased a length of blue velvet ribbon. Might I have a bit of it for one of my gowns? My maid has pointed out that the gown needs a freshening touch if it is to last another wearing. As it is quite my most favorite gown, I really do not wish to replace it at this time, particularly as I intend to squeeze every last groat that I can into our entertaining."

"Of course, Aunt Beatrice. I shall come at once to find it for you," Lydia said.

"Pray do not trouble yourself, Lydia. I can as easily ask your maid for it, and she will be the more likely to know where the ribbon has been put."

Lydia giggled. "Indeed, aunt! I do not think that I could put my hand on any one thing without my maid's aid."

"That is precisely what I was thinking," Lady Basinberry said before she swept out of the drawing room.

Lydia sat down to thumb through the latest issue of *The Lady's Magazine* while Michele wandered over to the window. Michele lifted the drapery so that she could look out. "I hope that Lady Basinberry does not plan grandiose entertainments, since I have no wish to make any more of a splash than I must," Michele said meditatively.

Lydia looked up from her contemplation of a fashion plate depicting an elegant walking dress. "The purchase of a dashing phaeton is just what one needs to enable one to fade into the background," she said affably.

Michele laughed throatily and conceded the point. "You are so right, cousin. I have erred indeed. But perhaps I shall not excite so much notice if I make a point of taking you up beside me to deflect any curious stares."

"I should like that. I wish to gather as much interest as I can," Lydia said frankly. When Michele laughed, she shrugged her slim shoulders. "It will be my one and only Season before I am wedded, you see, so I wish to dance and to be as merry as I can. Once I am a settled matron, it will not be respectable for me to kick up my heels."

Michele turned away from the window, dropping the drapery. She shook her head in amusement. "I wish I might see you a sober matron! Why, it is the height of improbability. You are nothing less than a whirligig when you become excited. I cannot imagine you in any other guise."

Lydia dimpled a shy smile. "Bernard says it was my liveliness that first attracted him to me."

"Then most definitely you should not become a sobersides, or Captain Hughes will become bored to tears with you," Michele said teasingly.

"He would not dare," Lydia declared. "I would kick up such a fuss that he would be forced to take notice of me. Indeed, he would wonder if he had not married a very vulgar female!"

"Perhaps you should try a little of that tactic on your unwelcome suitor. I doubt that his ardor would remain white-hot in that instance," Michele said. "He was always a proud man, and he appears to me to have grown more so."

"High in the instep is more like it," said Lydia. "I should be forced to suppress even my smiles if I were to wed that gentleman. His lordship is so controlled in his manners, so remote! I doubt there is even a dram of ardor in the gentleman."

Michele blinked at her cousin's sweeping statement. She could recall a number of occasions when Lord Randol had exhibited a strong sense of ardor. But she said nothing, not wishing to open yet another painful door in her past.

Lydia did not notice her silence, being busy with her own thoughts. She sighed as she looked over at her cousin. "It is not my nature or even my person that his lordship finds appealing, you know. Not long before your arrival, I overheard a loud gentleman tell my father that Lord Randol is on the lookout for a young lady with an impeccable bloodline who can be expected to fill his nursery with blueblood heirs. I suspect that any young lady would do, so long as she met his high criteria and could be expected to toe the line."

Michele felt every nerve within her protest against the picture that Lydia painted of Lord Randol. She forcibly reminded herself that he was no longer the gallant young officer that she had known and fallen in love with. She wrinkled her nose in a wry expression. "How can my uncle then be pleased at Lord Randol's suit? He appears such a doting parent. I am surprised that he would look favorably on a gentleman who does not bid fair to make his daughter happy!"

Lydia shrugged somewhat unhappily. "It is all because Papa is so dazzled by Lord Randol's condescension. After all, his lordship is a viscount. You would not think it, but Papa can be quite the snob. Why, Bernard is of particularly good family and he has excellent prospects quite apart from his military career. He is investing in the 'Change, you know. But Bernard is a younger son, whereas Lord Randol may bequeath a title upon his bride. Oh, how I wish that Lord Randol had chosen someone else!"

Michele said thoughtfully, "It becomes clearer to me every day that you must take fate into your own hands, Lydia. Lord Randol will not simply disappear. If it is Captain Hughes that you are resolved to have, then you are behaving unfairly toward Lord Randol. He obviously has not a clue to what you feel. The gentleman that I knew would have wanted to know."

"But I simply cannot talk to his lordship. You have seen how it is, Michele. He is so cold and forbidding that he discourages one's intentions."

"Do you wish to sit across the breakfast table from this gentleman you describe as forbidding for the remainder of your long life?" demanded Michele. She threw out her hands in exasperation. "Lydia, if you allow this indecision on your part to continue, you will discover yourself backed into a corner that you cannot escape, and you will end by wedding his lordship whether you wish it or not."

The thought of Lord Randol married to another assaulted Michele with unexpected pain. She muttered an incoherent exclamation. "Pst! I have not the patience to discuss the matter further. I am going upstairs to change for dinner. And I suggest that you become more of a woman, cousin!" She swept from the drawing room, leaving Lydia sitting with a shocked and betrayed look on her face.

The force of her emotion carried Michele up the stairs, but before she had entered her bedroom, her heart misgave her. She should not have flared up in such a fashion at her youthful cousin. She, too, had once been painfully young and was used to rely on the guidance and wisdom of others for her decisions. But that had come to an end more than a year ago, when she had resolutely turned down Sir Lionel Corbett's proposal of marriage.

Sir Lionel had made it known that he loved her passionately. He had said he was willing to marry her even though she was devastated by the news of Lord Randol's death, and he had expressed the hope that eventually she would grow to love him. But Michele had not wanted to be given everything by a man and be unable to return to him anything but kindness. Instinctively she had known it would have been unfair to Sir Lionel and to herself. In the end she had sent Sir Lionel away, and she had never regretted it. But she had yet to discover the full consequences of that momentous decision.

10

Michele had expected that Lydia would treat her coolly after the manner in which she had scolded her, but Lydia was in perfect spirits at dinner. She chattered and laughed much as usual, and if there was a hint of reserve in her eyes, it was only Michele who detected it. Certainly none of the guests at dinner thought anything was out of the ordinary.

Lady Basinberry had set up a rare convivial evening at home. She had invited a small number of guests to partake of dinner and to play cards or parlor games afterward, as took their fancy. The elder members of the party were a couple well-known to Mr. Davenport, which put him into an expansive mood. When the ladies had left the table, he asked that the best claret be brought out and served to his old crony, Mr. Hedgeworth, and the other gentlemen.

Afterward the gentlemen followed the ladies' example and retired to the drawing room. Mr. Davenport and his crony got up a friendly hand of piquet, establishing the bet at a penny at point, and settled down to business. There were three young gentlemen, one of whom had accompanied his sister, Elizabeth Hedgeworth. That young lady was a friend of Lydia's whom she had not seen in some time, and the two quickly put their heads together to whisper confidences. Michele was not left to her own devices, however, because Clarence Hedgeworth chose to make her the object of his clumsy gallantry. Not to be outdone, the two other youthful gentlemen followed suit. Michele treated their fulsome attentions with a good deal of laughter and kindness.

Meanwhile Lady Basinberry and her older companion, Mrs. Hedgeworth, enjoyed a quiet *tête-à-tête* beside the fire, each busily plying a needle to her embroidery. "I do not mind it very much, Winifred. I own that I am often tired, but squiring my nieces about gives me a certain satisfaction, much the same as I experienced with my own girls," said Lady Basinberry.

"But naturally you are not burdened with the same anxiety that one of them may end as an old maid," said Mrs. Hedgeworth, a twinkle in her eyes.

Lady Basinberry laughed. "Too true! They have their own parents, who may entertain that concern. My object is to introduce them into polite society and to maneuver opportunities for them to be in the company of eligible gentlemen."

"Then why ever have you brought this particular party together? Though I am naturally partial to my grandson, and the Murray boys are also well enough, I know that none of them fit your notion of a suitable match for Lydia. Why, she has known them all her life," Mrs. Hedgeworth said.

"Exactly so. The pressures of the Season have been such that Lydia and Michele have begun to deal with the gentlemen with almost an air of *ennui*. I hope to disarm them with this little gathering and renew their freshness of spirit. I have few concerns for Lydia. She is flighty enough to be easily influenced, though her persistence over a certain military gentleman does surprise me," Lady Basinberry said.

"Oh, my, has Lydia formed an attachment to someone completely ineligible?" Mrs. Hedgeworth asked with sympathy.

"He is not entirely ineligible, no. But my brother has greater hopes for her. I suppose it will do no harm in telling you, my dearest and oldest friend, but Edwin has been approached by a lord for Lydia's hand. Naturally he has granted his lordship permission to pay court to Lydia, but she, still in the throes of her infatuation with a uniform, has thus far declined to accept the offer," Lady Basinberry said.

Mrs. Hedgeworth chuckled. "You need not tell me Edwin's reaction to it all. The gentlemen are always such fools in these instances. Edwin denied the house to the soldier, did he not?''

"Very nearly as bad. He informed Lydia that her young military gentleman was unacceptable, which naturally set up her determination to spurn the offer from his lordship," said Lady Basinberry. "But I think that I have the situation well in hand. I have allowed Lydia to see her soldier, thus stripping him of unnecessary romance, and I am confident that his appeal must eventually pale beside that of other, more glamorous gentlemen. I anticipate a satisfactory ending with Lydia. However, my elder niece poses something more of a challenge. She has openly disclaimed any intention of marrying.''

Mrs. Hedgeworth shot a surprised glance toward the young lady in question, wo was laughingly disavowing the pretty compliments showered upon her in a spirit of competition by her group of admirers. "She does not appear in the least shy with the male sex. Whatever is the matter with the girl?''

"She lost her fiancé at Waterloo and ever since has steadfastly refused to accept any suit. My sister sent her to us in hopes that a change of locale might shake her out of herself. Michele goes along quite well in society and she has her share of admirers, but she treats them all quite impartially. You have only to look at the manner in which she orchestrates those three calflings to have a notion of how she deals with the gentlemen," Lady Basinberry said with a disgusted shake of her head.

Unaware that she was the object of such interest, Michele had succeeded for the most part in jollying her youthful admirers into thinking of her as their elder sister. She suggested a game of sticks and drew Lydia and Elizabeth Hedgeworth into the circle. In a very short time all six young people were absorbed in the nursery game, which was played with a great deal of laughter and bated breath as each tried his skill in picking up the tumbled sticks. Lydia was quickly seen to have the keenest eyes and nimblest fingers of the group, and after vanquishing all contenders, she was declared champion.

"I had no notion that you were so quick, cousin," Michele said, laughing.

Flushed and pleased, Lydia smiled. Her eyes were completely unshadowed as she looked over at her cousin. "I used to play quite frequently as a small child with my nurse. This was great fun. I do not know why we do not do such things more often. Actually, I enjoy all sorts of childish things, like the Tower Zoo and Astley's Circus," she said.

"Do you, by Jove!" exclaimed Toppy Murray, who had earned his unusual nickname for his unmanageable shock of fiery red hair. He impatiently brushed aside an unruly lock so that he could eye Lydia in approval. "We must go to Astley's, then. I never tire of the equestrian feats that are performed."

"Nor I," agreed his brother, Edward, who sported a less noticeable copper head.

"I should like it too, Edward," Elizabeth said, smiling hopefully at the young gentleman.

He reddened and made an awkward bow to her. "I shall be delighted to escort you, Miss Hedgeworth," he said with an assumption of formality.

"And you, mademoiselle? Do you also enjoy spectacles of horsemanship?" asked Clarence.

Michele smiled at the young gentleman, in whose eyes still lurked a good deal of admiration. "I enjoy anything to do with horses, Mr. Hedgeworth."

"Then I offer myself as an excellent escort, for I have been to the Royal Circus countless times and I daresay I may point out every subtlety of the performance," Clarence said loftily.

His pompous air earned him a good-natured shove from Toppy Murray. "What rot! But what can one expect of a Cambridge man, after all?" he said.

The evening ended nearly two hours later with much good humor and friendly good-byes. Promises were exchanged of planning a future outing to Astley's Royal Amphitheater. As the front door closed on the dinner guests, Lydia pronounced herself eminently satisfied with the evening. "I had such fun tonight," she said, giving a small skip.

"And I," Michele said. "Such informal company was a

breath of fresh air after the round of entertainments we have been attending. I shall be more able to bear the rest of it.''

Lydia nodded. ''I never thought a Season could be less than exciting, but after one meets everyone one should, and sees the same faces over and over, it becomes rather boring. Such stuffy functions! But I am actually looking forward to it again, especially since we are to go to Astley's Circus as well.''

''I am glad to hear it, for tomorrow we have several calls to make,'' said Lady Basinberry. She smiled as her nieces gave a mutual groan. ''Morning calls are a necessary evil, my dears, and we have neglected ours for too long. Even Edwin would agree, if he would but come out from behind his newspaper long enough to attend the conversation.''

Her acid tone caused her brother to give a guilty start. After saying good night to their guests, he had promptly settled himself in a wing chair before the fire and buried himself in the day's happenngs. He lowered the newspaper. ''Eh? What was that, Beatrice?''

But Lady Basinberry turned her shoulder on him. ''I fear that your visit to the Royal Amphitheater must be put off for a time, Lydia, since all our evenings have already been spoken for. However, if the anticipation will make the time pass more swiftly for you, I shall plan to leave one evening open so that you and your friends may have your little treat,'' she said.

''Thank you, aunt,'' Lydia said, much gratified.

''And now I shall say good night. Tomorrow will be a lengthy day and I wish to be well-rested for it. I might suggest the same for you, Lydia, and for Michele as well,'' Lady Basinberry said, rising from her chair.

''Of course, my lady. It will be a rare treat, indeed, to slip into my bed before the small hours of the morning,'' Michele said humorously.

''When you become as ancient as myself, Michele, you will have yet a keener understanding of what a luxury it is,'' Lady Basinberry said with a flash of tartness. She beckoned to her elder niece. ''Lend me your arm, Michele. I wish to speak with you on the way upstairs.''

Michele was surprised, but she willingly acceded to her aunt's request. She wondered what Lady Basinberry could possibly wish to discuss with her in such an odd fashion. As they walked together up the stairs, she waited for Lady Basinberry to open the subject that she had on her mind, but her ladyship said never a word. Instead she leaned on Michele's arm more significantly with each step.

Michele glanced at the elder woman's proud profile, vaguely perturbed by her ladyship's unusual dependence. Lady Basinberry stared straight ahead, her thin lips held firmly, and there was a remoteness in her expression that did not encourage conversation, so Michele held her tongue.

When she and Lady Basinberry parted at the head of the stairs, Michele turned aside toward her own bedroom. She discovered Lydia close behind her and paused. "I suspect that our aunt does not feel her usual self," she commented softly.

Lydia nodded in agreement. "I was astonished when she requested your support. Why, Aunt Beatrice is never ill and she positively abhors coddling, as she calls it. I wonder what is the matter with her."

"Her ladyship is growing older. Perhaps she simply finds that her energy is not what it once was," Michele suggested.

Lydia giggled. "I shouldn't wonder at it! Only think of the pace she has kept us at these past weeks. I began to doubt that I would be able to keep up with her."

Michele smiled, opening the door to her bedroom. "We may try to do so, cousin. But I suspect in the end that it will be you and I who are quite exhausted, while Aunt Beatrice remains standing and inquires what ails us." Lydia laughed and agreed, then went on to her own door as Michele entered her bedroom.

11

Lady Basinberry was true to her word. The following day she and her nieces called upon everyone that had recently left a card at the town house. When at last she was satisfied that their social duty was done, she requested the coachman to return home, just in time for a late tea. Afterward she left the younger ladies to their own devices and sought her own rooms, brushing aside their concern for her obvious tiredness with the comment that she was in need of a bit of quiet reflection after such a grueling day.

Michele rather agreed with Lady Basinberry's sentiment and asked if Lydia would be insulted if she attended quietly to some of her personal correspondence rather than just join her in the drawing room. ''I find that I am not in a conversational mood after this morning,'' she said apologetically.

''Of course not, Michele. Truth to tell, I am half-dead on my feet. I believe that I shall go upstairs to lie down for a few minutes,'' said Lydia, disguising a yawn behind her hand. She left Michele alone in the library.

Michele wrote letters to her parents and to a couple of friends in Brussels. When she finished, she glanced up at the clock on the mantel above the library's fireplace. She was astonished to see that it was still an hour or more before dinner, when she felt so tired. She decided to follow Lydia's lead and lie down before changing for dinner. She was glad that Lady Basinberry had committed them to only one function that evening. She did not think, otherwise, that she would be able to stay awake.

At dinner, Mr. Davenport commented that he had come home from the club to be greeted with the intelligence that all the ladies were resting. "I was surprised. I had thought that you would still be out shopping or whatnot," he explained before he savored a forkful of roast beef.

"Aunt Beatrice was a veritable taskmaster today. We must have called upon upwards of twenty personages, Papa. Michele and I were positively drooping. I thought we should never return home," Lydia said.

"Since Aunt Beatrice has not joined us for dinner, I suspect that she is regretting her determination to pay her respects to every one of her wide acquaintance. I hope that she has not overextended herself today," Michele said, concerned.

Mr. Davenport waved his hand. "You must not become anxious over your aunt, Michele. I have never been acquainted with a more tireless personality than my sister."

While Mr. Davenport was voicing his reassurance, Lady Basinberry was deciding that she was unable to accompany Lydia and Michele to the function for that evening. The concentrated activity earlier that day had taken its toll on the elderly lady and she reluctantly took to her bed after eating sparingly of the dinner tray that she had brought up to her rooms. Afterward she sent for her brother to wait on her.

He expressed shock at her tired appearance. "My word, Beatrice! What have you done to yourself? You look one foot short of the gravesheet."

"Thank you, Edwin. It is just what one wishes to hear when one feels as pulled as I do." Lady Basinberry glared balefully at him.

"My apologies, Beatrice. That was a most insensitive remark on my part," Mr. Davenport said hastily. "I am merely concerned for you."

Lady Basinberry was only partially mollified. She made an impatient gesture. "Never mind. What I have asked you to come up for is to inform you that I do not wish my nieces to miss the engagement for tonight. This ball will be one of the most celebrated of the Season. Edwin, you must escort Lydia and Michele."

Mr. Davenport stared at his sister in bulge-eyed horror.

"Surely you are joking! Beatrice, you know full well that I avoid formal squeezes like the very plague."

Lady Basinberry stared down her nose and said frostily, "My dear brother, it was you who wished a proper Season for Lydia and Michele. If you do not take a hand in this one instance, I cannot assure you that I shall have the inclination to see you through the remainder of the Season."

Knowing Lady Basinberry's nature as well as he did, Mr. Davenport had no doubt that she would carry out her threat. He sighed. "Very well. You may rest easy, Beatrice. I shall do my duty." The injustice of it was more than he could stand, however, and he said in an injured tone, "But it goes against the grain, so it does. I have had to give up my easy chair and my comfortable habits. I have had to seek refuge at the club, where one can blow a cloud in peace. All this I have accepted as a necessary evil. It passes all bounds, though, when I must rig myself out in evening dress and bear-lead a couple of misses."

Lady Basinberry was unmoved. She waved dismissal. "Go away, Edwin. You have little enough time to dress as it is." Mr. Davenport went, still fulminating, and placed himself into the hands of his valet.

An hour later he made his way downstairs to the drawing room, where Michele and Lydia had already been waiting for several minutes. They were astonished to see him in evening wear. "Papa, how magnificent you look." Lydia stood on tiptoe to kiss his cheek.

Mr. Davenport's annoyed expression lightened. "You are a good girl, Lydia," he said fondly.

"Is Lady Basinberry not accompanying us?" Michele asked.

The frown once more descended on Mr. Davenport's round countenance. "No, she shall not. Her ladyship is feeling under the weather this evening, so I am accompanying you and Lydia tonight," he said. He stood aside for them at the door. "The carriage awaits us at the curb. I do not want to keep the horses standing about, so be quick about it."

Michele and Lydia exchanged swift glances. It was obvious that Mr. Davenport was not at all pleased with the evening's arrangements. As one, the cousins set out to cajole him out of his sulks, with the result that by the time their carriage stopped at their destination, he was in a much more amiable frame of mind. He offered an arm to each young lady with the remark that he could not recall when he had been in such lovely company, and escorted them into the ballroom.

The ball was what was known as a squeeze, and therefore an assured success. Lydia and Michele quickly had their dance cards filled and began on a round of partners, while Mr. Davenport took refuge in a card room that had been set up for those who did not care for the dancing.

Michele was surprised and somewhat apprehensive when Lord Randol signed his name to her card. When it came time for their dance together, she was relieved that it was not to be a waltz, but instead a country dance. She took her courage in her hands and plunged for an explanation from him. "My lord, you have made it quite clear that you dislike me immensely. Why have you solicited my hand for this dance?"

Lord Randol looked down at her. The expression in his eyes was unreadable. "I am not certain, mademoiselle. Let me say only that I am intrigued by you."

Michele raised her brows. She said coolly, "I find that difficult to credit, my lord. If true, you would have communicated with me months ago."

His fingers crushed hers and she winced at the sharp pain. "You play a dangerous game, mademoiselle," he said softly. There were twin points of angry light in his hard eyes.

"On the contrary, I tire of this game that you set in motion when first I chanced to meet you at my uncle's home. With all due respect, my lord, you have behaved like an abominable child," Michele said.

"I think it time that we spoke privately, mademoiselle!" Lord Randol abruptly led her out of the dance, engendering surprised looks from those about them on the dance floor. His hand was viselike on her elbow as he strode along, and Michele half-stumbled in her effort to keep up with him.

Lord Randol swept aside the curtain from a window embrasure and ushered Michele in. She turned to face him, her breath coming quickly from between parted lips, as he stepped inside and dragged the curtain closed. The light from the ballroom was abruptly cut off and only the bright moon gave them illumination. He advanced slowly on her. There was a dangerous glitter in his eyes. "Now, mademoiselle. We shall have it all out in the open at last."

"I am happy to hear it," Michele said, holding her head high. Her pulses were leaping with the air of menace given off by her companion. She wondered fleetingly if she had been wise to antagonize him. But it was too late to undo. She gasped as his hands closed on her bare shoulders, and she involuntarily shrank from his devilish expression.

Lord Randol gave a bark of sharp laughter. "Do you fear me at last, mademoiselle?"

"Fear you?" Michele whispered. "I have never feared you, Anthony."

The use of his Christian name set flame to Lord Randol's barely checked emotions. "You are a jade," he breathed. He snatched her up in his arms. His lips came down to punish hers.

The sheer brutal force of the kiss was shocking. Her head was so bent that Michele began to fear that her neck would break from the force of it. Lord Randol's arms were constricting bands about her rib cage, through which she could barely breathe. After her first instinctive move to free herself, Michele endured the onslaught.

It ended as swiftly as it had begun. Lord Randol freed her so abruptly that she staggered and would have fallen except that her hand chanced to graze the balustrade. Michele caught her balance. She stared up at Lord Randol from wide eyes that appeared black in the moonlight. She gently touched the tips of her fingers to her throbbing lips. She was dazed by what he had done.

"Michele . . ." He made a move toward her.

She recoiled from his hand. "*Non!*" There was complete revulsion in the single syllable.

Lord Randol rocked as though he had been struck. Something akin to pain flickered across his face. Without a word he turned on his heel and dragged aside the curtain. His form was silhouetted briefly against the candlelight before he walked swiftly away. He was lost almost instantly to her sight in the milling crowd.

Michele leaned despondently against the balustrade. Silent tears coursed her cheeks.

A tall figure appeared beside the curtain. "Michele? Are you quite all right?"

She turned her back on the doorway, wiping surreptitiously at her face. "Of course, Sir Lionel. I . . . I am but admiring the moonlight," she said huskily.

He came forward to stand close behind her shoulder. "You need not pretend with me, my dear. I saw you and his lordship disappear behind the curtain. I witnessed the black scowl on his face when he came out so precipitately. Michele, I was concerned for you."

"Oh, Lionel!" Michele turned swiftly to bury her face against his shoulder. She felt his arms come up around her and she was grateful for the security thus offered to her. Foremost in her mind was the hateful manner in which Lord Randol had kissed her. With a catch in her voice she said, "He is not the same man that he was."

"I know it," Sir Lionel said. Above her head he smiled in a tender fashion. Softly he said, "Never mind. I am here for you, Michele. I shall always be near whenever you should need me." He allowed her to cry without further words from him.

After a moment, Michele straightened. She stepped back, brushing the back of her hand across her eyes. Sir Lionel let her go at once. He pulled out his handkerchief and without a word he offered it to her. Michele took the handkerchief to finish drying her eyes. When she was done, her expression was again one of assured composure. Sir Lionel nodded in satisfaction. "Good. I put myself entirely at your disposal, Mademoiselle du Bois." With a flourishing bow he offered his arm to her.

Michele managed to laugh through her embarrassment, and she accepted his escort with a gracious nod. As she placed her hand on his arm, she said softly, "I am grateful, Lionel. I feel compelled to apologize to you for—"

"Not another word, if you please." Before they had quite

left the shadows of the window embrasure, he stopped her. Still regarding her face, he brought up his free hand to warmly cover her fingers. "Pray consider the past few moments as never happening. We shan't speak of this instance again."

"Thank you, sir," Michele said gratefully.

He smiled then and led her out onto the dance floor. For Michele, the ball ended without further incident and she was grateful for it.

In the days following, she saw nothing of Lord Randol. He called but once at the town house, and she made certain that she was out of the drawing room before he entered it. Afterward Lydia expressed indignation that her cousin had deserted her, but Michele begged the excuse of the headache. Indeed, she had spent the remainder of the afternoon in her room, but more from fear of inadvertently coming face-to-face with Lord Randol as he took his leave than from any physical malady.

Lydia did not quite believe her cousin's excuse, but it was true that Michele had looked pale all that day. Following her thoughts, Lydia asked, "Did you not sleep well after we got in from the ball, Michele?"

"I spent an indifferent night, actually. Why do you ask?"

Lydia shrugged. "You do not act yourself today. Even Papa noticed how listless you were at luncheon. He asked me later if you were feeling off-color. I assured him that I did not think that you were falling ill."

Michele made an effort to smile. "I trust not, for Aunt Beatrice would insist that I was malingering only to spite her plans for me," she said offhandedly. Her attempt at humor raised a small laugh from Lydia, and Michele was able to turn the conversation into other channels.

However, she could not so easily shake her own oppressed spirits. She had been preoccupied with Lord Randol's shocking behavior the night before, and she had yet to reconcile herself. That he had shown her such complete lack of tender feeling had gone far in shaking those hopes she had cherished of breaking through his cold exterior and finding inside the man she had once known and dearly loved.

A message was brought up to Lydia's sitting room, where she and Michele were seated, that Captain Becher was below. "Oh, do you think that the captain has actually gotten your carriage for you?" Lydia asked, excitement entering her eyes.

"We shall see soon enough," Michele said, rising. As she and Lydia went downstairs, she felt anticipation give a much-needed lift to her spirits.

Captain Becher was in the drawing room. He bowed to the ladies, and once the pleasantries were done with, he invited them to step outside the front door in order to inspect the phaeton and team that he had found for the mademoiselle.

Michele and Lydia accompanied him outside, where he gestured expansively at the carriage at the curb. "There it is, mademoiselle."

Lydia drew in her breath. "Oh, it is beautiful."

Michele walked down the front steps, never taking her eyes from the phaeton. It was a perch phaeton, painted a bright yellow with black trim on the wheels, and to the front was hitched a perfectly matched team of blacks. Michele went to the leaders and delicately scratched their smooth noses, beginning the process of getting acquainted.

Captain Becher came to stand beside her. He was smiling. "Will it do, mademoiselle?"

"*Oui*, Captain Becher, very much so," Michele said, her dark eyes shining.

"I have taken the liberty of setting up a stable for your cattle in the next block. And if you wish it, I will recommend a couple of good lads, either of whom would make a decent groom," he said.

"Thank you, sir. I shall be glad to employ a groom of your recommendation. Your thoughtfulness has exceeded all my expectations."

"I was happy to oblige. You shall cut a dashing figure, mademoiselle," Captain Becher said. He gestured up at the driving seat. "Shall we tool about the block so that you may test their paces?"

"Only let me collect my bonnet, sir, and I shall be with you directly," said Michele, flashing an eager smile.

Lydia followed Michele back indoors and up the stairs to her bedroom, exclaiming enthusiastically all the while. She watched Michele put on her bonnet, and she sighed. "I do wish that I was accompanying you," she said wistfully.

"But of course you must, if you do not mind the rear seat," Michele said, picking up her driving gloves.

Lydia shook her head quickly. "Oh, no, I do not care two sticks for that! Wait for me. I shan't be a moment!" She dashed off to get her own bonnet.

The expedition was a successful one. Michele pronounced herself eminently satisfied with the team's smooth action. Captain Becher bowed his gratification. Once they were returned to the town house, he gave a hand to each of the ladies so that they could descend to the sidewalk. "In the morning I shall send round the two grooms for your inspection."

Michele gave her hand to him. Her smile was warm. "Thank you again, Captain Becher. I cannot begin to tell you how very much it means to me to be able to drive myself about."

During the drive, Michele's spirits had totally lifted. She thought that despite Lord Randol's horrid behavior, she would still like to try to reach him, and she could think of nothing more certain to capture his attention than driving her own equipage.

Captain Becher took his leave and drove away in the phaeton. Michele and Lydia walked into the town house to be met in the hall by Lady Basinberry. She nodded toward the closing door. "I glimpsed a phaeton. I take it that it was yours, Michele?"

"Indeed it was," said Michele cheerfully, drawing off her kid driving gloves.

"Aunt, it is the most beautiful carriage. So well-sprung, and the team are such smooth goers! I am positively green with envy that I do not know how to handle the ribbons as well as Michele, or I should order a phaeton for myself," Lydia said.

"I am certain your dear father would instantly grant such a whim," Lady Basinberry said dryly. At Lydia's grimace and quick shake of the head, she laughed. "Go along and rid yourselves of your bonnets. We have but an hour before dinner, you know."

The younger ladies exclaimed that they had had no notion that it was so late. "We have hardly left ourselves time to change," Michele remarked to Lydia, who matched her stair for stair.

Lady Basinberry heard her and called up, "Pray do not think that I shall ask Cook to hold back dinner, for I shall not. Punctuality is a virtue, unless one is as old as I. And then one may do as one pleases, of course." She went with firm step into the drawing room to wait for the rest of the family to assemble for dinner, completely recovered from her lapse of weakness of the day before.

12

Michele did not immediately set herself into the habit of driving. She wanted to make a certain impression with her phaeton, and to that end she visited the modiste to be measured for a new habit. It was a week before the habit was to be completed and she used the time to hire one of the grooms that Captain Becher had recommended. She also made herself known at the stables and became more familiar with her horses.

On the afternoon that Michele had chosen for her driving debut, she inquired whether Lydia would care to accompany her. "Oh, yes, I should like it above all things," Lydia promptly said. She dimpled at her cousin. "It is my duty, besides, for you expressed yourself unwilling to excite much interest this Season, and so I must save you from yourself."

Michele laughed and her eyes twinkled. "I shall be in your debt, then. I shall meet you in the front hall in a few minutes." She went upstairs to change into her new habit. When she returned downstairs, she was amused by Lydia's awed expression. As she drew on her driving gloves, she inquired, "Do I meet with your approval, cousin?"

Lydia let out her breath. "That is positively the most divine habit that I have ever seen," she said sincerely. "Somehow I do not think that I shall outshine you, Michele, for most definitely you are what Toppy Murray calls in all admiration a dasher!"

Michele inclined her head and suggested with a smile that they get on with their drive to the park. Lydia followed her out the front door of the town house and down the steps to the phaeton, where Michele's groom gave a supporting hand to each lady as she climbed up into the high carriage.

When Michele was seated in the yellow-and-black phaeton, attired in her stunning dove-gray habit, she knew that she presented a striking picture. She requested the groom to let go the leaders' heads and flicked her whip. With a flourish, she guided the horses into the traffic and set out for the park.

Lydia held on to the seat rail, made apprehensive by the heavy traffic that Michele was negotiating through, but she quickly realized that her cousin was an excellent whip. "I do wish that I could drive to an inch, just as you do," she said wistfully.

Michele glanced at her cousin. "If you wish it, I shall endeavor to teach you, Lydia. Once you have the technique down, it is not so very difficult."

"I think one must have a knack for it, actually. But perhaps with practice I might improve to the point that I do not tangle the ribbons," Lydia said. "I should like that, because a soldier's wife should know how to handle a team if she should ever need to."

"Quite true," Michele said as she turned the horses into the park.

"Oh, there is Aunt Beatrice's good friend Mrs. Angleton. She is an awful woman, but very clever for all that, and she did give us the name of that excellent bootier," Lydia said, smiling and waving to a grand-dame who stared at them from a slow-moving landau.

Michele gave a throaty laugh. "Then most assuredly we must do the polite. Shall we stop?"

Lydia stared at her in alarm. "Most certainly not! We should never get away from her. And you do not want your horses standing about forever." Michele allowed the truth of this observation and so she merely nodded to the good lady without slowing the phaeton.

Michele knew almost at once that her equipage was sparking a good deal of interest, from the stares of pedestrians and other drivers alike. She smiled and nodded to those who were known to her. Hats were reverently tipped in her direction by the gentlemen, and the ladies looked after her smart passing with varying degrees of awe and envy.

Lydia was not behind in noticing these reactions, and she giggled. "I think that we are making a definite impression, Michele. I have seen at least five dagger glances from ladies who puff themselves off as the height of fashion. Oh, I am enjoying myself!" She made an exaggerated bow to another lady and received a startled glance of recognition from the haughty woman.

There was only one individual that Michele actually hoped to make an impression upon, and she did not immediately see his phaeton. She was beginning to think that Lord Randol had chosen not to drive in the park that day when she suddenly met his astonished gaze. Automatically she slowed the pace of her team. She nodded in a cool fashion. "Good day, my lord." She would have breezed past him then, but he pulled on his reins to bring his team to a stand, and she did likewise. Her heart was beating incredibly fast, but nothing of her inner tension appeared in her serene expression.

"Lord Randol! I did not realize that you would be driving in the park this afternoon," Lydia said, a trifle dismayed.

"Miss Davenport, mademoiselle. I am usually found here, as most of my acquaintances know," Lord Randol said.

"How stupid of me not to expect it, when Michele has mentioned that you are a whip," Lydia said.

Michele flushed under his lordship's considering gaze. "Lydia is always most curious regarding anything to do with my life at home. She wished to know who had taught me to drive," she said quietly.

"Yes, and I was surprised to learn that it was you, my lord. I had not known before that you had such an interest in driving. We have never talked of such things," Lydia said.

The viscount did not appear to be listening to Lydia's chatter. Lord Randol allowed his gaze to travel slowly over the phaeton and the perfectly matched blacks before he again looked at the young woman in the dove-gray habit who sat on the phaeton's seat with such competent ease. "I see that you have set up a phaeton in your own style. My congratulations to your friends for their excellent choice of horse-flesh," he said.

"It is my phaeton-and-four, actually. I found that I missed driving myself about and I commissioned the purchase of this rig," Michele said calmly.

Lord Randol raised his brows in a surprised manner. "I see. That was a considerable expense to go to for a short visit, surely. Unless, of course, you mean to ship the equipage and team back with you. I assume that you will be returning to Brussels with the end of the Season?"

"I am not certain what my plans might be in a few months' time," Michele said. Lydia shot her a quick, speculative glance that she did not notice. She did not care for the direction of the conversation and attempted to lighten it. "I have noticed your own team, my lord. Your cattle look to be perfectly matched in their paces. Pray tell me, do you still wager your driving skills against all comers?"

Lord Randol smiled and a tiny spark of amusement lit the depths of his gray eyes. He was oddly relieved that she appeared to have forgotten the incident of a few evenings before. Each time he had recalled his behavior it had filled him with a sense of shame and disgust that he had not wanted to analyze. "I am no longer so imprudent. The war taught me that I am mortal and therefore I have learned a measure of humility in my abilities. And you, mademoiselle, do you still go about town setting all the other ladies to shame with your driving skill? I even seem to recall a race between yourself and another lady, an Englishwoman, who was quite put out at losing with such a broad margin."

Michele laughed shakily. "I had hoped that particular incident to have been long forgotten, my lord. It did not reflect well upon my reputation, as you may also recall," she said. Her hands trembled ever so slightly and the agitation was thus communicated to her sensitive horses, which stamped restlessly in place.

"It appears that your horses are still fresh. I will not keep them standing about any longer," Lord Randol said. He inclined his head to both ladies and gave the signal to his own horses.

Michele watched the viscount's phaeton bowl away, keeping her own team firmly under control. She could not believe how well their exchange had gone. Lord Randol had almost been his old self with her. Hope unfurled with frightening rapidity in her breast and she shook her head quickly in denial. It was too much to harbor that particular hope, especially when Lord Randol was courting her cousin, but oh, how pleasant it would be just to have his friendship again, she thought. With a flick of her whip, Michele put her horses in motion.

Lydia had been an interested spectator at the meeting between Lord Randol and her cousin. She had watched their faces closely and now she sat back against the seat with a contented sigh. She rather thought that her half-formed desire to throw her cousin back into Lord Randol's arms had made progress. "I do believe that is the most affable that I have ever seen his lordship. I was not at all as nervous as I usually am, and certainly you deal with him very well indeed," she said, sliding a glance from under her lashes at her cousin's profile.

Michele turned her head. "Whatever do you mean, Lydia?"

Lydia shrugged nonchalantly. "It is an observation only. I suppose the familiarity between the two of you can be accounted for through your past close association. Quite frankly, Michele, I begin to think that Lord Randol shows something of a partiality for your company."

"Pray do not be ridiculous. His lordship does not care for me in the least," Michele said, though without the heat that her words should have conveyed. She could not help but be caught up in the warm feeling of pleasure Lydia's comment had given her. "I think we should be getting back to the town house. Our aunt will be wondering where we have got off to," she said quietly. Lydia agreed, and instantly began talking about the various personages and carriages that they passed on the return home. Wiser than she had been just weeks before, Lydia did not once refer again to Lord Randol.

13

The following afternoon Clarence and Elizabeth Hedgeworth were visiting with the ladies when Lord Randol called. Lady Basinberry introduced Lord Randol to the Hedgeworths. Clarence recognized his lordship as a very knowing customer, someone that he would not care to tangle with. Elizabeth cast a fleeting glance up into his face before she colored and stammered a shy greeting, put out of all countenance by his grave and distant manners. In Lydia's confidence, she was already halfway persuaded that she should fear his lordship.

Lord Randol settled into a chat with Lady Basinberry and Lydia, while Michele played hostess to Clarence and Elizabeth. Lady Basinberry thought it time to give Lord Randol a little encouragement, since Lydia did not appear capable of doing so herself. "My lord, Lydia was but just telling me how much your visits mean to her," said Lady Basinberry. She glanced at her niece, whose mouth had dropped open slightly, and gave her a meaningful stare. Lydia closed her mouth and flushed, looking unhappy.

Lord Randol was not behind in noting the byplay, but he preferred to ignore it. He inclined his head to Lydia. "It is always a pleasure to call on you, Miss Davenport. I hope that we may spend a great deal more time in one another's company in the not-too-distant future."

Lydia took his meaning instantly. With a particular sinking feeling she heard her aunt assure the viscount that they were all anticipating that happy time. She realized what Michele had warned her of was coming true. She was inexorably being driven into a position where she would have no choice but to agree to marry Lord Randol. She swallowed convulsively, feeling ready to sink, but she knew that the moment of truth had come. "I am honored by your attentions, my lord. But I cannot ever accept your kind offer for my hand. You see, my heart quite belongs to another." Her clear voice crried to the others in the room, and all conversation abruptly ended.

Lady Basinberry was aghast. She threw a wild glance toward Lord Randol's shuttered face. "Lydia, you do not know what you are saying!"

Lydia tried to maintain contact with Lord Randol's penetrating gaze, but after a moment her lashes fluttered down. She made a helpless gesture. "I am sorry, my lord," she whispered.

"On the contrary, Lady Basinberry, I believe that Miss Davenport knows very well what she is saying," Lord Randol said. He wondered why his paramount feeling was not outrage, but instead one of immeasurable relief. Lydia looked up quickly, startled by his cool tone. He saw the anxiety lurking in her eyes. Lord Randol smiled, dispelling his grimness of expression. "You need not fear, I shall not eat you."

She flushed fierily. "Oh, I am sure that I never . . . what I mean to say is, thank you, my lord," she said in a shaking voice.

Lord Randol took her hand and raised it to his lips in a brief salute. "I think that I shall take leave of you now, Miss Davenport. You will admit that after such a leveler, a dignified retreat is all that is left to me," he said humorously.

"I am so very sorry, my lord," Lydia said breathlessly.

Lord Randol bowed to her and to Lady Basinberry. He took leave of the others in the drawing room and strode to the door. He was met in the doorway by Mr. Davenport, who stepped back to allow his lordship past. "My lord, surely you do not leave already?" Mr. Davenport asked genially.

"I have recalled another visit that I must make," Lord

Randol said. He exchanged a few more brief words and then he was gone.

Mr. Davenport looked around at those in the drawing room, and he was struck by the complete immobility of the small company and the varying degrees of shock or amazement on their countenances. "Whatever has gotten into the lot of you? One would think that an apparition had just passed through the room."

His bantering tone released Lady Basinberry from her stupefaction. "Edwin! Your daughter has just given Lord Randol the roundabout."

"What!" Mr. Davenport turned startled eyes on his daughter.

Lydia was pale and somewhat awed by her own temerity. "It is quite true, Papa. I have told Lord Randol that his suit is unacceptable to me," she said in a low voice. She turned toward her aunt. "I am sorry, Aunt Beatrice. I know that you are as disappointed as Papa. I did try to like his lordship, I did truly."

A strangled sound issued forth from Mr. Davenport's throat, swinging the attention of all to him. They watched fascinated as he opened his mouth once or twice. His face was becoming suffused with an alarming shade of puce and he appeared to swell with the strength of his emotion.

At the unmistakable signs of a grand rage, Michele stepped quickly to Lydia's side. She slipped a supporting arm about her cousin's slender waist. She could feel Lydia trembling. She was soothingly, "My cousin was civil about it, uncle. Lord Randol took the disappointment quite well. I do not think that there will be repercussions from that quarter."

Mr. Davenport found his voice at last. "That will be enough, Michele. There can be no creditable defense." Mr. Davenport stared angrily at his erring daughter. "I wish to see you in my study at once, Lydia!" he said awfully. He stood waiting for her in the doorway.

Lydia quailed before her father's anger. "Yes, Papa." She slipped quickly past her father, and Mr. Davenport closed the drawing-room door with a distinct snap. Those left in the drawing room heard, a moment later, another door shut.

Clarence and Elizabeth Hedgeworth exchanged horrified glances. With one accord they rose to take their leave. "We . . . we really must be going," said Miss Hedgeworth.

"That I readily understand," Lady Basinberry said in a tone that brought quick color into Miss Hedgeworth's cheeks. Lady Basinberry held out her hand to the younger woman. "I apologize for the awkwardness of the past several moments, Elizabeth. I know that I may rely upon your discretion."

"Oh . . . of course, my lady," Elizabeth said, acutely uncomfortable. She seemed to have difficulty in meeting Lady Basinberry's eyes.

Her brother managed to rise to the occasion with an aplomb at variance with his young years. "Rest assured of it, my lady," he said firmly.

"Thank you, Clarence. Do, pray, give my regards to your dear grandmother," Lady Basinberry said graciously.

The Hedgeworths promised to do so, and Michele offered her hand to each of them in turn. "Good-bye. I hope that I may visit with you both again," she said.

Elizabeth pressed Michele's fingers, saying with repressed agitation, "Pray tell Lydia for me . . . I am so very sorry! But I am her friend. Assure her of that, please. And . . . and I shall be happy to do anything . . ."

Michele smiled at the embarrassed young woman. "Certainly I shall do so, Elizabeth." After taking brief leave of Michele, Clarence took hold of his sister's elbow and the Hedgeworths got themselves out of the drawing room without a moment's loss.

When they were gone, Lady Basinberry shook her head. She was already past her own agitation and was prepared to shrug off the unfortunate incident. She picked up her embroidery hoop and began to place smooth unhurried stitches. "It is an extremely bad piece of work. I had thought Lydia better-mannered than to do such a thing, but at least she did not blurt it out during an assembly. It is fortunate indeed that only the Hedgeworths were present, for I am confident that we may actually rely upon their discretion."

Michele was paying scarce attention to Lady Basinberry's observation, having discerned even through the closed door the angry rise and fall of her uncle's voice. Disturbed, she asked, "My lady, what shall my uncle do? I can hear him even now. He is so very angry with Lydia."

Lady Basinberry paused in her embroidering to consider the matter. "It is true, I have rarely seen Edwin in such a taking. I suppose I should not have sprung it on him as I did, but I was so rattled myself that . . . . I still can scarce believe Lydia's ill-breeding! It passed all bounds of propriety, and I suppose that is what has so struck Edwin. I suspect that once he has finished shouting at Lydia, however, everything will be back to normal. Edwin dotes on Lydia, as I am sure you have noticed. He will not remain angry with her for long, I promise you."

"I hope that is true," Michele said. She perched on the arm of the settee and began to pleat and repleat her muslin skirt. She could not help wondering if it had been the scolding she had given Lydia that had led her cousin into such a disastrously public declaration to Lord Randol.

Lady Basinberry glanced irritably at her. "Pray do stop fidgeting, Michele. If you must be doing something, come sit beside me and sort my colors for me. My eyes are not as sharp as they once were."

"I do not believe that for a moment, ma'am," Michele said, managing a laugh. Obediently she sat down beside her aunt and picked up the tangle of multicolored yarns. She had barely begun to separate the colors when her quick ears caught the sound of a door being thrown open, to be followed instantly by distressed weeping and running steps on the hall tiles. The yarns dropped from Michele's lap as she leapt up.

Lady Basinberry only tilted her head. "What can you do, my dear? Lydia will be the better for a good bout of tears in the privacy of her bedroom, you know."

Michele wavered. Finally she sighed and sat down again. She bent to retrieve the yarns that had tumbled to the Aubusson carpet. "You are right, of course."

"I invariably am," Lady Basinberry said. She then introduced a casual topic and Michele made an effort to

uphold her end, but it was a lagging conversation. Lady
Basinberry gave up on her, defeated by Michele's
abstraction, and allowed silence to fall until just the slow
ticking of the mantel clock was heard. Michele waited for
what seemed to her a decent interval before she excused
herself from the drawing room. She went upstairs to knock
on Lydia's door, but there was no answer, which did not
particularly surprise her. Undoubtedly Lydia preferred to be
alone after such a miserable scold.

Michele managed to fill the remainder of the long afternoon
in the library, writing letters to her parents and to several
of her friends in Brussels. She had left the library door open
and she raised her head when she heard Mr. Davenport request that his sister join him in the study.

Through the open library door Michele saw Lady Basinberry precede her brother into the study. "I find this whole
episode preposterous," she said as she entered.

"No more than I, Beatrice. And that is what I wish to
discuss," said Mr. Davenport. He shut the study door with
a decisive snap. From her place at the writing desk in the
library, Michele stared meditatively at the closed door. Her
uncle was obviously still upset by Lydia's surprising
announcement. She hoped that Lady Basinberry could
persuade him to a calmer state of mind.

Michele returned to her letters, but it became increasingly
difficult to concentrate on her task because she heard Lady
Basinberry's angry exclamations, forcibly matched by Mr.
Davenport's deeper voice.

Michele was becoming uncomfortable and had just gotten
up to close the library door when the door opposite opened.
Unaware of his niece, Mr. Davenport stomped down the hall.
Michele heard him tell the butler that he would be dining
at his club and that he did not know when he would return.
Lady Basinberry came out of the study to stand in the hall
looking after her brother with the coldest expression that
Michele had ever seen on that lady's countenance. The outside door slammed. Lady Basinberry turned on her heel and
walked swiftly away, her skirts swirling about her ankles.

Michele slowly closed the library door. She finished her

letters quickly, not feeling able to convey enjoyment on paper when she was so perturbed. She felt a strong sense of guilt, which she knew was irrational. But she was convinced it had been her advice that had made Lydia make known her feelings to Lord Randol. If she had not urged Lydia to it, perhaps the entire incident would never have happened. And too, she had felt such a leap of her pulses when she realized what Lydia had done, for it meant that Lord Randol was free to pursue another young woman as his bride. Michele knew that what she was thinking was fanciful in the extreme. There was still that bitter wall between herself and the viscount and there could never be more until the unexplained bitterness was dealt with.

Michele moved restlessly about the library, picking out a title here and there, then replacing the volumes on the shelves. Finally irritated by her own behavior, she decided to change early for dinner. She swept up her letters to give to the butler to post for her and went upstairs.

An hour later, when Michele went down, she discovered that only Lady Basinberry awaited her. "Good evening, my lady." Lady Basinberry stared at her and then returned to what appeared a grim contemplation of the flower arrangement. Quietly Michele asked of the footman in attendance, "Is Miss Davenport joining us this evening?"

"No, miss," the footman said woodenly.

"I see. Thank you." Michele followed Lady Basinberry into the dining room and seated herself opposite the older lady. Michele summoned up a smile for her aunt's benefit. "It seems that we are alone tonight."

"Quite." Lady Basinberry's tone was short. She seemed disinclined for polite conversation, her expression showing her to be preoccupied with rather unpleasant thoughts.

Michele was relieved to be spared the effort of making polite conversation. She had attempted to talk to Lydia before coming downstairs, only to be informed by her cousin's maid that "miss is not wishing to see anyone at the moment." Despite the unencouraging message, Michele had hoped that Lydia would at least make an appearance at dinner. She felt horribly responsible for the entire matter, and her conscience would have been somewhat eased if Lydia had chosen to come down.

The first course was served, but neither of the ladies seemed to favor the soup, nor were they roused to enthusiasm by the vegetables. The roast beef was brought to the table accompanied by the butler's hopeful comment that Cook had gone to lengths to make certain it was done to taste, but Lady Basinberry spurned the meat course, partaking only of small amounts of the potatoes and gravy, peas in cream sauce, and bread. Michele thought that she had never had less appetite as she toyed with a small meat pie.

The subdued atmosphere was unabated through the meal, both ladies merely picking at their plates. Lady Basinberry preserved her silence, only occasionally breaking it to exclaim under her breath, "That idiot!" Her scornful mutterings did nothing to assuage Michele's increasing unhappiness with her own role in Lydia's disgrace. When the desserts were offered, Michele waved the selection aside and requested a cup of hot sweet tea. She cast a glance in her companion's direction. Lady Basinberry had accepted a dish of bread pudding. Michele well knew that bread pudding was a favorite with Lady Basinberry, but after a mouthful or two, her aunt pushed it away.

When the covers were removed and the ladies rose from the table, Lady Basinberry roused herself out of her black reverie to thank Michele for her forbearance. "I am bad company this evening, my dear, and I know it. I would as lief snap off your nose as not," she said with a wintry smile.

Michele was touched by Lady Basinberry's apology. "It is just as well that we are engaged for only a musical soiree this evening. Perhaps you will find the selections soothing," she said.

"I am not a colicky infant that I need soothing," said Lady Basinberry sharply. At her niece's startled expression, she sighed. "I am sorry, my dear. Indeed, the music will be quite nice." She allowed the footman to drape her cloak about her shoulders, and after assuring herself that Michele was also ready, she swept out of the front door to be handed up into the carriage at the curb.

The ladies arrived at their destination and said all that was expected of them to their hostess, explaining that Lydia's absence was owing to the headache. Then they took their seats and assumed composed expressions of interest for the several languid airs that were performed on harp and pianoforte. But later neither Michele nor Lady Basinberry could have said what the selections had been.

At last the soiree drew to an end and the ladies exchanged compliments with their hostess, hiding their thankfulness that the long evening was done. They returned to the town house in silence, and their good-nights to one another were brief.

Before retiring, Michele thought again of knocking at Lydia's door, but she decided against it. Perhaps a night's lonely reflection would make Lydia more amenable to company.

Michele slipped into bed. Her maid blew out the candles before softly closing the door as she went out. Michele stared into the blurred white of the canopy overhead. Lydia could not mean to remain in her bedroom. Michele hoped she would be at breakfast in the morning.

14

At breakfast there was no sign of Lydia. Michele was disappointed, but not really surprised. It was otherwise with Mr. Davenport. He watched the door with a frown, more than once drawing out his pocket watch to glance at it. "Where the devil is the girl?" he asked finally.

Lady Basinberry had been watching her brother silently for several minutes and she now took the opportunity to show her disdain. She curled her upper lip in derision. "Surely you do not expect Lydia to bounce in to breakfast as though nothing has happened."

Mr. Davenport threw his sister a glance of dislike. "I expect my daughter to know better than to indulge in a fit of the sulks, Beatrice."

"The sulks! Is that how you view it, Edwin?" Lady Basinberry's eyes snapped with an angry light. "You have turned her life upside down. How did you expect a young girl to react to such ridiculous dicta?" she inquired scornfully.

Mr. Davenport threw down his napkin, a harassed expression on his plump face. He got to his feet and with heavy dignity said, "I am going to my club."

"You were always a craven," Lady Basinberry shot at his retreating back.

For reply, Mr. Davenport crashed the door shut. There was a short silence. Michele broke it with a hesitant question. "My lady, what has happened? Lydia refuses to see me or, for that matter, anyone else but her maid. And what you have just said to my uncle—what is it about?"

"You may well ask! My brother has finally and irrevocably proved his idiocy. In his words, since Lydia has seen fit to whistle down such an eligible offer as Lord Randol's, then she may end her days a spinster. Edwin has forbidden Lydia to attend social functions for the remainder of the Season or to receive callers. If any inquire after her, she is to have the influenza, if you please," Lady Basinberry said bitterly.

Michele exclaimed in horror. "This I cannot believe! Why, Lydia is a prisoner, *en effet*! How can my uncle do this thing when he is, before all else, a *bon âme*?"

Lady Basinberry sighed, suddenly tired in her demeanor. "Edwin is indeed a genial man. But like most mild-mannered sorts, he simmers and stews and sometimes boils over when one least expects it. Unfortunately for Lydia, as it happens," she said. Lady Basinberry stared at the remainder of her breakfast with almost a look of revulsion on her face. She pushed aside her plate. "I cannot swallow another mouthful. Edwin's stupidity has positively curdled my stomach."

Michele stared into her teacup, swirling the hot dark liquid. "I hold myself utterly responsible for Lydia's disgrace."

Lady Basinberry was startled. "Nonsense! How could you be responsible? Michele, I warn you. If you mean to turn maudlin on me, I shall not be held accountable for my actions. My temper is frayed almost beyond endurance as it is."

Michele looked up. Her gaze was straightforward but unhappy. "But it was I who advised Lydia to make known to Lord Randol her true feelings regarding his suit. It never occurred to me that she would do so in such a way."

Lady Basinberry regarded her with suddenly narrowed eyes. Her voice was soft, controlled, yet nevertheless acid. "You must have been very persuasive, to be sure. Lydia is such a biddable, good-natured girl, not at all given to freakish starts."

Michele was astonished by the patent hostility in her aunt's voice. She hastily sought to reassure Lady Basinberry. "On the contrary, it was but a passing comment. Lydia had again complained of her anxiety regarding the match. I merely pointed out to her the consequences of continuing to allow

Lord Randol to assume that his suit was entirely agreeable to her.''

Lady Basinberry's eyes glittered. "Pray tell me, my dear, do you intend to have Lord Randol for yourself?''

For a frozen second Michele stared at the elder lady. Lady Basinberry's caustic shot had hit uncomfortably close to the fabric of her fantasy. She said quietly, answering Lady Basinberry as well as her own inner questionings, "I could not have his lordship even if I meant to undercut my cousin, my lady. Lord Randol despises me.''

Lady Basinberry put up her brows in exaggerated surprise. "Indeed! I find it passing strange that a gentleman with whom you are scarcely acquainted could have developed such a strong distaste for your company, my dear niece. Surely you exaggerate.''

"I was acquainted with Lord Randol in Brussels. Our friendship did not survive his return to England,'' said Michele shortly, not wishing to go any deeper into her former relationship with the gentleman in question.

"It becomes better and better. Your friendship with Lord Randol must have been a strange one to result in such animosity upon the part of his lordship. Tell me, did your dear mother and François know of this . . . friendship?'' Lady Basinberry asked.

Michele stiffened. Her eyes flashed. "I beg your pardon, my lady! Perhaps you will speak more plainly.''

Lady Basinberry smiled, but the coldness of her eyes did not lighten. "I warn you, my dear. Take a care that you do not meddle further in Lydia's affairs, or you shall have me to contend with. And I can be an extremely formidable enemy.''

For a heartbeat Michele stared into Lady Basinberry's hard eyes. Then she placed her napkin carefully on the table. Her eyes had darkened almost to black with the insult that she felt. Rising to her full height, she said coldly, "Excuse me, Lady Basinberry. I have some errands that I must attend to this morning.'' She swept out of the breakfast room.

Michele went directly upstairs and rang for her maid, who came running at the unusually urgent summons. The maid

saw at once that her mistress was in a rare temper, and she
inquired with concern what was required. "I am going
driving. Get me my habit. . . . No, give it to me. I wish
you to go downstairs and tell the footman that I want my
carriage," Michele said tersely. The maid dropped a curtsy
and left on her errand. Michele scrambled into her habit.
Twenty minutes after leaving Lady Basinberry in the drawing
room, she was rolling away from the town house to the park.
Inside the gates she saw Sir Lionel Corbett in the distance
on the green, and that he was raising an arm in greeting.
But she pretended not to see him and drove on at a spanking
pace. She knew that Sir Lionel's heavy gallantries would set
her teeth on edge. There were other acquaintances of hers
in the park, but Michele stopped for none of them, instead
inclining her head and flourishing her whip as she passed.
Her smart progress was noted and commented upon with
admiration by those who knew something of driving.

Lord Randol had taken up a friend beside him in his own
phaeton and they were engaged in a discussion on horseflesh
when Michele's distinctive yellow-accented carriage swept
past. Lord Randol watched the paces of the team and the
expert handling of ribbons with a detached interest.

His friend was not so forbearing. "A damn fine sight, is
she not? The whole town talks of her driving, you know.
I should like to make her acquaintance one day," he said,
ogling the disappearing mademoiselle through his fob.

Lord Randol glanced at his friend in some surprise.
"Ferdy, I had no notion that you were in the petticoat line."

The Honorable Ferdinand Huxtable-Taylor flushed and
dropped his fob. "No such thing. In any event, that is hardly
a proper way to speak of a lady."

Lord Randol merely smiled, declining to air his thoughts
about Mademoiselle du Bois. But he did stare thoughtfully
after the easily recognized phaeton with its matched blacks.
He had had a fleeting impression of the driver's lovely face
and he had gathered in that instant that something had upset
her. He did not know why he should care, and it rather
annoyed him that he did. He flicked his whip, and the tip

nipped his leader's ear. The team's paces quickened in instant response.

"By Jove, you have the deadliest eye that I have ever seen," Ferdy said appreciatively. He glanced at Lord Randol. "You were luckier than most, Anthony. You were always at home using either hand, while some poor bastards ended unable to even feed themselves properly."

"I am fortunate, indeed. My wounds deprived me of very little of moment." Lord Randol's voice was controlled, but there was a queer twist to his lips. His instinctive sympathy for the unhappiness that he had glimpsed in Michele's face evaporated as though it had never been.

Michele spent the better part of an hour tooling her carriage, and the familiar exercise served to cool her anger. She made up her mind that she would remain civil toward Lady Basinberry, but she intended first to make quite clear that she would not put up with such insult as her ladyship had given her that morning.

Michele heard herself hailed and she turned her head. Recognizing Mr. Hedgeworth and Elizabeth in their carriage, she pulled up her horses. She greeted them with a smile. "How do you do? It is a fine morning for driving, is it not?"

"Quite. Oh, I say, mademoiselle, that is a spanking team," said Mr. Hedgeworth, admiring the blacks.

"Thank you, sir. Perhaps one day you shall try their paces."

Mr. Hedgeworth flushed, speechless with gratification. His sister laughed at him and tweaked his sleeve. "You have quite bowled Clarence over, mademoiselle. His most passionate wish is to own just such a showy team. Grandmama's horses are a bit plodding for his taste, you see," Elizabeth said.

Mr. Hedgeworth was embarrassed by his sister's confidences and he made haste to turn the subject. "We were wondering whether you and Lydia should like to set a day for an expedition to Astley's Circus. It would be jolly good fun."

"I am sure of it. I have no objection myself, but I fear

that Lydia is indisposed, so perhaps we may put off the treat for a while,'' Michele said.

Miss Hedgeworth thoughtfully regarded her. "It has to do with that ghastly scene, doesn't it?" When Michele hesitated to reply, she leaned forward and said earnestly, "Mademoiselle, pray do tell me the truth. I am Lydia's staunchest friend and I should like to know."

Michele sighed. "Very well. I cannot hide the matter from you, since you were present during that unfortunate announcement of Lydia's. As you are aware, Mr. Davenport was very angry with my cousin. I learned this morning that he has forbidden her to leave the house or to receive callers."

"How incredibly gothic," said Elizabeth, indignation in her gentle voice. Soft pink flew to her cheeks, and an unusual spark of anger lit her eyes.

"I must say, that is coming it rather too harsh on poor Lydia," said Mr. Hedgeworth. Upon meeting Michele's eyes, he coughed deferentially. "I beg your pardon, mademoiselle. I meant no disrespect toward your uncle."

"I have not taken offense," Michele said, smiling. "However, I am certain that my uncle must relent. One cannot put it about that one's daughter has the influenza for the remainder of her natural life, can one?"

The Hedgeworths laughed at that and agreed. They exchanged a few more words with Michele before she told them good-bye. When she returned to the house, she was told that Lady Basinberry had gone out. Since Mr. Davenport had not returned from his club and Lydia chose to stay closeted in her bedroom, Michele had the dining room to herself for luncheon.

She heard the sounds of Lady Basinberry's return outside in the hall, and her ladyship's query to the manservant, who answered, "Yes, my lady. The mademoiselle is at luncheon." Michele sighed and set down her teacup. It appeared that Lady Basinberry also wished to speak to her. Perhaps it was just as well to have everything brought out aboveboard as soon as possible. The door swung open and Michele looked around.

Lady Basinberry paused on the threshold, her eyes meeting Michele's cool gaze. She stepped forward and the door fell shut. "I have requested that fresh tea be brought in," she said, pulling off her gloves. She sat down at the table and her eyes rose to meet Michele's once more. "I am very bad at apologizing, my dear. However, I am fully aware that I did you an injustice this morning. I hope that we may put such unpleasantness between us to rest."

Michele was silent a moment. "I think that would be the best course, my lady. Otherwise the atmosphere in this house would be truly intolerable."

Lady Basinberry grimaced, but she did not immediately reply, since the butler had entered with fresh tea. She waited until they had been served and the butler had withdrawn from the room before she said, "You have hit it precisely, Michele. The atmosphere in this house . . . It is but a poor excuse for my own behavior, however. I have always prided myself upon my personal control. But I anticipate that it will be severely tried until my foolish brother abandons his idiotic stance. I have just come from making a call on Mrs. Hedgeworth. She asked me of Lydia, and it was immediately obvious that pair of hers told her something of what has occurred. Winifred is too knowing to swallow whole that story of Lydia ill in her bed. I was forced to reveal Edwin's folly. She assured me of her complete discretion, naturally. I think that I can trust her to keep to her word."

"Even if Mrs. Hedgeworth does so, I cannot believe that there will not be talk. My cousin cannot simply disappear from society without comment. Eventually there will be those who will guess much of the truth, and the rest will spur the rumors to idiotic proportions," Michele said.

"Yes. I wonder what new ailment Edwin plans to concoct for Lydia when her influenza must have run its natural course," Lady Basinberry said sarcastically. "I do not intend to let the matter rest, I assure you. Edwin shall rue the day that he ever hit upon this preposterous scheme of his to punish Lydia."

"I cannot understand what it is that my uncle hopes to

accomplish by it. Even if Lydia were to regret her decision, she now stands no chance of wedding Lord Randol,'' Michele said.

Lady Basinberry raised her brows. ''Indeed, my dear, that is true. Unless Edwin is playing a deeper game than we know. But that is impossible. He is not so devious. And certainly Lord Randol is too proud to reconsider.''

''Then let us hope that you are able to persuade my uncle to a more compassionate stance. I should not like to think what Lydia might do if she is forced to continue as she is,'' Michele said. ''My cousin is a spirited young woman. I know that in the same circumstances I would not sit tamely in my bedroom for weeks, assured that my future held only more of the same!''

Lady Basinberry did not reply, but there was a thoughtful look in her eyes.

15

For a fortnight after Lydia announced her disinterest in Lord Randol's suit, Mr. Davenport stood firm against Lady Basinberry's unflagging arguments. On several occasions Michele heard their raised voices, and once she inadvertently entered the drawing room in time to catch Lady Basinberry pithily informing Mr. Davenport of his shortcomings. "I tell you to your head, Edwin, that you are all kinds of fool to sacrifice any chance of Lydia's making a decent match to your own fit of disappointed pique," she said roundly.

Michele paused in the doorway, dismayed. Before she could retreat, her uncle looked up and saw her. His mouth was drawn in a thin stubborn line that eased only slightly as he tried to summon up a smile. "Come in, Michele. There is no need for you to run off," he said with a shadow of his former geniality.

"I do not wish to intrude," Michele said, loath to join her feuding relations. She had endeavored to stay as much out of their way as possible for several days—not an easy goal to accomplish, when on most evenings they had dined together. Her only relief from their tense company had been the social events that she and Lady Basinberry had continued to attend.

"Nothing of the sort. We have done with this conversation," said Mr. Davenport, coming forward to take her hand in a gentlemanly gesture.

"You may have said all that you wish to, but I have not done with this subject, Edwin," Lady Basinberry said.

"You shall never persuade me, Beatrice," Mr. Davenport said shortly. He turned his shoulder on his sister. "Michele, allow me to hand you in to dinner."

Michele threw a glance at Lady Basinberry's angry expression, uncomfortably aware that her uncle was using her as a buffer against her ladyship's continued importunities. However, she really had no choice but to accept her uncle's escort into the dining room. Mr. Davenport seated her at the mahogany table, completely ignoring his sister, who had followed them. He did not do the proper thing and seat his sister, but instead took his own chair.

Lady Basinberry was left standing, and her mouth worked, though nothing issued forth. An appalled footman leapt forward to hold Lady Basinberry's chair. She, obviously furious at her brother's broad lack of courtesy, made a point of thanking the manservant.

Dinner was served, and only the clatter of cutlery broke the antagonistic silence observed by Mr. Davenport and Lady Basinberry. Michele tried to start up a conversation, but each attempt failed dismally and she thought with irritation that Lydia showed great good sense in taking her meals in her room. It was an incredibly uncomfortable hour before Michele was able to excuse herself from the table and flee. That evening she was engaged to the Hedgeworths to see a theater play, and she was never more glad in her life to escape the town house.

Mrs. Hedgeworth inquired in her gentle way after Lydia's health, and Michele replied evasively that her cousin was still keeping to her rooms. She despised herself for the lie, especially when she caught the exchange of glances between Clarence and Elizabeth. Michele sighed and tried hard to concentrate on the play.

At Mr. Davenport's insistence, the story that had been put about that Miss Davenport was indisposed with the influenza and was unable to receive callers continued to be enforced. Lydia was to all intents and purposes a prisoner to her father's stil-smoldering anger. Lady Basinberry performed her social duties with a certain brittleness. Whenever she had occasion to speak to Mr. Davenport, she treated him with the scorn that she had always before reserved for willful fools.

The household was generally affected by the unhappy atmosphere. Lydia was said to be indulging in frequent bouts of weeping. Michele tried to offer what comfort she could, but more often than not Lydia sent her away without seeing her. Under the circumstances, and without Lydia to accompany her, Michele was not particularly interested in attending the social activities. But Lady Basinberry pointed out that for both young ladies to drop out of society would arouse a furor of comment. Reluctantly Michele heeded her ladyship's argument and tried to appear as usual, but it was difficult to smile and laugh off her cousin's absence whenever a mutual acquaintance chanced to ask about Lydia's convalesence.

Those who called at the town house to visit with Lydia were turned away from the door unless they were quick enough to ask for Mademoiselle du Bois or Lady Basinberry. Clarence and Elizabeth Hedgeworth called several times, always to ask if the situation had changed any for the better, and Michele was unable to give them that assurance.

On Mr. Davenport's orders, Captain Hughes was denied entrance to the house altogether. But Captain Hughes was not easily discouraged, and hardly a day passed that he did not try to gain admittance. It chanced that as Michele was returning from a drive in her phaeton, Captain Hughes was coming down the steps of the town house. He wore a disconsolate and bewildered expression that roused Michele's sympathies. He did not appear to notice her, and started to walk away down the sidewalk. When she hailed him, he turned and took a quick step over to the phaeton. "Mademoiselle du Bois!" he exclaimed, his face lighting up.

"Pray step up, Captain. I wish to speak with you," Michele said.

Captain Hughes swung himself up into the phaeton and seated himself beside her. "This is well-met, mademoiselle. I had hoped to call on you today."

Michele guided her horses back into the carriage traffic

before she replied. "We shall take a turn about the block. It would not do to be seen with you by the servants, you see," she said with a quick smile.

Captain Hughes did not return her smile. Her words tore away any semblance of polite reserve that he might have maintained. He half-turned on the seat so that he could see her face. "Mademoiselle, I must crave your indulgence. What has happened to Lydia . . . to Miss Davenport? I am not allowed into the house or even to leave a note for her."

Michele sighed. "I am most sorry, Captain Hughes. My uncle unfairly blames you for a stand that Lydia has taken. He apparently hopes to persuade Lydia to forget you by these uncivil tactics."

Captain Hughes's taut face reflected his upset. "What can you mean, mademoiselle? I have not spoken to Lydia in days, and then our conversation was nothing untoward. Believe me, I have never incited her to anything that her father could possibly dislike."

Michele slanted a glance at him from her extraordinary midnight-blue eyes. "You have caused Lydia to fall in love with you, Captain. That is your sin."

He was momentarily bereft of speech. He shook his head helplessly. "But it has always been so between us. From the instant that our eyes met, I knew that Lydia was meant for me. And she assures me that it was the same for her. We have never disguised our feelings for one another. Mr. Davenport has known for some time of my hopes in Lydia's direction, even as I have known and accepted his understandable wish for a more exalted offer for her, and placed my confidence in our love for one another, which must win out in the end. What I do not understand is why suddenly he should kick up such a dust."

"He is angry because Lydia informed Lord Randol in front of several witnesses that she would not accept his lordship's suit because her heart was given to another," Michele said quietly.

"Oh, my word, the foolish girl," Captain Hughes said softly.

Michele laughed, though not lightheartedly. "Quite! My

uncle was so enraged that he has denied Lydia to everyone, and he has put it about that she has the influenza. Needless to say, it is not a very happy house at the moment." She sighed, hardly noticing when she had to correct her team's paces in order to let by a flashing barouche. "I had hoped that my uncle would have relented by now, but he remains obstinate despite Lady Basinberry's unceasing campaign on Lydia's behalf."

"But what will happen to Lydia?" Captain Hughes asked. "He cannot mean to keep her shut up forever!" He was appalled by the thought of his beloved in such straits. It was all he could do not to give in to a strong impulse to return at once to the town house and storm the doors.

"Of course he cannot. I still believe that he must relent, and it but takes patience until he does so," Michele said. She glanced at her companion, whose face was cut by a deep frown. "I did wish you to be aware of the facts, Captain."

Captain Hughes gave a fleeting smile. "I thank you for your kindness, mademoiselle. That explains everything. I wish that there was something I could do. I fail to see what course I might follow, short of shaking some sense into Mr. Davenport."

Michele laughed in genuine amusement. "If ever anyone needed a good shaking, it is my uncle," she agreed. She thought a moment. "If you like, I will carry a message from you to Lydia."

Captain Hughes's eyes lighted up. "By Jove! Will you, mademoiselle? You are kindness itself. I shall scribble one on the instant that I procure a pen." He pulled out one of his calling cards while Michele directed her team over to the curb. Captain Hughes jumped to the sidewalk and disappeared into a book vendor's stall. In a very few moments he reemerged and climbed back up into the phaeton. He handed the calling card, now tightly folded in half, to Michele. "You may read it if you wish," he said diffidently.

Michele flashed him a smile. She put the calling card safely in her reticule. "I trust you, Captain. I know that you are not the sort to urge Lydia to any action that could place her in jeopardy."

He was moved by her trust in him. He lifted her gloved hand to his lips. "Thank you, mademoiselle."

"Pray call me Michele, Captain. We are co-conspirators, after all," she said with a laugh. Her eyes twinkled at him.

Captain Hughes smiled. "Very well, and I am Bernard, if you please. I shall leave you here. I am not so very far from a friend's lodgings, and I believe that I shall drop in on him."

Michele nodded her understanding. Captain Hughes climbed down from the phaeton to the sidewalk. Michele gathered the reins and raised her whip in a brief salute to him before she directed her team back into the traffic and headed toward the Davenport town house. She thought about the note she carried in her reticule. She was a little uncomfortable to be in the position of go-between, but she had felt so badly for Captain Hughes, who was obviously frustrated and disturbed by the turn of events. The role of conspirator was not one that fitted her well, but she promised herself it would be for but the one time. Her uncle would surely relent soon and Lydia could then communicate directly with Captain Hughes.

As it happened, Mr. Davenport was already wavering. He had at first spent the better part of his waking hours at his club so that he could escape his sister. But he quickly found it awkward to accept the sympathy that his acquaintances offered when they learned of his daughter's unfortunate lapse in health. When he could no longer look anyone in the face, he began to hide at home in his office and began to feel as much a prisoner of his fit of anger as was Lydia.

On only one occasion did Lydia come downstairs for dinner, and that was when Mr. Davenport declared that he would not have his daughter stewing in the sulks. But Lydia's woebegone face, her subdued manner, and her obvious loss of weight so greatly affected him that he did not demand her presence at the dinner table again.

However, Mr. Davenport remained haunted by the memory of his daughter's unhappiness, and began to have his first misgivings over the way he had treated her. When next Lady Basinberry taxed him over Lydia, he made a grudging show of giving his permission for Lydia to accept and to go on morning calls if she so wished. "However, I still will not have that Hughes fellow in my house, and so you may tell her, Beatrice. He is to blame for this and I'll not have him poisoning my little girl's mind anymore," he said firmly.

"Very well, Edwin," Lady Basinberry said, signaling her disapproval with her chilly tone. But she considered her brother's concession a small triumph, brought about by her own unceasing efforts. She turned her hand to the next step, which was to coax Lydia out of her rooms and put her into her father's company as much as possible, for as she told Michele, "I wish Edwin to positivily swim in guilt."

Upon giving over Captain Hughes's note to Lydia's maid, Michele had not been surprised when she saw a change for the better in her cousin's overall demeanor. However, she had not expected Lydia's initial euphoria to sustain her for very long. Michele found Lydia's sudden calm acceptance of her circumstances odd, until it crossed her mind that her cousin, by using her personal maid as a go-between, could have remained in clandestine communication with Captain Hughes. Michele felt her suspicions justified when Lydia did not seem particularly affected by her father's continued barring of Captain Hughes from the house. Michele wondered if she had given more credit to Captain Hughes's sense of honor than it deserved, for if ever there was a young lady who was ripe for forbidden assignations, it was Lydia.

Mr. Davenport was unable to withstand the pressures of his own stinging conscience and his daughter's subdued manner. He gave in and rescinded his ultimatums over Lydia, forgave her for her waywardness, and finally resigned himself that she would never be Lady Randol. However, he remained adamant against Captain Hughes, unreasonably sticking to his belief that that gentleman was solely to blame for the rift between himself and his beloved daughter.

16

One morning Michele entered the breakfast room to discover Lady Basinberry already at the table, deep into the contemplation of the morning's stack of invitations. Michele seated herself, replying to the footman's soft query that she would like eggs and a slice of ham from the sideboard. She then served herself coffee. "Good morning, my lady," she said.

Lady Basinberry was sipping her morning tea and waved in reply. When she put down her cup, she gestured at the pile of invitations on the silver salver. "We have several new invitations, as you see. I wished to consult with you and Lydia which of these would most suit you, for they are all of the same ilk, not frightfully important but assuredly entertaining."

Michele had picked up one of the gilt-edged cards, but at Lady Basinberry's statement she glanced up quickly. "Did you say Lydia?" she asked, surprised.

Lady Basinberry smiled. There was a look of satisfaction in her eyes. "Yes. I spoke quite sharply to Edwin again yesterday evening. He has relented at last."

"But this is marvelous news!" Michele exclaimed.

"I have sent word up to Lydia, and . . . Ah, there you are, my dear. Michele and I were just discussing these invitations. Pray join us, Lydia," Lady Basinberry said, holding out her hand to her younger niece.

Lydia took her aunt's hand and dropped a kiss on her alabaster brow. "Thank you ever so much, Aunt Beatrice!"

137

She sat down at the table, looking fresh and lovely, and she laughed when she met Michele's smiling gaze. "I am to be free again, cousin!"

"So I understand. I am happy for you."

Lydia asked the footman for her usual toast and chocolate before she turned again to her aunt. "I am so grateful to you, Aunt Beatrice. I know that if it had not been for you, Papa still would not have come around. I am so looking forward to getting out into society again, you can have no notion," she said excitedly.

Lady Basinberry held up an admonishing forefinger. "You are not out of the woods yet, my girl. I have wrung a concession from your father that you may attend such assemblies as I deem suitable, and you may now receive callers at home. However, he remains quite adamant against Captain Hughes, and the house remains closed to that particular gentleman."

Lydia's face fell. "I might as well return to my room, then."

Lady Basinberry chided her with an unusual show of gentleness. "Come, Lydia. Such a poor show of spirit is unworthy of a Davenport."

"Oh, can you not understand, Aunt Beatrice? I love Bernard, and to be parted from him is more than I can stand," Lydia said despairingly. There was the sheen of tears in her eyes.

Lady Basinberry had disagreed with her brother's refusal to have Captain Hughes in the house, feeling that Lydia would be the more driven toward him. She had not been able to alter Mr. Davenport's mind, however, and now she said, "I do not agree with your father's policy toward Captain Hughes, but it would not be proper of me to countermand his orders in his own house. However, I shall allow you to speak with Captain Hughes if you should chance to meet him in society. Not to do so would almost certainly cause comment, since it is well-known that he is one of your most persistent admirers."

Lydia's expression brightened immediately. "May I truly, aunt? You are so kind, Aunt Beatrice! Truly the very, very best of aunts!"

Lady Basinberry snorted at such an accolade. "I must warn you not to show a hint of partiality to Captain Hughes, Lydia. Your father is bound to hear that I have allowed you to converse with the captain, and I cannot defend my benevolence on the grounds of its being only common civility to speak with the gentleman if you subsequently throw yourself at Captain Hughes's head. In such circumstances, I would wash my hands of the entire matter."

"I will be circumspection itself," Lydia said, only too happy to make such a promise if it meant she would be allowed to speak with her beloved military gentleman. She plucked a card from the stack of invitations, and her eyes lighted up once more. "Oh, famous! We are invited to a masquerade on Tuesday next. I have always wished to attend one. Michele, have you ever been to a masked ball?"

Michele, who had quietly listened to the conversation that had transpired, nodded. "Indeed I have. It was a vast masked company, lent mystery and romance by the pretense of anonymity. It was all very outrageous and completely delightful. I enjoyed myself immensely." She laughed at Lydia's envious expression. "You are of a mind ripe for such frivolities, cousin, I can see."

"I cannot think of anything more delightful," agreed Lydia. She read the invitation again, a smile on her lips and anticipation in her eyes. "What delicious fun we shall have."

"I am sorry that I must disappoint you, Lydia. We will not be attending the masquerade. The hostess is not of the best *ton*," said Lady Basinberry without looking up as she perused another invitation.

Lydia's mouth fell open in dismay. "But why ever not, aunt? Even if the hostess is not quite the thing, I know that simply everyone will be there."

"Precisely so, Lydia. The guests at these sorts of functions are a mixture of gentlefolk and the vulgar. It is not the sort of company that I wish you to be associating with." Lady Basinberry saw that her niece was drawing breath to argue, and she said firmly, "Not another word, Lydia. My decision is quite final."

Michele watched the disappointment come over her

cousin's face and she regretted that she had described her own experience of a masked ball with such enthusiasm. She wished that Lydia could be brought back to her former light-hearted self. Her cousin had had so few nice treats in the last fortnight and more. Michele turned to Lady Basinberry. "My lady, perhaps I may offer a compromise."

"Not you also, Michele. I had thought you past such frivolous entertainments," Lady Basinberry said, sighing.

Michele laughed. "I admit to a taste for frivolity, then. A masquerade is always amusing in the proper company. Perhaps Lydia's wish for an evening in masks may be met by a masquerade night at Vauxhall Gardens."

"Oh," breathed Lydia. She turned a hopeful gaze on Lady Basinberry. "Pray say that we may go, aunt. I should like it excessively."

Lydia's pathetic eagerness was patent. Lady Basinberry could not find it within her to again dash the gathering anticipation in her niece's eyes. She pursed her mouth thoughtfully. "I have no real objection, Lydia, if it is to be a small private party."

Lydia clasped her hands together in an excess of happy emotion. "The party will be all that is respectable. It shall be Michele and I and you and dear Papa—"

Lady Basinberry snorted. "I wish that I might see Edwin draped in a domino with a mask over his face. What a ludicrous thought!" Her thin lips turned up in a slow malicious smile. "And it is one that I find undeniably entertaining. I shall speak to your father, Lydia. I believe that a masquerade night at Vauxhall will be quite an unexceptionable outing."

Lydia was radiant. She jumped up from the table. "How fortunate that I planned to go to the shops on my first day out, for I do not own a domino and I must order one at once."

Michele rose as well. "Do you mean to go immediately? I think that I shall bear you company, for I did not bring a domino with me from Brussels."

Lydia looked somewhat startled. "Oh! That is, I had meant to take my maid with me. I expect it to be a rather dull outing, you know."

Michele raised her brows, feeling somewhat surprised. "I beg pardon, cousin. I did not realize that you would prefer your own company."

Lydia flushed, aware that Lady Basinberry was regarding her with speculative curiosity. "It is not that, of course not! I suppose that I am so used to being alone these days that I did not express myself well. Pray do come, Michele, and we shall leave my maid at home. Then we shall not be crushed among the packages in the carriage, for I mean to spend every last farthing of my pin money."

Her dark eyes dancing, Michele said, "I doubt that my uncle would approve of such a plan."

Lydia tossed her head, her expression defiant. "Papa can hardly expect me to toe the line when he has behaved so abominably." She swept out of the breakfast room, leaving her cousin and her aunt staring after her.

Lady Basinberry poured herself another cup of tea. "I think Edwin made a graver error than even I realized," she commented with a shade of satisfaction. Lydia's show of independence had pleased her. She had not thought the girl capable of such spirit.

"I shall try to curb Lydia's worst impulses," Michele said.

"I do thank you, my dear. But perhaps it would be best simply to allow Lydia her head. I would rather that she express her resentment by buying out the shops than cast her energies into less acceptable avenues. Captain Hughes is not out of the picture, after all."

Michele contemplated her aunt's expression. "I take your meaning, of course. However, I promise you that Lydia shall behave with decorum while in my company."

Lady Basinberry smiled. "You are a staunch ally, Michele. I am grateful. Lydia will be waiting for you. I expect that I shall not see either of you again until tea." Recognizing that she was dismissed, Michele left her ladyship alone to drink her tea.

Lydia insisted that they first visit a glover and a milliner before going on to the modiste's shop. "My white gloves are quite soiled even after laundering. I simply cannot reenter society with yellowed gloves," Lydia said as she chose a pair and handed them to the saleswoman.

"And the milliner?" asked Michele. "I know full well that you have already a hat for every occasion."

Lydia dimpled and slid a mischievous glance at her cousin. "I do, of course, and some I have not yet worn. But I should like to present Papa with a truly outrageous bill for behaving in *such* a way." Lydia tripped out of the glover's with Michele laughing in her wake.

The visit to the milliner proved to be a very pleasant half-hour of browsing among ribbons and feathers and bonnets of straw, lace, and velvet. While Lydia did her determined best to discover the most opulently trimmed and frivolous bonnet that she could, Michele found herself succumbing to temptation as well. The hat she chose was one of chip straw, trimmed in blue satin and lace and white feathers. She set the bow jauntily under one ear.

"How very becoming it is on you, Michele," said Lydia, coming up behind her cousin and inspecting Michele's choice with approval.

Michele glanced past her own reflection in the mirror to smile at her cousin. What she saw made her eyes widen. She spun around on the seat. "My word!" she exclaimed, ogling the befeathered and beaded creation crowning Lydia's head.

Lydia giggled and raised her hand to brush the wide brim of the bonnet she wore. "It *is* frightful, is it not? Papa will have a fit," she said cheerfully.

"Indeed he will," said Michele, awed. She waited until her cousin had given the huge bonnet over into the reverent care of the saleswoman. She said urgently, "Lydia, you do not truly mean to buy that ridiculous contraption, surely!"

"Most definitely I do. And I shall wear it, too," Lydia said.

When they left the milliner's, it was to give into the care of their driver two large bandboxes. Lydia next directed the driver to the address of the modiste, and she and Michele alighted to enter the shop. The modiste instantly recognized the young ladies and rushed over, waving aside the lesser attentions of her assistant. "Miss Davenport, Mademoiselle du Bois, it is a pleasure! Is the gracious Lady Basinberry not accompanying you this morning?'' she said, her bright eyes darting toward the door.

''We are on our own today, madame,'' said Michele with a smile. ''And we have come on a special quest. Miss Davenport wishes to attend a masquerade at Vauxhall and we shall each require a domino.''

''Ah! The masquerade! It is a *divertissement* incomparable. Of a certainty I shall assist in discovering for you the most enchanting of silks for the dominoes,'' the modiste said enthusiastically. She begged the ladies to be comfortable and began to bring bolts of silk for their inspection. Lydia was dazzled by the rich colors and the fluid feel of the fabrics. She was unable to make up her mind which shades she preferred, and the modiste, smelling an opportunity to guide a client into a particularly dear purchase, bent her efforts in guiding Lydia to a decision of mutual satisfaction.

For several minutes Michele was left to her own devices, and in short order she chose a silk of shimmering slate blue. She brushed her fingers over the cool fabric, a faint smile of remembrance on her lips. The last time she had attended a masquerade it had been in the company of a rakish gentleman who had taken liberties of her very willing lips. Michele sighed and shook her head, able to laugh a little. Her memories seemed always filled with enchanted moments. It was a pity that the gentleman in question no longer cared for her in just that way.

''A most marvelous shade, mademoiselle. I salute your cleverness, for such a blue shall blend with whatever your escort may choose,'' the modiste said, coming to Michele's side.

Michele flashed a smile, her eyes twinkling. ''And I had thought that I chose it to complement my coloring,'' she said humorously.

''Certainly it does. What do you think of my selection?'' asked Lydia.

Michele looked at the delicate rose pink that her cousin indicated and she said sincerely, ''You will be perfectly adorable in it.''

Lydia flushed with pleasure. "Handsome indeed, cousin! We have been quite successful in our outing, I think. Indeed, if we had done nothing else all the morning, I would be satisfied."

"What, and give up that monstrous hat of yours? Fie on you for your caprice, Lydia," Michele said. Her cousin owned that she had forgotten the hat. With a few more words to the modiste, the price of the dominoes that were to be made up from the silks was settled upon, as well as a time of delivery, and the ladies left the shop.

Lydia cast a glance up at the blue sky. "Michele, it is such a beautiful morning. Let's not waste a moment more of it tooling about to the shops, but instead let's go for a promenade in the park."

"I admit to a liking for the notion. Very well, you know best where to direct the driver, Lydia," Michele said, settling herself in the carriage amidst the various packages that had accumulated.

Lydia happily did so, and for the few minutes it took to reach the park, she chattered in her former sunny way. Michele was content to allow her cousin to carry the livelier end of the conversation, finding simple enjoyment in Lydia's return of high spirits. Indeed, Lydia's eyes had brightened almost to stars, and the becoming color had returned to her cheeks. Michele thought she had not seen Lydia look so lovely in some weeks.

The carriage stopped and the driver handed the ladies down. Lydia and Michele started down one of the green walkways that meandered under the arching branches of the trees. With each passing moment Lydia appeared to become more animated. She spoke in breathless accents and her eyes darted constantly ahead as though in anticipation. Michele became concerned about her cousin's barely suppressed excitement, but she did not have long to wonder at the reason for it.

A gentleman detached himself from a wide tree trunk and stepped out of the deep shade. Michele instantly recognized him. She glanced quickly at her cousin's face, which was registering radiant gladness. "Oh Lydia!"

But Lydia was deaf to her cousin's tone of dismay. She ran quickly to meet Captain Hughes, who caught her hands and reverently raised each in turn to his lips. They spoke briefly before closing the distance between themselves and Michele, who stood watching the meeting with disbelief and anger. Her eyes were darker than normal with her outrage. Michele found it difficult to accept that Lydia had used her to cover a rendezvous with Captain Hughes, especially when she had assured Lady Basinberry not two hours past that this sort of meeting would not take place under her aegis.

Lydia was not insensitive to the anger in her cousin's flashing eyes. She said quietly, "I do apologize, Michele. It was not my intention that you be involved. My maid was to have been with me today, you see, and there was not time before we left the town house to send a message to Bernard."

"Of course. I understand perfectly. I am the red herring, *en effet*," Michele said coolly. Her nod for Captain Hughes was barely civil. "I had not expected this of you, sir."

Captain Hughes reddened, but his frank gaze did not waver from her accusing stare. "Believe me, I acquiesced in this abominable subterfuge with the utmost reluctance. But Lydia was obviously in such dire need of my ear that I could not gainsay her."

Michele was unmoved. "You are a man of little backbone and less honor, sir."

"I shall not allow you to insult Bernard in such a fashion, cousin," said Lydia, her own temper rising. At Michele's swift negative gesture, she realized that she could not afford to further antagonize her cousin. With an effort Lydia caught back her anger and tried a faltering smile. "Pray try to understand, Michele. I am not allowed to see Bernard. I have been perfectly distracted at the pain of not seeing or speaking with him. Can you not allow me just a few moments? I beg you, cousin."

Looking into Lydia's tearful eyes, Michele was shaken by a sudden surge of sympathy. It was true, Lydia had been torn from the man she claimed to love and had been forbidden his company. Never mind that she had managed to be in some sort of communication with him; it was hardly the same as seeing his face or hearing his voice. Michele thought she more than anyone else must appreciate the importance of such small joys. She sighed, nodding in defeat. "I shall wait here for you, Lydia. But pray do not leave my sight. I should not like to be obliged to chase you down."

Lydia flashed a heartfelt smile. "I do thank you, cousin!" Her escort nodded his thanks as well, and the couple turned to walk slowly up the path, their heads close together and their conversation low. They stopped several paces ahead and turned to face each other, conversing still.

Michele pretended an inordinate interest in a patch of flowers, but she kept one eye on her cousin and Captain Hughes. Her sense of duty would not be still, voicing the insidious suspicion that Lydia and her lover meant to fly for a destination unknown. She shuddered when she envisioned returning to the town house without Lydia and attempting to explain to her uncle how she had been hoodwinked and that his daughter had eloped with the one man above all others that he held in abhorrence. But her imaginings came to nothing after all, as Lydia and Captain Hughes parted at last, he to walk quickly away in the opposite direction while Lydia rejoined Michele.

"Thank you, cousin. I can never repay you for your faith in me," Lydia said.

"Can you not? I will tell you, then. Promise me that you have not made arrangements to elope with Captain Hughes."

Lydia stared at her in astonishment and gathering hurt. "Michele! As if I could ever contemplate such a scandalous thing. Why, it would go against everything that I have been taught."

Lydia's obvious surprise both relieved Michele and made her ashamed of her base suspicions. "I am sorry, Lydia. Of course you would not. But I was so taken aback, and, yes, angered, at being used as your unwitting confederate that I did not think clearly. Lydia, since you have reassured me that this meeting was harmless, I shall say nothing about it, for the knowledge of it would surely hurt you in my uncle's eyes. But I do not wish to be a party to any such thing again."

"You have my word on that, cousin. Shall we return to

the carriage? I am certain that it must be coming on luncheon,'' Lydia said.

Michele agreed that the hour had become late, and as they returned to the carriage, they spoke on indifferent topics. The rendezvous with Captain Hughes was never referred to again.

17

Lydia celebrated her freedom by diving into a whirl of social functions. The long-awaited trip to Astley's Circus in the congenial company of the young Hedgeworths and the Murray brothers was but the first and most sedate of her outings. She insisted upon accepting as many invitations as she possibly could, and when Mr. Davenport remonstrated with her, saying that she was attempting too much, Lydia, with an unusually mulish look in her blue eyes, said, "I have no intention of letting any more of the Season pass me by, Papa. Especially since it is expected of me to make a brilliant match!"

Mr. Davenport was silenced. He beat a bewildered retreat, not at all understanding the new streak of firm determination in his formerly sweet and biddable daughter. "It is all the fault of that Hughes fellow," he muttered.

Lady Basinberry was less astonished than her brother by Lydia's behavior. "I do not know what Edwin expected. Anyone else with the wit God graced him with would have been unsurprised by this rebelliousness of Lydia's. But that is Edwin all over. He never looks past his own nose," she said.

Michele did not reply to Lady Basinberry's irritated observation, keeping her own counsel. She also had thought it unrealistic of Mr. Davenport to assume that his relationship with his daughter would remain the same after the manner in which he had treated her. But Lydia's present course was becoming extreme, and she observed Lydia's almost feverish

intensity with growing concern. Even now as she watched
from across the ballroom, Lydia was flirting outrageously
with every gentleman who came within her vicinity. Her
cousin was swiftly becoming touted as a dreadful flirt,
Michele thought. She glanced at Captain Hughes, who made
up one of Lydia's circle of admirers, and she saw from the
stoniness of his expression that he at least was not enjoying
Lydia's newfound popularity. Michele started making her
way unobtrusively toward her cousin with the object of
whispering a word of advice.

Lydia's change in character when she reentered society
had at first been viewed with astonishment and had quickly
become something of a minor scandal. Not all were disapproving, however, for Lydia sparkled with laughter and
her quick teasing glances had served to attract several new
admirers. When Michele approached her, she stood laughing
amidst half a dozen gentlemen who vied for the favor of her
hand in to dinner.

"Why, sir! How very witty of you, to be sure. You almost
persuade me," said Lydia. She glanced archly toward a
gentleman who stood slightly apart. "And you, Captain
Hughes? Do you not also have any witticisms to put forth
on your own behalf?"

"I fear that I am not of the same caliber of wit," Captain
Hughes said quietly. He excused himself from the group.
An expression of acute disappointment flitted across Lydia's
face as she saw him walk away, but she turned a determined
smile on another of her suitors.

Captain Hughes saw Michele and approached her.
"Mademoiselle du Bois, good evening."

She gave her hand to him. "Captain Hughes, it is always
a pleasure to speak with you. I have been hesitant in
attempting to capture your attention, not wishing to call you
away from Lydia."

Captain Hughes smiled, a shade of grimness entering his
eyes. His glance traveled to his beloved, who had apparently
made her choice of escort and was bestowing her hand upon
the winner amidst the good-natured complaints of the rest.

"I do not think that Miss Davenport shall much miss me," he said.

Michele looked up at him with earnest concern. "You must not think so, sir. Lydia is still very much in love with you."

Captain Hughes turned his gaze on her. He shook his head, though his smile did lighten. "You are loyal and softhearted, mademoiselle. But I do have eyes in my head. Miss Davenport has learned to care less for me, and the most honorable course left to me is to perform a graceful exit from her circle of intimates."

Michele caught at his sleeve. "Captain, you must believe this when I tell you. Lydia has played the part of the flirt these last weeks because she hopes to punish her father for his shameful conduct. Believe me, Mr. Davenport has been made much bewildered and anxious by these tactics, but I do believe that Lydia honestly means nothing by her actions."

Captain Hughes covered Michele's hand with his own and smiled rather sadly. "I wish that I could believe you, mademoiselle. But Lydia—Miss Davenport—vouchsafes me the veriest commonplaces when we meet. I am not allowed to call, and she will not come apart with me for even a few minutes at a ball to grant me a few private words. What am I to think?"

Michele realized that the case was more desperate than she had known. Apparently Lydia had not chosen to tell her beloved of the close watch set on her by Lady Basinberry, who had insisted that Lydia should not encourage Captain Hughes by the least sign. "Captain, allow me to explain—"

He interrupted her, saying softly, "It would be of little use. I cannot continue as I have, with but a glance from her or the slightest pressure of her fingers on mine when I greet her . . ." His voice shook, and he paused to gather his control. He said gravely, "I think it best that I withdraw from the lists. Pray convey to . . . to Miss Davenport my eternal admiration and my regrets." He bowed and quickly walked away, despite Michele's entreaty to remain and hear her out.

Michele was on the point of following the captain, but she was frustrated in her decision by the appearance of Sir Lionel

Corbett, who commented as he observed Captain Hughes's hasty retreat, "Now, what is the matter with our dear captain? He was wearing the gloomiest expression that I have ever chanced to encounter on his bland countenance."

Michele forced back a sharp retort, knowing better than to offer anything that might be food for the gossip mill. She gave the slightest of shrugs and said in an indifferent voice, "Is he? I had not particularly noticed. Sir Lionel, have you come to take me in to dinner?"

He flashed a brilliant smile, all interest in Captain Hughes dissolving. "Indeed, mademoiselle, I would be most honored to do so," he said warmly.

Michele smiled as she placed her fingers on his arm. "Then let us go in, sir." Sir Lionel escorted her into the dining room and seated her with a flourish at their table, at which Lydia was already waiting. Sir Lionel left to fill plates for Michele and for himself. Michele knew that Lydia's escort must be on the same errand, and she seized the opportunity to talk with her cousin. "Lydia, I spoke to Captain Hughes but five minutes past. He is convinced that you no longer care for him because of your abominable behavior this past fortnight."

"Oh, no! Bernard *could* not believe such a thing," Lydia exclaimed, dismayed.

"What else could he think, when you have played him fast and loose these last several days without any explanation? It was obvious that you had not told him everything of your present circumstances," Michele said.

Lydia restlessly played with her fan. "I thought he understood. About Papa, I mean. That day in the park I told him that I . . . Oh, Michele, Aunt Beatrice watches and listens so! I cannot say more than two words to Bernard before she sweeps down on me. I had hoped by being present at every function I would see more of Bernard, but even then I dare utter only the most insipid pleasantries for fear I may be overheard. We are always in the midst of a crowded assembly. I cannot say what is truly in my heart. As for my flirting, I had hoped that if I attracted several admirers, Bernard's attentions would not be as noticeable to our aunt."

She snapped shut her fan and looked across the table. Michele was startled by the sheen of unhappy tears in her cousin's eyes. "Michele, Bernard is the only one who matters to me. I pretend to be gay and lighthearted to cover my true feelings. It has all become intolerable to me! I do not know that I can go on in this fashion much longer."

Lydia's voice held a desperate note that Michele had never heard before. She reached over to give a sympathetic squeeze to her cousin's hand. "That is just what Captain Hughes said. We must contrive something before all is lost," she said. Lydia stared at her, startled and shaken. Her lips parted on a question. Michele saw that the gentlemen were returning to the table and she gave a warning shake of her head. "We shall finish our conversation later, cousin."

"What's this? I do believe the lovely ladies are telling secrets, Mr. Thorpe," Sir Lionel said jovially. His intelligent eyes took in Lydia's downcast eyes and then traveled to Michele's bland expression.

"Of course we are, sir. That is a lady's prerogative," retorted Michele. "And no, we shall not enlighten you."

Mr. Thorpe laughed. "That is a set-down if ever I heard one, Sir Lionel."

"Quite. My ears are scorched," Sir Lionel agreed. Under cover of the ensuing laughter, Michele smiled encouragingly at her cousin. Lydia straightened and made an obvious attempt to appear as usual, even smiling at Mr. Thorpe's gallantries.

Sometime during the dinner hour Michele chanced to glance over the crowded tables about them. She met Lord Randol's somber gaze. There was something speculative, even questioning in his eyes that rattled her composure. She felt the heat rise in her face. He raised his wineglass in acknowledgment of her and then allowed his glance to drift past.

Michele swallowed. She glanced around at her dinner companions, wondering if any had noticed her discomfiture, but the gentlemen were laughing at some artless witticism that Lydia had uttered. Michele was thus afforded a minute of reflection. She did not know what to think of that peculiar expression in Lord Randol's eyes. His initial antipathy toward her seemed to have abated remarkably since the occasion of his last visit to the town house and Lydia's clear reununciation of his suit. He had not called there since, and whenever he had met Lydia, Lady Basinberry, or herself, he had merely bowed and made a courteous remark or two in passing before he sauntered on to join other companions. He never remained long in their company, except perhaps for form's sake to solicit a set with Lydia.

Michele knew that she should be grateful that he no longer goaded her with hateful words, but perversely she would have preferred his active dislike to his present formal indifference. The hope she had held that her driving of the phaeton would elicit an ongoing response from him had not advanced past their one conversation. She had seen him several times out in his own carriage, but he had not again indicated by word or look that he desired to speak with her. Michele was forced to the unwelcome conclusion that he really did not care for her in any way. When she glanced at Lydia, she thought that her cousin's romantic troubles were but a counterpoint to her own unhappy state.

"Is anything troubling you, Michele?"

Michele looked up at Sir Lionel quickly, and she considered him dispassionately. He was generally acknowledged to be a handsome gentleman of polished address and style. He had proved himself to be completely devoted to her. Michele knew that she could not ask for more in a gentleman, but even so, she could not love Sir Lionel Corbett. She wondered whatever could be wrong with her that she still loved a gentleman who obviously wanted nothing to do with her. "Troubling me? Why, nothing at all, Sir Lionel," she said. At once she saw the disbelief in his keen blue eyes. She smiled faintly and made a very Gallic gesture. "Oh, very well, I shall admit to the slightest of migraines. But it is of little consequence, I assure you."

"On the contrary, I will not have it recalled later that I played part in a dreary evening. I insist that you go home at once, Michele," Sir Lionel said. He smiled at her, raising her fingers briefly yet warmly to his lips. "I am thoroughly selfish, you see. I wish that every moment in my company be remembered as pleasant. Come, I shall escort you myself."

Lydia had been listening to the exchange, giving but half an ear to her dinner partner's latest extravagant compliment, and now she interjected, "Michele, I would feel badly if you were to go home alone. I shall accompany you, I think."

Despite Mr. Thorpe's well-bred protests, Lydia was firm in her decision. Within a very few minutes Lydia and Michele had excused themselves to their hostess and notified Lady Basinberry of their intent, promising to send the carriage back for her ladyship, to be available when she had tired of the soiree.

Sir Lionel and Mr. Thorpe saw the ladies to their carriage. Sir Lionel promised to call on Michele with the mysterious assurance of having something that he wished to lay before her for consideration. "I believe it as auspicious a time as any to talk with you on a subject close to my heart," he said.

Michele felt her heart sink. She put him off as best she could, but she knew it to be inevitable that he would declare himself once more. And she wondered whether she could again reject him with the same confidence that she had before. She was no longer so certain that she wanted to live her life entirely alone. However, the decision was being brought on her too suddenly, and she made Lydia promise not to leave her alone with Sir Lionel whenever he should choose to call.

Lydia looked at her in the flickering of the passing lamplights. "I understand, of course. And I shall do as you ask. But are you certain that it is what you want?"

Michele shook her head. "I no longer know what it is that I hope for. I know only that I need time to choose."

"Do not leave it so long that you choose wrongly. Only see what has happened to me with Bernard, all because I assumed that he would understand my purpose in flirting with other gentlemen," Lydia said bitterly.

Michele forgot her own dilemma in the face of her cousin's wretched unhappiness. "I shall speak with Captain Hughes, I promise you, Lydia. It will all work out, you will see." She was not so confident as she sounded, but she hoped that for Lydia's sake she was right.

18

Lord Randol looked every inch the fine gentleman that morning. His beaver was set on his head at a rakish angle, well-starched points rose out of his perfectly executed cravat, the fit of his coat was superb, and his legs were encased in buff pantaloons that smoothed without a marring wrinkle into black Hessians of immaculate polish.

He was driving his phaeton down the crowded street when he chanced to sight a familiar figure on the walk. He gave only half his attention to the task of guiding his phaeton safely between a bowling tilbury and a heavy wagon while he wondered what Michele du Bois was doing afoot. Without at once realizing the significance, he saw a roughly dressed individual jostle against her. An instant later another man had stripped her of her reticule and shoved her into the path of a draycart.

Lord Randol shouted. He came to a stand as quickly as he could haul his team to the curb. Snubbing the reins, he leapt down and thrust his way through the crowd that was already beginning to form. Michele sat on the pavement, half-supported by a burly gentleman. Her face was extremely white. "Michele!" Lord Randol exclaimed sharply. He went down on one knee beside her.

She looked up quickly at the sound of his voice. A glad light sprang into her eyes. "Anthony."

The burly gentleman, who was becoming acutely embarrassed by the presence of a lady in his arms, was greatly relieved that the lady seemed to know the well-dressed gentle-

157

man. "It were a pair of hooligans, sir. Took the young lady's purse, they did, and pushed her into my cart deliberate-like."

"I saw it from the street," Lord Randol said shortly, sparing a brief nod of thanks for the man. He held out his hand peremptorily to Michele. "Let me help you stand."

Michele bit her lip. Her eyes appealed to him. "I have twisted my ankle, my lord."

"It were a bad tumble, guvnor. Like as not the ankle be broken," the drayman said helpfully.

Lord Randol was irritated by the man's pessimistic prediction when he saw that Michele's face whitened to an even greater degree. He said brusquely, "There is nothing for it, then." Without further ado he lifted Michele up into his arms and carried her toward his phaeton, several of the curious onlookers trailing in his wake. Lord Randol was surprised by how light she felt in his arms. She was pressed close against him and her breath was warm on his cheek. When he turned his head, he met her midnight-blue eyes. The dark color, just short of true black, had never ceased to amaze him, and he remembered likening her eyes to a dark velvety sky. The whimsicality of his thoughts annoyed him, but not as much as his own feelings. The sensations stirring in him had little to do with acting the good Samaritan. Quite the contrary, he thought grimly. More harshly than he intended, he said, "You must let go my neck and grasp the rail if I am to help you into the phaeton."

Michele's face flamed and she averted her wide gaze, depriving him of the wonder of her marvelous eyes. She said not a word until she was settled on the seat and he was preparing to climb up beside her. "I . . . I dropped some books, my lord?"

Lord Randol grunted. He turned, to find the drayman with the volumes already in hand. He thanked the man and handed the books up to Michele. Then he sprang up into the phaeton. Taking up the reins and his whip, he pointed his horses into the milling traffic. Only then did he glance again at Michele. "I apologize for my rough tone earlier. It was uncalled-for."

She made a dismissive gesture, not looking at him. "It was nothing, my lord," she said formally.

He saw that she favored her right foot, resting it on top of her other foot, and that she winced when the phaeton took a particularly hard jolt. "If it is any comfort to you, I do not think that your ankle is broken, but only sprained."

"Your consideration is appreciated, my lord."

Lord Randol felt a spurt of annoyance that she did not meet his eyes. "What the devil were you doing walking at all, and unchaperoned to boot? You should know better than to go traipsing off without your maid, at the least."

"My maid has the cold. And I was walking only a few blocks to the lending library. I never thought that—" Michele bit off what she had started to say, realizing of a sudden that she was not required to answer to him. She turned an indignant expression on him. "What gives you the right to censor me, my lord?"

"As a gentleman I have the duty to express concern for a lady of my acquaintance," Lord Randol said stiffly.

"Your concern is noted, my lord. Pray let's leave it at that, for you have made it plain these months that any claim that once lay between us no longer exists," Michele said with a touch of bitterness. "There is the town house. I wish to be let down at once, if you please."

Lord Randol swung the phaeton over to the curb and snubbed the reins, his thoughts revolving about the odd catch in her voice when she had spoken. It could not be entirely owing to the pain she was suffering, he knew. He leapt down from the seat and went around the phaeton to offer his aid to Michele. She had already risen from the seat and started to maneuver herself down, when her ankle seemed to give way. She practically fell into his waiting arms. She made a determined movement to be set down, but he tightened his hold about her and carried her up the steps to the front door, which was opened by the porter. "My lord! Mademoiselle, what has happened?" the servant exclaimed.

"Mademoiselle du Bois was set upon by a pair of thieves," said Lord Randol shortly. He strode toward the drawing room, and the porter, realizing his intent, ran ahead to thrust open the door.

Lady Basinberry started up from her seat beside the fireplace. Her embroidery hoop dropped from her hands as she stared in astonishment. "Lord Randol! Michele, child! You are white as a sheet. My lord, what has happened?"

He set Michele down on a convenient settee. She averted her face from him and he looked across at Lady Basinberry. "I shall allow Mademoiselle du Bois to explain. Perhaps in future you will see that she does not go walking about unattended, my lady," he said. "I have left my team standing. Pray excuse me, my lady. A pleasure, as always." He bowed himself out of the drawing room and left the town house.

As he drove away he could not stop recalling Michele du Bois's white face and his own bewilderingly protective feelings upon seeing her attacked. He tried to rationalize that he would have reacted in the same manner regardless of the lady's identity, but deep down he knew that the unholy rage he felt toward those who had set upon Michele was greater than any he would have felt on another lady's behalf. He was an intelligent man and it did not take long before he acknowledged that he regarded Michele du Bois with very different emotions than he had once attached to her. He had deliberately and painstakingly fed his hatred of her, but the encounters between them and her manner toward him had served to consistently rob his banked fury of its potency. "Damn her beautiful dark eyes," he muttered.

His expressed interest in Lydia Davenport had thrust him into close proximity with Michele, a situation that he had quickly discovered to be intolerable. There had been a certain measure of relief for him when he was able to distance himself from Lydia Davenport's circle after the young lady's unexpected disclosure.

Lord Randol was still immeasurably grateful that he was no longer obligated to offer for Lydia Davenport. He could not recall why he had ever chosen to press his suit with her when she was not at all what he required in a bride. Miss Davenport was too biddable and too sweet-natured; her hair and eyes were too light; her speech lacked a certain nearly intangible Gallic lilt; her figure, though quite good, lacked the dash and allure of that of another lady. In short, Miss Lydia Davenport was not Mademoiselle Michele du Bois and could never replace her cousin in his affections.

Lord Randol shook his head, a black frown forming on his face. He was still in love with Michele du Bois and it did not please him to realize it. The thought was distinctly unpalatable and he reacted by seeking physical release. Upon reaching the park, he whipped up his team and gave the horses a good run. Then he returned them to the stables that he patronized and sauntered through town.

Lord Randol whiled away an indifferent day, paying a visit to Gentleman Jackson's Saloon to watch other sporting bloods, who were not constrained by stiffened and damaged physiques, to spar with the master. On catching sight of the viscount, Jackson made a point of speaking with him and offered some private advice on working his shoulder. Lord Randol quietly thanked the pugilist, aware that the clumsy words were meant in the spirit of friendship. He left the saloon soon afterward and made his way to his club to indulge in a few hands of piquet. He lost for the most part, which seemed to fit his mood exactly.

When he returned to his house, he picked up the cards in the tray and carelessly flipped through the invitations that he had accepted for that evening. None appealed to his jaded, restless spirits until he came across the dinner party at the Earl of Kenmare's town house. He recalled the earl as a pleasant gentleman, quiet but shrewd, who had been a steadying influence in the hectic days before Waterloo, when many of the English tourists in Brussels had been made nervous by Napoleon's last march. As for the countess, she had always shown him a graciousness that was difficult to resist. All in all, the Kenmare dinner party was exactly what he needed to take his mind off his dour thoughts.

Lord Randol called for his valet, and when the man appeared, the tedious business of dressing began. His coats were cut fashionably close-fitting, and with his stiff shoulder he required assistance in getting in or out of the garments.

Lord Randol stepped out of his town house attired for the

evening in a dark blue coat with flat gilt buttons, over a ruffled shirt and silk waistcoat, and pantaloon trousers that strapped under the arches of his Spanish leather dress shoes. He settled inside his carriage, and his driver whipped up the horses for the short ride to the Kenmare town house, which was situated in the most fashionable part of London.

When he arrived, Lord Randol entered the ballroom and was greeted by the Earl of Kenmare and the countess. Lady Kenmare was particularly warm in her greeting. "I recall you very well, my lord. A most dashing and romantic figure you struck in your regimentals," she said, a dimple appearing in her cheek.

Lord Randol smiled. "You are too kind, my lady. It all seems very long ago."

"Indeed it does. Such a stirring and terrible time. I hope never to see its like again in my lifetime. There were so many bright young lives lost," Lady Kenmare said somberly. She shook her head, and her smile returned. "I do apologize, Lord Randol. For a moment I fell into memories that are best left to one's solitary reflection. On a happier note, I must tell you that I have paired you at dinner with an old friend. I trust you will forgive my matchmaking instinct, but I shall be honest and confess that I did not try very hard to resist the impulse." Her gray eyes invited him to share in her amusement at herself.

Lord Randol laughed. He made an elaborate bow. "Of course, ma'am. I hold myself completely at your service."

She held out her hand to him once more. "Thank you, my lord. I know how awkward it is when one is placed in such a position, but just this once I thought I would give fate a gentle nudge."

The earl had listened to the exchange with some amusement. "Mary, I suspect that his lordship is beginning to regret his coming tonight. I think I shall take him off with me before you render him completely a *blancmange*."

Lady Kenmare was not at all offended by her husband's dry manner. "Yes, do; but do not allow Lord Randol to stray too far. I have high hopes for him this evening." She waved them off and turned to greet another arriving guest.

Lord Randol spent a congenial half-hour with the earl and several other acquaintances before dinner was announced. He was in a mellow frame of mind when Lady Kenmare came up and presented to him his table partner. When his eyes fell on the countess's companion, all his enjoyment in the evening fled. Michele stared at him, and her expression was as incredulous as he knew his must be. Lord Randol made an effort to appear indifferent. He took Michele's nerveless hand and raised her fingers to his lips. "Indeed, this is a surprise. When you mentioned an old friend, Lady Kenmare, I had no notion how dated the acquaintanceship would be." He felt rather than saw the shudder that went through Michele, and his lips tightened.

Lady Kenmare's smile wavered. A slightly anxious look appeared in her eyes. She had caught the twin looks of astonishment that had been in their faces before polite masks came down over their expressions. There was none of the quick delight in their eyes that she had anticipated seeing. "I suppose I should have informed each of you of the other's identity. It was such a silly trick, really. But after the manner in which Michele clung to hope in finding you again, only to learn that you were among the dead, my lord, I assumed that . . ." Her voice faltered way in dismay.

Michele gave a swift smile of reassurance for Lady Kenmare. "It was a kind thought, my lady. Lord Randol and I are both conscious of it."

Despite the shock that he had just sustained, Lord Randol was not to be outdone in courtesy. "Indeed, Mademoiselle du Bois and I should have much to talk about over dinner. I anticipate a most interesting evening."

Lady Kenmare was relieved. For a moment she had had the sinking sensation that she had committed an unforgivable *faux pas*. "I am so glad. For a moment I wondered . . . But that is neither here nor there. Pray enjoy yourselves." She was gone in the next instant, to find her own escort, and Lord Randol and Michele were left standing awkwardly together. They looked at each other for a long moment. Then he offered his arm to her and they followed the other guests in to dinner.

19

The day after the Kenmare dinner party, boxes delivered from the modiste arrived while the ladies were idling away the afternoon. Lydia insisted that the boxes be brought directly into the drawing room, and when Michele gently remonstrated, she said, "Oh, what can it matter? We have not had a visitor in hours." Without further ado, she lifted the lid of one bandbox and tore through the white tissue. A folded domino of pale rose was revealed. "How lovely it is!" she exclaimed. Lydia freed the silken garment from the box and slipped it over her day dress. She went to look at herself in the large mirror that hung above the fireplace mantel, and was immensely pleased at what little of herself she could see. "It goes marvelously with my blue eyes and my blond coloring. Not that my hair will show when I have drawn up the hood, but one must think of these things," she said.

"Quite true," Michele said, undoing the strings of the other bandbox. She lifted the lid and moved aside the top layer of tissue paper. She noticed that Lydia had drawn near to watch with avid curiosity. She laughed and offered the bandbox to her cousin. "Would you like to unbox it, Lydia?" she asked teasingly.

Lydia smiled sheepishly. "You know me so well, Michele." She carefully laid her own domino across the settee so that its long folds cascaded down over the seat before she took the bandbox from Michele's hands. Lydia lifted the domino from the bandbox. White tissue fell away from its silken folds to drift to the carpet. The domino of slate blue shimmered in the sunlight. Lydia drew in a delighted breath. "The color is even more beautiful than it was on the bolt!" She flung the domino about her cousin's shoulders and stepped back, clapping in approval of the effect. "It suits you perfectly, Michele."

"I rather think it does," Michele agreed, fingering the domino. The silk was cool and smooth to the touch. She was surprised how much she was anticipating the masquerade night at Vauxhall.

The drawing-room door opened and a gentleman stepped in. He paused at sight of the drifting tissue and the dominoes. "I hope that I am not intruding."

"Oh, it is you, Sir Lionel! Of course you are not. Is not Michele's domino perfectly lovely?" Lydia said, gesturing proudly at her cousin as though she had conjured up a delightful vision.

"It is indeed." Sir Lionel sauntered in and greeted Michele, who had hastily removed the domino and folded it over her arm. He raised Michele's fingers to his lips. Still retaining her hand, he smiled down at her. "I take it that you and Miss Davenport will be attending a masquerade."

"We are going to Vauxhall Gardens. Lydia had a desire to experience a masked ball, which activity Lady Basinberry frowned upon. This expedition is to be Lydia's reward for giving way so graciously," said Michele, smiling at her cousin. She unobtrusively regained her hand as she turned from Sir Lionel to refold the domino into its box.

Lydia blushed and protested what she felt was a slur on her youth. "Sir Lionel, surely you of all gentlemen must understand. A masquerade is so romantic, so out of the common way."

Sir Lionel seated himself across from the ladies. He crossed one knee over the other and swung his booted toe gently. "Quite so, Miss Davenport. I myself have a definite fondness for such an entertainment. Perhaps I may see you at Vauxhall. When will this party of yours take place, Miss Davenport?"

"Oh, it shan't be a party precisely. My aunt considers

masquerading a rather frivolous and forward entertainment, so it will be just the family and perhaps a few friends. But do join us for dinner in our box if you should find yourself at odds, Sir Lionel. I believe that Papa means to take us to the first masquerade night in June,'' Lydia said. She cast another admiring glance at her domino and fingered it with satisfaction.

''A fitting capstone to a fine Season,'' Sir Lionel said, nodding in his pleasant way. He slanted a laughing glance in Michele's direction. ''And you, mademoiselle? Do you also anticipate this summer evening's entertainment?''

''Certainly, Sir Lionel. I was always one to enjoy to the fullest whatever entertainment was offered,'' Michele said quietly.

''So I recall,'' Sir Lionel said in a warm voice. He glanced at Lydia. ''I had hoped that you might indulge me for a few words, Michele.''

Lydia looked up quickly. She met Michele's gaze of appeal and knew that her cousin wanted her to remain. She began to fold her domino carefully, as though oblivious of whatever else was happening in the room.

''Certainly, Sir Lionel. What is it that you wish of us?'' Michele asked, her tone cool and inquiring.

Sir Lionel appeared reluctant to begin. He threw another glance toward Lydia, but it was obvious to him that she had not taken the hint. He said blankly, ''Do you know, I have forgotten. How very awkward of me, to be sure. But I am certain it will come to me again, perhaps at a more propitious time.'' He stayed for only a few minutes and then took his leave.

When he was gone, Lydia shook her head at her cousin. ''I do not know why you do not give Sir Lionel some encouragement, Michele. It is patently obvious that he still adores you. And you must wed sometime.''

Michele's eyes sparked with laughter. ''You sound so like a determined lady of our acquaintance, Lydia. Do not tell me that you have joined Lady Basinberry's camp and have become determined to marry me off!''

''It is not precisely that, but I do wish you happiness. I

know that you still cannot reconcile Lord Randol's indifference. But, Michele, you must consider the remainder of your life. Here is Sir Lionel—and I daresay I can name one or two others as well—who positively dotes upon you and who could make you very comfortable. Pray, what should stop you from accepting the best that any of these other gentlemen can offer to you?''

Michele's smile held a touch of sadness. ''Perhaps I do not encourage any of these fine gentlemen because their best falls short of what I once had. Lydia, I do not think that I can settle for comfort when once I loved to the depths of my soul and that love was returned in full measure.''

''But—''

''Lydia, after knowing the tenderness of your passion for Captain Hughes, could you willingly pledge yourself to another?'' Michele asked.

Lydia was silent. She began to fold one of the dominoes so that it could be replaced into its bandbox. ''You are right, Michele. It would be impossible, I think. Since we have made peace, I see ever more clearly that Bernard and I are perfect for each other. No one else could possibly fill his place.'' She looked up, pity in her gaze. ''How I wish that it was different between you and Lord Randol. I had hoped . . . I suppose there is no harm in telling you now, but I had hoped that your constant presence at my side would induce his lordship to transfer his attentions from me to you. I had visions of playing the fairy godmother and of bringing the separated lovers back together. I see now that was a rather idiotic notion.''

''On the contrary, it was well-meant,'' Michele said, thinking of Lady Kenmare's attempt to accomplish the selfsame goal. She hugged her cousin. ''Thank you for caring so much, Lydia.''

That evening the Davenport household remained quietly at home instead of leaving the house to attend a social function. After a companionable dinner they settled themselves in the drawing room. The younger ladies decided upon a game of piquet. As Lady Basinberry embroidered, she expressed herself relieved to have nowhere in particular to go. "But I do not complain at our shocking pace these last weeks. You have managed to attach quite a handful of admirers, Lydia. I have not spent such a busy Season since my last daughter was at home. It has been most gratifying," she said complacently.

Mr. Davenport grunted and turned the page of his newspaper. "You have probably not spent so much blunt in one Season, either," he muttered.

"What was that, Edwin?" Lady Basinberry asked challengingly.

Mr. Davenport peered around the edge of the newspaper. "I said nothing at all, dear Beatrice. I merely commented on the shocking price of corn. We shall have rioting one day, mark my words." Lady Basinberry subsided, mollified.

Lydia giggled, sliding a glance at her cousin. Michele bit her lip. She recommended that Lydia give greater attention to her cards. "For I am already some points ahead of you, cousin," she said.

Lydia was immediately put on her mettle, and she straightened in her chair. "We shall see who accumulates thirty first," she said, tossing her head.

There was a stir originating from the front hall, a sharp voice, and swift hard steps. Lady Basinberry looked toward the drawing-room door. "I wonder who that might be," she said. She was not long left to her curiosity.

The door opened and the butler showed in a gentleman whose overcoat swirled with the impatience of his movements. "Lord Randol, sir."

Mr. Davenport got quickly to his feet, amazement writ plain upon his countenance. "My lord! I had not expected to see you again. That is to say, this is indeed a most welcome surprise." He found that he still clutched his newspaper, and he tossed it aside so that he could take the hand that Lord Randol had extended.

"Davenport, ladies. I am glad to have found you all at home." Lord Randol turned to make his bows to the women. As he did so, the candlelight shifted across his face, revealing high on his brow an open gash from which came a dark trickle of blood.

Lydia squeaked in alarm. "My lord, you are bleeding!"

"Am I? It is of no consequence," Lord Randol said with supreme indifference.

"My dear sir, I shall ring immediately for a sticking plaster. It appears a nasty cut indeed," Lady Basinberry said, moving toward the bellpull.

"Great heavens, man, have you been attacked by footpads? The scoundrels are roaming the street at will, I have been told," Mr. Davenport said.

"Whatever has happened, my lord? Was it indeed footpads?" Lydia asked.

Mr. Davenport had poured a glass of wine and now offered it to Lord Randol, who politely declined it. "No, nothing so dramatic as that. It was only a rock thrown up by a passing carriage." His eyes searched out and found Michele. She stood quite still, her face a shade paler than usual. She had not uttered a word since his entrance. Lord Randol firmly turned down Lady Basinberry's urgent request to seat himself. His eyes still on Michele's face, he said, "Thank you, but no, my lady. I wish for nothing. I have but come to speak privately with Mademoiselle du Bois."

There fell a startled silence as several pairs of eyes fixed upon his inscrutable face. Lady Basinberry found her voice first. "Speak privately with Michele? Why, this is a highly irregular request, my lord. Indeed, it is quite shocking," she said with haughty disapproval.

"Nevertheless, I fear that I must insist," Lord Randol said. The candlelight flickered over his scarred face and the gash on his brow. He appeared dangerous, and his insistence was strange, coming from one who had rarely shown the least degree of carelessness in his manners.

"I am not certain . . ." Mr. Davenport faltered. He looked toward his niece, a doubtful inquiry in his eyes. After the briefest of hesitations, Michele nodded in acquiescence. Mr. Davenport rocked on his heels, and his stays creaked. "Of course, my lord. Perhaps the back parlor will be an appropriate place," he suggested.

Lord Randol opened the door and with a peremptory gesture invited Michele to leave the drawing room. She went past him with a wooden expression. None of the curious trio left behind could have guessed from her manner that her heart thumped violently in her breast.

When Lord Randol and Michele were safely out of earshot, Lady Basinberry rounded on her brother. "I do not know what you are thinking of, Edwin! Our niece should not be closeted alone with his lordship. It is most improper."

"I know it, Beatrice," Mr. Davenport said, perturbed. "But what was I to do? I am not Michele's guardian. She is her own mistress and she has every right to form her own decisions."

Lady Basinberry snorted in disgust. "I shall not deign to comment upon *that*! I merely hope that Michele is aware of what it is she dares in agreeing to this most unorthodox meeting. It is shocking, indeed. I tell you, François du Bois has much to answer for in his daughter's handling of herself. A properly schooled young lady would never agree to a *tête-à-tête* for any reason." She added a few more pithy remarks that drove Mr. Davenport to take refuge behind his newspaper.

Lydia paid little heed to her aunt's sweeping denouncement of Michele's upbringing. The romanticism of youth made her hope for something of wonder, but she thought regretfully that she had seen too much of Lord Randol's chilly nature for such hopes to be practical. But still her curiosity was rampant, and she asked of no one in particular, "I wonder what it is he has to say to her."

Her question served to silence Lady Basinberry, and Mr. Davenport lowered his newspaper. They all studied one another, but no one was prepared to offer a theory.

20

Michele could not imagine why Lord Randol had demanded to speak privately with her. She had not seen him since the dinner party given by the Countess of Kenmare, and there had certainly not been any indication then that he wished further concourse with her. She cast a look up at his face as she preceded him into the back parlor. She could read nothing but severity in his expression, and she very nearly regretted her impulse to satisfy her curiosity and go with him.

When Lord Randol closed the door behind him, he stood for a moment with his hand at rest on the brass knob. Michele regarded him from a few steps away, waiting for him to break the silence. At last he left the door, intending to usher her to a chair. But he stopped before he had quite closed the distance between them. He looked at her for several long seconds, then said abruptly, "Since the countess's dinner party, I have been unable to forget her words about you."

"Can you not? How odd, to be sure," Michele said coolly. Her heart was continuing its pounding. She still did not know what he wanted of her, but there was an odd little lift of anticipation within her.

"I have come to demand the truth of you," Lord Randol said.

His voice was harsh. A tiny muscle jumped in his taut jawline, always in the past a certain sign of some strong emotion. But even so, Michele felt an uncoiling of the tension that had her in its grip. "Have you indeed?" She noticed that the blood that trickled from his brow threatened to mar the pure white of his high shirt collar. She pulled her handkerchief free from her sleeve cuff and reached up to press it against the deep cut on his brow.

With an oath Lord Randol knocked aside her hand. His eyes blazed as his lips curled in an unpleasant smile. "I am amazed, mademoiselle! Do not the sight and smell of blood offend your fine sensibilities?" he demanded harshly.

"Pray do not be stupid! I have tended those who lost limbs, my lord. Why should I faint now at the sight of a little blood?" retorted Michele, not understanding the cause of his blaze of bitterness. She could only guess that it had something to do with his own old wounds.

Lord Randol barked a laugh that was totally devoid of amusement. "Why should you indeed, if that were true? Oh, you hoodwinked the Countess of Kenmare finely. But I have cause to know better, do I not? You could not find the stomach to bear the sight of my wounds. That was why you did not come. Instead you had delivered that nauseating apologetic note to free yourself of any ties to a probable cripple!"

Michele recoiled from the venom in his voice. "What are you accusing me of? I have done nothing to you that you should hate me so!"

"Do you dare to deny it? I have kept the proof of your perfidy, mademoiselle. I have kept the damning letter to remind me of your treachery and your shallow love," Lord Randol snapped. He reached into his pocket to draw out his leather purse, and from it extracted a much-folded sheet. He thrust it before Michele's wide eyes. "There, mademoiselle! Your own words are come back to condemn you!"

Michele took the sheet and unfolded what proved to be a letter. Its top was ragged, as though it had been hurriedly torn from a notebook. It was stained and permanently creased by repeated readings. Undeniably the handwriting was her own. Michele read the well-remembered words over and over, her brows drawn in confusion. "But I do not understand. It is my penning, yes. But how did it come into your possession? I had written it to Sir Lionel after he . . ." She looked up quickly, awful comprehension dawning in her eyes. "*Mon Dieu*, Anthony! I refused Sir Lionel's offer for me, and this . . ." She raised the letter in the air. Her hand dropped slowly as she looked at him in gathering horror.

For a long tense moment Lord Randol stared at her. His very breathing seemed to have stopped. "It was Sir Lionel who brought me that damnable note," he said hoarsely.

A horrible weight constricted Michele's chest as she whispered, "He told me that he had seen you die."

"So he did," Lord Randol said grimly. "When I read that letter, something within me shriveled away. When Sir Lionel left me, I lay broken in body and spirit. I thought I would lose my mind, until I learned to hate you. It was my hatred for what you had done—what I thought you had done—that gave me the strength to survive. God, how I fought to live! I wanted at least that much revenge upon you for casting me aside." He smashed his fist against the mantel. "Damn his black jealous heart! Damn him!"

Alarmed by the viscount's barely suppressed violence, Michele caught at his arm. "Anthony. Calm yourself or you will do yourself an injury," she commanded quietly.

Lord Randol half-turned. His arms closed tight about her, as a drowning man might grasp a floating spar. His voice was muffled against her sweet-smelling hair when he said, "My God, Michele. When I recall what I have said to you . . . what I have done to hurt you!"

Michele felt tears burn her eyes. She raised her head and laid trembling fingers against his lips. "Hush, my love. It is in the past. We have survived, have we not?" When he attempted to speak, she shook her head. "No, Anthony. We shall never mention again the terrible things we have thought or said to each other. I forbid it."

Under her fingers, she felt his lips curve in a smile. She took away her hand. Her voice wobbled. "Good. You are not to be an intractable husband, then. I shall like that, I think."

Lord Randol looked down at her with a gathering light in his eyes. "On the contrary, I plan to be the most demanding of husbands. And I intend to begin this instant." He caught her up and his lips found hers in a hard, demanding kiss.

His arms tightened about her so that she could barely breathe. With an inarticulate sound she wound her arms about his neck and gave back to him the same fierce passion.

When at last they broke apart, they were trembling with the force of emotion that had been unleashed. Lord Randol raised a shaking hand to brush aside a curl from Michele's half-closed eyes. "I shall never let you go again," he said in a low, intense voice.

Michele was shaking. She felt certain she would fall if she did not cling to his strong frame. "I hope that is a vow of the highest order, my lord," she whispered throatily, endeavoring to smile at him.

"You may rest assured of it, my dearest love," Lord Randol said. "And I shall make it official as soon as I can procure a special license."

Michele drew back to the extent that his arms would allow. "We are not going to Gretna Green, surely?"

Lord Randol denied it. "I do not intend that our long-past-due marriage should finally take place under a cloud of scandal. You shall have your uncle to give you away and Lydia to be your maid of honor," he said.

"I wish that my mother and father could be present," Michele said a shade wistfully.

Lord Randol looked down at her face, his gaze slowly tracing each beloved feature. "You shall have them with you, then."

Michele looked at him, startled. "But you spoke of a special license. I did not think that you wished to wait so long. It will take some time for my parents to free themselves of their obligations and journey to London."

"I have set aside the thought of a special license." He smiled suddenly, his eyes bright. "My very dear lady, what is another month if it means that I may bestow upon you some measure of happiness? By all means, we shall have your father and your mother at the wedding. Write to them at once. We shall post the banns when you have a reply from them. That will give you time to put together a trousseau. I do not want my bride coming to me in just any old shift."

Michele blushed fierily. She laughed, a sensation of

incredible happiness in her heart. "You are far off in your thinking that a mere month is enough for a proper trousseau, my lord! But I suspect that with Lydia and Lady Basinberry to aid me, I shall manage to pack a proper gown or two."

"Good. It is settled, then. I, too, have business to finish before we may embark on our honeymoon." He thought about Sir Lionel Corbett's perfidy and all the anger and hurt and betrayal that he had endured over the long months of his convalescence crystallized. There was a dangerous, hard expression in Lord Randol's eyes, but it was quickly gone when he met Michele's questioning gaze. "Shall we tour Europe for our honeymoon?"

Without thinking over her response, Michele said quickly, "Oh, no, I do not wish to share you with anyone." Lord Randol burst out laughing, and she reddened. She punched him lightly. "Do not make fun of me, Anthony. I do not intend to sound indelicate, but it is true. I do not wish to share you with society, not when I have longed to be with you so very much."

He crushed her to him and his lips again found her willing. After a tender moment he set her away from him, but retained hold of one of her hands. He gently swung their clasped hands back and forth. Michele's breath caught in her throat, for his eyes held the devilish carefree light that she remembered from long ago. "I believe that you have hit on the most admirable of schemes, mademoiselle. After the ceremony we shall hide ourselves away at my country estate, and society be damned."

"It will create something of a stir, my lord," Michele said happily.

Lord Randol raised her hand quickly to his lips. "What matter? Come, it is time that we returned to the others."

When Lord Randol and Michele returned to the drawing room, their clasped hands and general demeanor of contentment immediately communicated to the party that something of moment had occurred. Lydia sprang up, her eyes brightening. "Michele! Is everything at last as it should be?"

Michele laughed happily. She left Lord Randol's side to hug her cousin. "Very much so, dearest Lydia."

Lydia fervently returned her embrace. Tears sprang to her eyes. "I am so very glad. I knew when you first told me about Lord Randol that you still cared for him. That was why I threw you together as often as I could contrive it."

"Thank you a thousand times, cousin," Michele said softly.

Lydia turned to hold out her hand to Lord Randol. She dimpled at him. "I am far better off without you, my lord."

Lord Randol smiled, not at all offended. He kissed her fingers lightly. "I would have made you the very devil of a husband," he agreed.

Lady Basinberry and Mr. Davenport had been listening in various degrees of amazement and shock. Lady Basinberry found her voice. "Am I to understand that Lydia's engagement to Lord Randol was dissolved over Michele?" she demanded in freezing accents.

Lydia rounded on her aunt. "On the contrary, Aunt Beatrice! I had never accepted Lord Randol's most flattering suit. And once it became known to me that his lordship was previously affianced to my cousin, I could not in good conscience have ever accepted his offer."

Mr. Davenport sat down abruptly. His eyes were fairly staring from his head. "Michele affianced to Lord Randol! That is impossible! Why, that was done with long ago."

"Nevertheless, it is true, sir. I hold myself entirely responsible for the confusion of these past weeks. I should have withdrawn my suit for Miss Davenport's hand immediately upon learning of Mademoiselle du Bois's presence in your household," said Lord Randol. "It was ill-done of me not to do so. My only excuse must be that I was laboring under an old misunderstanding between myself and your niece that blinded me to my duty and my honor."

"I do not understand any of this," complained Mr. Davenport, bewildered by the turn of events.

"Pray do not act such a fool, Edwin. It is as plain as a pikestaff that Michele has stolen his lordship right from under poor Lydia's nose. And *she* has not the wit to see it!" Lady Basinberry said, twin spots of angry color staining her high cheekbones.

"It is no such thing!" Lydia exclaimed indignantly. "Michele and Lord Randol pledged themselves to one another on the eve of Waterloo. They did not even know of my existence then. Tell them, Michele!"

Lady Basinberry snorted her patent disbelief. "I am sure it is a vastly romantic tale concocted for just such shatter-brains as yourself, Lydia."

Michele sat down on the settee beside her aunt, whose stiff disapproving posture did not encourage such proximity. She said gently, "However, it is the truth. Dear ma'am, you cannot be any more shocked at this turn of events than I am. When I walked into the drawing room with Lydia that first day, I could scarcely believe the evidence of my eyes. I had thought Lord Randol to be dead. Indeed, I was told most definitely that he had died." She looked across at Lord Randol, at the scar that slashed his face, and a smile curved her lips. "I was never more glad of anything in my life to discover that I had been deceived."

"Deceived? What do you mean?" Lady Basinberry asked sharply.

Michele hesitated, unwilling to open up to scrutiny the pain and humiliation of the past. But Lord Randol chose to step into the breach. "Just that, ma'am. It seems that a mutual friend, for reasons of his own, chose to lie to us both in an effort to keep Michele and me apart. Michele was told that I had died, whereas I was persuaded in a most convincing manner that Michele renounced her claims on me because she could not abide any sort of disfigurement." He gestured toward his face with the odd shortened movement of his right arm that had become characteristic of him.

Lord Randol's explanation was met by profound astonishment. "What rot!" Lady Basinberry exclaimed.

"Diabolical!" said Mr. Davenport, marveling and horrified. "But what man in his right mind would conceive of such a thing?"

Lydia's fertile mind leapt intuitively to the truth. "Sir Lionel!" She saw the swift exchange of glances between her cousin and Lord Randol and said in amazement, "I am right. It is written all over your faces. But why? Sir Lionel is such a perfect gentleman. And anyone can see that he positively dotes on Michele.''

Lady Basinberry had also seen the quick look pass between her niece and his lordship. It was that, more than anything that could have been said, that convinced her of the validity of what she had heard. ''I suspect that you have hit it exactly right, Lydia.'' She turned an interrogating gaze on Michele, her own sharp memory at work. ''Did you not once turn down Sir Lionel's offer for your hand?''

Michele nodded unhappily. ''I bungled it horribly. He . . . he proposed an instant after informing me of Lord Randol's death, and I was not gentle in my rejection. Afterward I felt badly. He seemed so downcast and horribly wounded. I wrote him a letter . . .'' Her voice faltered and she appealed to Lord Randol with a helpless gesture.

''A letter which Sir Lionel used to convince me of his assertion that Michele no longer cared for me,'' Lord Randol said in a hard voice. There was a cold look in his eyes that made Lydia shiver.

''My word,'' Mr. Davenport said inadequately.

''In that case, I am most sorry that I have encouraged Sir Lionel's attentions toward you, Michele. I hope that you will accept my profound apology for adding to an uncomfortable situation,'' Lady Basinberry said.

Michele smiled mistily at her, hearing the softened tone of her aunt's voice for the first time directed toward her. ''It is of no moment, my lady. I have been able to fend off Sir Lionel's pursuit with Lydia's help. He is a very tenacious gentleman, however.''

A martial light appeared in Lady Basinberry's faded blue eyes. ''I shall have something of consequence to say to the gentleman when next I have occasion to see him,'' she said grimly.

Michele placed her hand on the elder lady's thin arm. ''My lady, I believe that must be my place,'' she said quietly.

Lady Basinberry met her steady gaze for a long moment before she slowly nodded. ''Very well, it will be as you wish. You have more courage than I would have had at your age.''

Michele laughed. "I find that difficult to believe, dear ma'am."

Lydia gently tugged at her father's sleeve. "Come, Papa, you cannot remain sitting there when there is a toast to be made."

Mr. Davenport heaved himself out of his chair with the usual creaking of stays. "Quite right, Lydia. I was so flabbergasted by the moment that I forgot my manners. We must certainly toast the happy couple."

Wineglasses were filled and handed around the circle. Mr. Davenport looked at the small assemblage as he lifted his glass. "To his lordship and Michele, who have found one another again despite incredible odds," he said.

"Hear, hear," said Lord Randol. He slipped an arm about Michele's waist. Lady Basinberry lifted her brows at his lordship's shocking display of familiarity, but she said not a word.

After the toast was drunk, Michele slipped free of Lord Randol's embrace, laughingly scolding him for his lack of proper decorum. She had seen her aunt's glance and she had a wish to satisfy that lady's stiff code of etiquette. Lord Randol allowed her to go. His eyes reflected the devilish light that had attracted her from the beginning and promised her retribution. He turned courteously to Lady Basinberry and Lydia when Michele approached her uncle. Michele said quietly, "Do you mind too awfully much that it is I rather than Lydia who will wed Lord Randol?"

Mr. Davenport smiled at his niece. "I admit to a small twinge of regret at losing a title for my daughter. I suppose the title was never meant to be Lydia's at all, and I have a shrewd notion that Lydia remains blind to everyone but her soldier. If the truth be known, I am reluctantly admiring of her steadfastness. In the end I shall probably resign myself to a daughter who insists upon following the drum. But do not tell her that I said so." He winked at Michele, and she smiled, glad that at last the clouds over her cousin's life seemed to be lifting.

But Lydia had heard her father, and she whirled,

exclaiming, "Oh, Papa, do you mean it? May I see Bernard again?"

Mr. Davenport rolled his eyes and sighed his resignation. "Aye, my dear. I cannot remain hard against you forever. Captain Hughes has my permission to pay court to you. You may tell him so for me. I shall await his formal call on me."

"Thank you, Papa," Lydia said rapturously. She smothered her father in a fierce hug, from which he emerged somewhat bemused.

"Edwin, I believe you have finally let your mind go begging," said Lady Basinberry. "What has been the point of this Season if you will allow Lydia to bestow her hand on that young soldier after all?"

"True, the fine hopes that we cherished are quite dashed. But I am not altogether displeased, Beatrice," Mr. Davenport said as he regarded not only the light in his niece's eyes as she gazed up at Lord Randol but also his daughter's transparent happiness.

Lady Basinberry opened her mouth to deliver a cutting remark, but she found that she could not do so. She was not so unaffected by the shameless sentimentality of the moment as she thought she should be.

The following morning, Lydia rushed into the library, where Michele was engaged in writing the most important letter of her life to her parents. "Michele, it is too horrible for words!" she exclaimed. "I have just seen Bernard and I have asked him to be my escort to Vauxhall. What do you think? His domino is purple! *Purple!* And it is far too late to have another done up." She threw herself into a chair, and a profound look of gloom settled on her countenance.

Turned slightly away from the desk, Michele laughed at her. "My dear cousin, surely there is nothing in that to cause such distress."

Lydia straightened abruptly. "How can you say so, Michele? My domino is rose pink! Why, we will clash hideously. I simply cannot abide the thought. Everything must be perfect now that we are to be together again."

"Then I shall propose a solution. You shall wear my

domino and I shall wear your rose domino. We are of a height and may easily switch.''

"Thank you, cousin!'' Lydia said fervently. "I shall send a note round to Bernard directly to let him know that he need not scour London for another domino after all.'' She danced out of the library, once more serenely happy.

Michele returned to her letter. She chewed on the pen thoughtfully as she scanned what she had already written. She dipped the quill into the inkwell and added a few more words. Satisfied, she sanded the sheet dry. A smile curved her mouth. She imagined that it would come as a surprise to her parents to learn of her approaching nuptials, but the greatest surprise to them would be to read the name of her intended. Her loving parents had packed her off to England to forget Lord Anthony Randol, and instead, she had found him again. The irony made her laugh aloud in an unclouded peal of merriment.

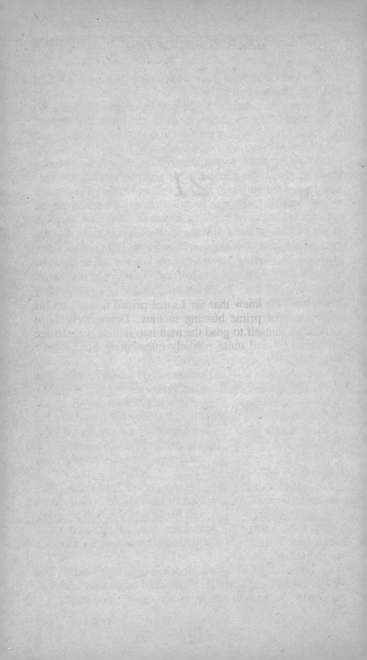

21

Lord Randol had looked for an opportunity to bring Sir Lionel to book for his betrayal. But he did not want to create a scene in society because he did not want Michele involved in any way. He finally ran Sir Lionel to ground at Tattersall's, amongst the purely male social circle of sporting gentlemen. He knew that Sir Lionel prided himself on his ability to spot prime hunting mounts. Deliberately Lord Randol set himself to goad the man into issuing a challenge by derisively and quite publicly questioning Sir Lionel's expertise in judging horseflesh.

Sir Lionel was of a temperament quick to take affront at any dispersions cast on his judgment, and Lord Randol's insulting remarks cut him to the bone. But though anger clouded Sir Lionel's eyes, it did not completely haze his intellect, and he refused to be drawn. "I am not such a fool, my lord. What would be said of me if I challenged a cripple?" He nodded in a condescending fashion toward his antagonist's stiff shoulder.

Lord Randol smiled. His eyes were bright hard agate. "Sir, you are a coward." With a flick of his wrist he cut his riding crop lightly once, twice, across Sir Lionel's face. There was a gasp from among the onlookers that had gathered about them. Two thin lines of blood beaded up across Sir Lionel's spare bronzed cheek.

Sir Lionel stood with fists clenched tight at his sides. The skin of his face had purpled. "You shall name your seconds, my lord!" he ground out from between gritted teeth.

185

"Done," Lord Randol said promptly. He named two gentlemen from the group of onlookers, who nodded their acceptance. The viscount looked blandly at Sir Lionel. "I believe it is my choice of weapons. It shall be pistols."

"My seconds will call on yours to determine the time and the place," Sir Lionel said gratingly. He turned on his heel and thrust his way through the exclaiming crowd.

Lord Randol watched Sir Lionel stalk away, a faint cold smile playing about his lips. His arm was grabbed by a friend who had witnessed the extraordinary exchange.

"Are you mad, Anthony?" the gentleman demanded.

"On the contrary, Ferdy. I am quite sane. I mean to even an ancient score," Lord Randol said coolly, removing his friend's hand from his sleeve and smoothing the fabric.

"What could be of such importance that you would force a duel on that man?" asked the Honorable Ferdinand Huxtable-Taylor.

Lord Randol looked at him. "My life." He walked away, leaving the onlookers talking in excited speculation.

The duel took place five days later and was attended by upwards of ten witnesses. Among those were the four seconds and two grave men of medicine. The others were merely along to be able to report the odd event. None knew what was at the root of the long-standing insult rumored to have made Lord Randol press the fight on Sir Lionel, but there was little doubt that the principals regarded one another with great enmity. Upon reaching the designated dueling ground, Lord Randol and Sir Lionel had exchanged but one glance, a glance so palpably full of hatred that one spectator declared his opinion that there would be a killing.

It was noted that both antagonists had forgone colored coats, having chosen instead dark, somber attire, even down to black cravats. It was attire that befitted a funeral, said one wag, but his witticism did not engender merriment. A chill pall seemed to hang over the gathering quite apart from that of the characteristic damp of the early-morning hour. White fog laced the air, alternately hiding and revealing those who measured off the proper dueling distance.

The principals were brought together to choose their weapons, Sir Lionel given precedence since the choice of weapon had gone to Lord Randol. The gentlemen took their places back-to-back, the barrels of their respective weapons held alongside their heads and pointing toward the dreary sky. The paces were counted out. The principals stepped away from one another, one pace at a time. On the count of ten, the command came to turn and fire.

Sir Lionel spun about. His pistol came down to level on the front of his opponent's coat. He squeezed the trigger. There were a flash and an explosion. A puff of smoke eddied into the cool morning air.

Lord Randol felt the whistling passage of the ball past his ear. The shot had missed him completely, he noted in detachment. He stared across the fog-shrouded green at Sir Lionel, who stood with his head up in a defiant attitude. His discharged pistol hung from his hand at his side.

Deliberately Lord Randol took aim. Another crashing report and billow of acrid smoke. Sir Lionel staggered a step, a peculiar expression crossing his face, before he crumpled to the ground. There were shouted exclamations. Several gentlemen ran to the fallen man.

Lord Randol calmly gave his pistol into the care of one of his seconds. With Ferdy's silent help, he began to shrug into his greatcoat in preparation for driving himself back to town.

Two gentlemen separated themselves from those standing around Sir Lionel's inert body and the busy medical men. They approached the viscount, examining him curiously. "Good news, my lord. You merely creased his skull," one said.

"Damnation. I meant to kill him." Lord Randol pulled on his driving gloves. "I'm for breakfast, gentlemen. Pray join me." He strode off with his seconds, leaving the messengers with their mouths agape.

"Cold-blooded bastard, ain't he?" one of the onlookers remarked.

Another nodded. "Coolest thing I have ever witnessed.

His lordship simply stood there, his pistol raised, and allowed Sir Lionel to shoot at him. That takes a remarkable nerve. One must respect his lordship for it.''

"Aye." The first gentleman reflected a moment as he turned to watch Sir Lionel's unconscious body being carried toward a carriage. "I'd give my teeth to be privy to what lies between those two gentlemen."

"We aren't likely to discover it now. The field of honor has seen justice done. The matter is finished with, I'd say," said the other, almost regretfully. His companion nodded agreement and they walked to their carriage.

By late afternoon all of London knew that a duel had been fought between Lord Randol and Sir Lionel Corbett. Speculation ran rife over its cause, but those at the Davenport town house had no trouble in distinguishing the matter.

The news was brought by Captain Hughes, who, since the understanding between Lord Randol and Michele had been announced, had been more warmly welcomed to the town house than in the past. As Michele listened to him tell what he knew of the duel, she sank down on the settee.

After a sharp glance at her white-faced niece, Lady Basinberry recommended that Michele be given a glass of water, a service that Lydia immediately took upon herself. "I do not know why you should look so puling, girl. According to Captain Hughes, his lordship came off without a scratch," her ladyship said bracingly.

Michele shuddered. "It is all so very barbaric."

Surprisingly enough, Lydia agreed. After giving the glass of water to Michele, she sat down beside her cousin and placed a comforting arm around her. "It is horrid. What if Lord Randol had been killed?" she asked.

"Lord Randol was more fortunate than you know," Captain Hughes said, and proceeded to point out a possibility that the ladies had overlooked. "If his lordship had managed to accomplish his announced intent of exterminating Sir Lionel, his own life would now be forfeit and he would be forced to flee the country into exile."

Michele shook her head. "It is unimaginable. I cannot

believe that Anthony could have done something so idiotic,'' she said in a low shaking voice.

Lady Basinberry snorted derision. ''Notwithstanding the good captain's presence, I shall tell you to your head, Michele, that the male sex are notorious for their stupidity.''

''Here, now!'' objected Captain Hughes unwisely.

Lady Basinberry arched her brows and haughtily stared down her thin nose. Her blue eyes were chilly in expression. ''Well, Captain?''

Captain Hughes found himself in the position of giving offense by any reply he might make, and diplomatically he chose to appear tongue-tied before her ladyship's challenging stare.

Lydia laughed at her beloved. ''Bernard, you are such a coward! Why, I would have come right back at anyone who made such a sweeping statement about my own fair sex.''

''Undoubtedly. However, I hope that I have too much respect for her ladyship to ring a peal over her head,'' retorted Captain Hughes. He slid a glance at Lady Basinberry and made her a respectful bow. ''That is, I shall endeavor to curb my opinions, at least until Lady Basinberry becomes my relative.''

Lady Basinberry laughed, pleased by his show of spirit. ''I begin to like you very well, Captain.''

Lord Randol put in an appearance not many minutes later. Michele instantly requested a private word with him in the back parlor. His lordship made his bows to the company and then followed Michele into the privacy of the next room. He looked at her with a faint lift of his brows. ''Yes, my love?'' Michele uttered an unflattering word in French. ''My dear lady, how very ungenteel,'' he laughingly protested. He attempted to pull her into his arms, but she shook him off.

''Do not treat me as though I were a green girl, Anthony!'' She spoke in swift, furious French. ''How dare you expose yourself in such a way? You could have been killed. I would have lost you again, and for what? Your damnable pride!'' she said bitterly.

''It was not pride, mademoiselle. The duel was a necessary

catharsis for me. Sir Lionel betrayed us in a fashion wholly devoid of compassion. I could not allow him to walk away without satisfying some part of my fury. I would not have been able to live with myself otherwise. The hatred would have eaten away at me until it threatened our very happiness,'' Lord Randol said quietly.

"Sometimes I wish that I did not love you quite so much,'' Michele said, a break in her voice. Lord Randol put his arms around her, and this time she did not rebuff him. She turned her face into his shoulder. "Promise me that you will not risk yourself again in such a fashion,'' she whispered.

"You have my oath on it. It would be extremely unsporting to go after the same man again,'' Lord Randol said, ending on a deliberate teasing note. He was satisfied when he saw the lifting of the shadows in her extraordinary dark blue eyes. He kissed her lingeringly before he said, "We have the future for our own, Michele. The past is finally dead.''

In the idyllic weeks following the duel, Mademoiselle du Bois and Lord Randol were seen much together. Society in general marveled at the change in Lord Randol, who seemed to have utterly forsaken his mantle of cold hauteur and to have become each day visibly more carefree and prone to laughter, while Mademoiselle du Bois was said to positively radiate happiness when she was in his lordship's company. The gossips spoke confidently of an impending announcement.

Lord Randol and Michele often drove one another about town. Because he was a notable whip, his unconcern in giving over the reins to her was seen as a testimony to the mademoiselle's own obvious driving skill. "After all, his lordship would hardly allow her to tool his own high-stepping cattle if he were not confident of her ability,'' said the Honorable Ferdinand Huxtable-Taylor, who had conceived an even greater admiration for the lady.

One golden afternoon when Michele returned from a drive with Lord Randol, the butler gave her the long-awaited letter from her parents. She asked Lord Randol to stay while she read it, and when she was done she cast herself into his arms with a happy laugh. "Mama writes that she and Papa are delighted that you are alive and we are to marry at last. They are setting out instantly for London."

Lord Randol swung her about, also laughing. They were quite oblivious of the gathering servants outside the open door of the drawing room. Lady Basinberry arrived on the scene, and at a baleful look from her, the servants hastily withdrew.

Lady Basinberry raised her brows in exaggerated astonishment. "One need not attend Astley's Circus to witness astounding spectacles of aerial grace," she said loftily.

Grinning, Lord Randol put Michele down. "I am all contrition, my lady," he said, which statement earned him a snort of disbelief from Lady Basinberry.

Michele was becomingly flushed. She held out the letter to Lady Basinberry, her eyes shining. "Aunt, I have a letter from Mama. She and Papa are coming as quickly as they may."

"I am happy to hear it. The sooner that you and his lordship are wedded, the better. With such a display, you have set the servants' tongues wagging and I shall have no proper work out of them for the rest of the evening," Lady Basinberry said tartly. She grasped the knob to the drawing-room door. Surprisingly, she smiled. "I shall just go and consult with the housekeeper and the cook on the preparations to be made for the coming visitors." She closed the door, leaving Michele and Lord Randol alone in the drawing room.

They looked at each other in astonishment. "I believe that Lady Basinberry becomes human at last," Lord Randol observed.

Michele choked on a throaty laugh. "Really, Anthony!" She walked into his waiting arms.

22

The following week, an announcement was inserted in the *Gazette* to quietly publicize the engagement of Mademoiselle Michele du Bois to Lord Anthony Randol, Viscount Callander. It did not go unnoticed, and there was open talk at how fortunate Mademoiselle du Bois had been to snare for herself a title. The felicitations received by Michele expressed genuine hopes for her happiness, especially those she received from acquaintances who had known her and Lord Randol in Brussels. A particularly warm note came from the Countess of Kenmare, who added the footnote that she had become the proud grandmother of a baby boy and was traveling to Scotland to be with her daughter, but hoped to return in time for the wedding. Dashing off a reply to Lady Kenmare, Michele expressed her happiness for her old friend Abigail. She privately hoped that it would not be long before she, too, could present an heir to her husband. The passing thought brought a pleasing warmth to her face and curved her full mouth in a soft smile.

"Whatever are you so pleased about, Michele?" Lydia asked, noticing her cousin's expression. "You look like the cat that swallowed the canary."

Michele blushed and evaded her cousin's inquisitiveness with less than her usual skill. Lydia eyed her, and would have pursued her inquiry except for Lady Basinberry's command to leave Michele to the privacy of her own thoughts. "Unless you wish to share your daydreams of your soldier, Lydia?" Lady Basinberry asked, her brows raised. Flushing,

Lydia took her aunt's point and subsided with her magazine.

Sir Lionel made a slow recovery from his wound. He still suffered from the headache, so he kept close to his rooms, and it was therefore late in the week before he read the *Gazette* notice of the engagement. He threw down the paper with a virulent curse. Pacing his bedroom, he hesitated over his course of action. It took him several moments of reflection before he decided what he should do. Throwing off his quilted dressing gown, he called for his manservant. While the valet assisted him into his day clothes, he scowled into space. The valet wondered at his master's foul temper, but knew better than to offer anything more than a selection of freshy starched cravats when Sir Lionel was in one of his dark moods.

Sir Lionel took an inordinate time in tying his cravat. At the end of thirty minutes, with half a dozen mangled attempts lying at his feet, he was at last satisfied. The valet helped him to slip into his tightly tailored coat. Sir Lionel picked up his hat and his gloves and left his rooms with but one object in mind.

When word was brought up to the upper sitting room to Michele that Sir Lionel awaited her downstairs, she hesitated. She was uncertain whether she should receive him. Lady Basinberry, whose arrival in the sitting room had coincided with a pot in steaming tea and a pattern book containing several examples of wedding gowns, looked at Michele with delicately raised brows. "My dear, shall I send him away for you?" she asked.

Michele swiftly made up her mind. She shook her head, and her mouth became firmly set with determination. "I shall meet with him. It is for me to send him away."

Lady Basinberry closed the pattern book. "I shall go down with you and hover about the door. If it appears too terribly uncomfortable, I shall be available for you."

Michele caught up Lady Basinberry's withered hand and held it for a moment against her cheek. She was constantly astonished by how close she had become with the proud elderly woman since her engagement to Lord Randol. "Thank you, dear lady," she said quietly. She rose from her seat, and after a swift glance at herself in the cheval glass, she turned to leave the sitting room. Lady Basinberry accompanied her down the stairs. In the entry hall Lady Basinberry paused beside the footman and quietly requested that he remain close beside her.

Michele opened the drawing-room door. She went in, closing the door, but remained standing with her hand still on the knob.

Sir Lionel turned quickly from the window. He did not approach her, but instead studied her face from across the room. What he saw made his lips tighten. He turned again to stare out the window. "So you know at last," he said.

Michele came further into the room. She stopped and placed her hands on the back of a chair. "Why did you do it, Lionel?"

Sir Lionel was silent for such a long time that Michele began to think he was not going to answer her. At last he said, "I hardly recognized Lord Randol when I stumbled over him in the hospital tent. His face was laid open to the bone. It appeared as though his entire right side was but a mass of bloody tissue and broken bone. He was nearly mad with pain. I truly thought he would die."

He turned away from the window to regard Michele's whitening face. There was a plea for understanding in his clear blue eyes. "Later, when I saw you, so strained and white but wanting to know any news, I could not bear the thought of you going to him and seeing him in such a ghastly state. It was unthinkable. I thought he would die. So I told you that he had."

Michele's fingers tightened painfully on the wooden chair back. She said slowly, "Did you not know . . . did you not realize that I would not have cared? I would have gone even though I knew he was to die in my arms!"

Sir Lionel stepped quickly toward her. "Michele! It was to spare you that anguish that I lied. Don't you see? I loved you too well to stand by while you stepped into a nightmare."

"That should have been my choice, Lionel," Michele said quietly. She drew breath and plunged into what was for her the most difficult part. "After I had turned down your proposal, I was so shaken by the depth of your disappointment that I wrote a letter to you.''

Sir Lionel's hands bunched into fists. ''You pitied me! I! Who loved you more than my own life.''

''Or your honor, Lionel?''

He stared at her, taken aback. Then he threw back his head to laugh uproariously. When he looked at her again, his eyes glittered. ''Aye, my honor! In very truth, I traded it for revenge. Can you even begin to fathom my feelings upon receiving that scrap of paper? Such noble sentiments, such understanding words! But laced throughout was the unmistakable odor of pity. I think I went a little mad. I tore off my name from the top and I took that letter to his lordship. He had not had the decency to die after all, you see. I gave him to understand that you knew of his wounds but you could not bear the thought of seeing him like that, half-crippled and almost certainly blinded in one eye. He read the letter and he, too, gathered the overwhelming scent of pity. It gave me a sense of fierce satisfaction that I had not misconstrued your words.''

At some point in his recital Michele had pressed the back of one hand to her lips against the sick feeling that rose within her. Now she dropped her hand and stared at him, appalled. ''*Mon Dieu*. How could you leave him like that?'' she whispered.

Sir Lionel flushed. ''Leave him to wallow in tortured thoughts, do you mean? Those same thoughts were mine, Michele! In my madness I chose not to bear the pain of them alone.'' He sighed as he scraped a hand across his face. ''When I saw you here, that first day in the park, all the old ghosts that I thought laid to rest forever rose to haunt me once more. I discovered to my devastation that I still loved you.'' He came toward her. ''Michele, I cannot help myself. You are more beautiful than ever. Your eyes, your mouth . . . The thought of holding you in my arms taunts me day and night.'' He reached out for her.

''Do not touch me!'' Michele said sharply, taking a step backward. She was trembling in every limb. ''How can you claim to love me? You betrayed me, Lionel. You tried to destroy all that I held most dear. Once—yes, once—I cared for you. I cared for you as my dearest of friends. But I do not think that I ever truly knew you. I realize that now.'' Her throaty voice was even lower than before. ''And I do not wish to know you.''

For several seconds there was silence. Sir Lionel slowly drew himself up. His eyes, hard and bright, did not waver from Michele's face. Then without a word or a backward glance he strode out of the drawing room.

Michele heard the outer door slam. Her inner tension snapped and her cheeks were suddenly washed with tears. She sat down abruptly in a chair.

Lady Basinberry saw Sir Lionel stride angrily out of the drawing room and from the house. She immediately entered the drawing room. At sight of her niece's bowed figure, she paused. Then she went up to lay a gentle hand on Michele's shoulder. ''My dear.'' Her hand was caught in a painful grip and Michele turned toward her. Lady Basinberry put her arms about her niece. ''It is over, my dear. It is over at last.''

In the days following, Michele was haunted by the dread that Sir Lionel would again approach her. But as the days slipped past and there was no sign of the gentleman, she was gradually able to put him out of her mind. She was aided to this happy state by Lord Randol's constant company, and when Mr. Davenport mentioned that the promised excursion to a masquerade at Vauxhall Gardens was to take place at last, it seemed the most natural thing in the world for her to request of Lord Randol that he act as her escort.

His lordship raised his brow. ''My dear lady, a masquerade? I would have considered us both far too jaded for such entertainment,'' he said teasingly.

''I shall take leave to inform you, my lord, that I am not in the least *jaded*,'' Michele said with some spirit. ''On the contrary, I discover an enthusiasm in myself for such frivolity. However, if you do not wish it, then I must find for myself another escort.''

Lord Randol raised her hand to his lips, but instead of saluting her fingers, he turned her hand over and kissed her sensitive palm. He smiled when he felt her shiver. "I shall not disappoint you in any way, mademoiselle."

Michele's face grew warm. "You are a perfect beast, Anthony," she exclaimed, pulling away her hand. She knew that Lady Basinberry watched them from across the drawing room. "You have put me out of countenance. I wish that you had never come to call today."

"But then you could not have begged my indulgence."

"Your indulgence?" Michele started to give him a much-needed set-down, but she could not withstand his laughing eyes. Instead she put out her hand to him. "Anthony, how very much I missed you."

"You shall never have to miss me again, my girl," he said, still smiling, but he spoke with a somber undercurrent to his voice. He clasped her hand in his, and thus they sat, quite intimately situated on the settee despite the others in the room.

"Isn't it perfectly marvelous?" Lydia sighed, touched by the romantic picture.

Lady Basinberry sniffed. "I hope never to see you display such open manners, Lydia. It is quite disgraceful." But she smiled a little as she spoke. At a thought, her smile turned a shade malicious. "Pray enlighten me, Lydia. Whom has your father approved as your escort to Vauxhall?"

Lydia turned bright red, but she answered her aunt with composure. "Papa has agreed to allow Captain Hughes to join us, Aunt Beatrice." She stared as her aunt began to laugh. "You already knew! How infamous of you to tease me, aunt!"

"It is my wicked nature. I do not apologize for it. Age does give one certain licenses, you see," Lady Basinberry said complacently.

The masquerade night at Vauxhall Gardens was more expensive than ordinary nights, and Mr. Davenport grumbled about the foolishness of youth. But once the party had crossed the river and stepped into the gardens, even he had to admit that it was a pretty sight. A thousand lamps illuminated the gardens so that the walkways appeared lit with enchanted fire.

The company wandered down the long avenues of trees, admiring the fountains, the cascades, and a fine statue of Mr. Handel. Strains of music drifted from the orchestra pavilion. "It is all simply too marvelous for words," Lydia exclaimed ecstatically, her eyes showing bright in the slits of her mask.

"Perhaps, my dear. But I for one should like to take refreshment. I am not used to all this walking about. Edwin, pray find our supper box," Lady Basinberry said. She had not deigned to wear a mask, but held one mounted on a stick. Now she used the mask in the manner of a fan and waved it gently before her face.

"Of course, Beatrice." Mr. Davenport led the way to a small supper box set in a leafy arbor and politely seated his sister. Lord Randol and Captain Hughes performed the same office for the younger ladies, and the party settled down to arrack punch, powdered beef, custards, and a fine syllabub laced with wine. It was a lovely summer evening and the warm air was caressing. More than once it was remarked how pleasant the gardens were that evening.

After the dinner was done with, Captain Hughes said, "I think that another turn about the gardens is in order to work off that splendid meal. Would anyone care to join me?"

"Oh, yes!" Lydia said at once. Recalling herself, she turned quickly to her father. "That is, if you have no objection, Papa."

Before Mr. Davenport could form a reply, Michele said, "I, too, would like to see the gardens again. I shall accompany you and Captain Hughes, Lydia." She smiled at Lord Randol. "My lord, I hope that I may prevail upon you to offer me escort."

Lord Randol bowed his acquiescence. "I will be honored to do so, mademoiselle."

Mr. Davenport smiled fondly at the younger set. Since his niece had become engaged to Lord Randol, he had become completely reconciled to Lydia's *tendre* for Captain Hughes. "Certainly you should walk about again. It is a very pretty night. However, I think that Lady Basinberry and I shall stay here to enjoy the fine music and to watch the promenaders.''

"Indeed I shall," Lady Basinberry said. "I am too old to match such energy. Besides, I am feeling decidedly sleepy from the punch.''

The two couples left the supper box, laughing. Their concealing dominoes and masks made them anonymous among the other promenaders and lent a spice of excitement to their outing.

Captain Hughes kept to a measured pace so that he and Lydia quickly fell behind their companions. He stopped before an unlit walkway and Lydia looked up at him inquiringly. He grinned down at her, the flash of his white teeth rakish beneath his mask. "Here is the Dark Walk, my fair lady. Do you dare to enter it with me?''

"Oh!" Lydia eyed the opening of the darkened walkway, from which could be heard giggling squeals and laughter. Feeling herself blush, she nodded. "Let's go!''

With a flourish Captain Hughes led his beloved into the infamous Dark Walk, where young ladies venturing alone could be certain of being accosted by impudent young gentlemen. When the leafy dark closed about them, their steps slowed and finally stopped. Lydia turned into her chosen gentleman's arms with a soft sigh. He lowered his head and Lydia closed her eyes in anticipation of his kiss.

Instead, she heard him give a peculiar grunt. His arms slid away and he fell against her. She staggered under his weight and pushed at his chest. "Bernard!" He dropped sprawling to the ground, his eyes rolled up in his white face. Lydia screamed.

Over Captain Hughes's body stood a dark figure holding a thick branch in gloved hands. The hulking apparition laughed softly. It turned its masked face toward Lydia. Recognizing her peril, Lydia whirled. But she had not gone two steps before strong hands clutched her. She fought frantically as a peculiar-smelling cloth was pressed over her mouth and nose. Instinctively she tried not to breathe, but she could not escape the sweetish odor. The blood pounded in her head. Her last conscious thought was one of despair.

Lydia's head lolled limply as her captor swung her unconscious body into his arms. Without a thought for the man moaning and stirring feebly on the ground behind him, he said, ''Now we are for Gretna.'' He strode swiftly down the walk. The dark swallowed him and his burden.

23

Michele and Lord Randol made a circuit of Vauxhall
Gardens before turning their leisurely steps back toward the
Davenport supper box. The disappearance of their companions somewhere along the way had not surprised them,
nor had they been displeased. The privacy gave them an
opportunity to speak as freely as they wished, and if they
lingered more than once in the shadows to snatch a sweet
kiss, none who passed were able to recognize those who
indulged in such shameless exhibitions. Indeed, there were
few who actually cared. It was tacitly understood that
masquerade nights allowed licenses that were not otherwise
tolerated.

Michele and Lord Randol were in sight of the supper box
when a dominoed figure staggered into their path. The
gentleman clutched the back of his head. He had lost his
mask, and in the lamplight his chalk-white face was easily
recognized.

"Good God! It's Hughes!" exclaimed Lord Randol. He
leapt forward to catch the other man, whose knees had begun
to buckle, and carried him safely to the ground. Supporting
the wounded man in his arms, Lord Randol said urgently,
"Hughes! What has happened?"

Quickly Michele knelt beside him. She pulled down
Captain Hughes's hand and saw the dark blood staining his
fingers and palm. She sucked in her breath. Her gaze shifted
swiftly to his head to discover the seeping wound that matted
the hair about it. She pulled out her handkerchief, squared

it, and pressed it to the wound. "Where is Lydia?" she demanded sharply.

Captain Hughes had difficulty focusing his eyes, and his reply came slow and stumbling. "Lydia . . . Took her. Said . . . said Gretna Green."

"But who . . . ?"

In a single horrible instant, Michele watched through her mind's eye as Lydia lifted the slate-blue domino from the bandbox, and in memory heard her say in her clear sweet voice, "It will suit you perfectly, Michele." The drawing-room door had stood open and a visitor had come in. "Oh, it is you, Sir Lionel! Is not Michele's domino perfectly lovely?"

With sick certainty Michele knew who had abducted Lydia and why. Her eyes flew to Lord Randol's face. "Sir Lionel—he knew that I was to wear the blue domino."

Lord Randol's jaw tightened. A dangerous glitter came into his eyes. "The bastard," he breathed.

Captain Hughes tried to haul himself upright, clutching Lord Randol for support. "Must . . . after them . . . at once."

Over his head, Michele met the question in Lord Randol's eyes. She shook her head. "He has taken a hard blow to the skull," she said quietly.

Lord Randol gave a sharp nod. "You are in no fit shape to chase after those two, Hughes. I shall go. Come, we must get you to the supper box." Lord Randol supported the injured man to the supper box, with Captain Hughes weakly protesting his fitness the entire distance.

Michele rushed ahead. She discovered Lady Basinberry alone. "My lady! Where is my uncle?"

"Why, he stepped out for a moment," Lady Basinberry said, astonished. She said sharply, "Michele, you have gone pale as a ghost. Are you quite all right?"

Michele waved aside her aunt's concern. "Captain Hughes has been attacked and Lydia is gone—abducted!"

Lady Basinberry started up from her chair, alarmed queries tumbling from her lips. Michele told her hurriedly what little was known, as Lord Randol and Captain Hughes reached the box. She stood aside for them to enter, and Lord Randol lowered the ashen-faced man into a chair.

His lordship was breathing a little quickly from the exertion as he glanced from Lady Basinberry's appalled expression to Michele. "You have told her? Then I am off." He started to leave the box.

Michele stepped quickly after him and caught at his arm. "I am coming with you."

Lord Randol impatiently shook his head, frowning. "I shall make better time alone. God knows how far along the road it will be before I catch them."

Michele said lowly, "He has done this out of spite. When he discovers that he has Lydia instead, and that you have followed him, he will be in a killing rage."

"Michele, let's not argue over this. I shall bring her back, but alone."

Michele shook his lordship's arm and said furiously, "Do you think that I have found you only to lose you again? *Non*, I am going!"

Lord Randol covered her hand with his and warmly pressed her tightened fingers. He smiled at her tenderly, understanding at last. "Come, then." He nodded to Lady Basinberry, and with Michele pressed close behind him, stepped out of the box.

"My lord!"

Lord Randol turned. Ignoring Lady Basinberry's sharp rebuke, Captain Hughes had managed to drag himself up. The man's face was white as a sheet. "Bring her home safely," he said hoarsely.

Lord Randol smiled, his expression one of grim purpose. "I swear it."

A scant half-hour later, Lord Randol tooled his phaeton through the London streets toward the Great North Road. Beside him, Michele sat ramrod straight on the seat. She clenched the seat rail tightly with one hand. The breeze brushed her face and tugged insistently at the hood of her domino. She had long since discarded her mask, but there had not been time to change her attire and she was grateful for the warm lap rug that Lord Randol had thrown over her

knees. Her light gown had not been donned with any thought
to a fast, cool midnight drive.

Michele turned her head to glance at Lord Randol's hard
profile. His lips were set in a grim line and his body was
poised to the job. The reins were handled expertly between
his strong fingers.

He appeared to concentrate solely on his driving, yet he
seemed to feel her regard, because he threw her a gleaming
glance. The silver moonlight was kind to his scarred face.
"Do not look so anxious, my love. The moon is nearly full
and it lights our way well enough. We shall catch them."

"But Sir Lionel will expect to be followed. He will not
linger on the road," Michele said, voicing her apprehension.

Lord Randol flashed a smile that looked positively fiendish.
"I'll wager my team against any jobber cattle that Sir Lionel
could have hired. We've reached the edge of town. Hold
on, my dear. I mean to spring 'em!" He lifted the reins in
the lightest of commands, signaling his leaders.

Michele grasped the rail beside her tighter as the well-
matched team of four accelerated to a pounding gait. The
wind rushed to meet them and at last succeeded in snatching
off her hood. Her hair was whipped about her head, but
Michele never gave a thought to the havoc wrought to her
appearance. She could only think of her cousin, terrified and
alone, somewhere ahead.

The miles passed quickly. Lord Randol alternated the pace
of his team time and again to draw all the distance that he
could from the horses. Michele discovered that it was
wearying to shout against the wind, and so conversation with
her companion was almost nonexistent.

Michele was aware of the passing hours as her body grew
fatigued by its enforced bracing against the movement of the
phaeton. She could hardly have been more tired than Lord
Randol, however, she thought as she glanced at his lordship.
Even though he still maintained his alert posture and his
driving was as skilled as ever, there was a deepening frown
that bracketed his mouth and contracted his brows. His right
shoulder and side, though mended, were not as strong or
limber as formerly and had to be paining him. Michele did

not know how he kept at it without at least shifting his position on the seat.

Finally she shouted, "My lord, how much longer?"

Lord Randol spared her a quick glance and pitched his voice above the wind. "We should have gained on them considerably. I hope to run them to ground within the hour."

Michele had to be content with his supposition. She strained her eyes for any glimpse of a chaise-and-four, which was the most likely means of transport that Sir Lionel would have chosen.

Lord Randol again pulled his team down to a slower pace and she had to fight the impulse to urge him to retain their former speed. She knew perfectly well that the team's strength had to be husbanded or the horses would be blown before ever they came upon their quarry. After a few minutes she spoke the thought that had been plaguing her for some time: "Perhaps they have stopped for the remainder of the night."

Lord Randol laughed shortly. "I do not anticipate it. Sir Lionel, unless he has already discovered the mistake in identity that he has made, will be more than anxious to cover the distance to Gretna before first light." He glanced at the lady beside him. "You see, he will want to present a *fait accompli* whenever I should arrive."

Michele absorbed the implication of his words. She shook her head, wondering how an engaging gentleman like Sir Lionel could come to harbor such hatred that he would wish to inflict the utmost pain on those whom he despised so dreadfully. For that was what Lord Randol meant. A man driven by such obsessive black emotion was capable of nearly any act. She shivered, glad that it was not she who rode in that carriage ahead. She could only hope that Lydia, since she was not the object of Sir Lionel's hatred, would not come to immediate harm while in his power.

"Ah, there they are!"

Lord Randol's triumphant exclamation startled her out of her reverie. Michele stared at the chaise ahead of them. It bowled along at speed, and a horseman loped beside it. The set of the shoulders of the rider was familiar to Michele, causing her to draw in her breath sharply. She knew beyond the shadow of a doubt that the rider was indeed Sir Lionel.

The distance between the chaise and the phaeton closed. The horseman glanced over his shoulder and then gestured wildly to the driver of the chaise. A whip snaked black in the moonlight, the crack loud even above the pounding of Lord Randol's horses. The chaise began to draw away from its pursuer.

"They are outdistancing us!" Michele exclaimed, beating her fist against her thigh with the angry frustration that welled up inside her.

Lord Randol laughed. His hands rose once more, sending the lightest of commands to his leaders. His horses increased their efforts, flattening out to an astonishing speed. Michele clutched the rail with both hands, fearing for her life. She threw a startled glance at his lordship. There was a faint smile curving his lips. His hard gray eyes glittered in the bright moonlight. He had lost his hat and his dark hair was whipped by the wind.

Michele looked wildly ahead, and her stomach contracted in sudden fear. Lord Randol had drawn the phaeton off to the far side of the chaise on the narrow road, so that it was in direct line with any oncoming traffic. As the distance was inexorably closed between the vehicles, there came to be but inches to spare between the phaeton and the chaise. Out of the corner of her eye she saw the blur of Lord Randol's hands. She knew in that same appalling instant that his lordship meant to pass the chaise. Just as certainly, Michele knew that they would be overturned and killed. As the phaeton drew level with the chaise, she snapped her eyes shut.

24

It was over in a flash. Michele felt a surge of air; heard the double pounding of hooves, and then the phaeton was past. She opened her eyes in time to witness the precise way that Lord Randol turned the phaeton so that it blocked the road. Then he snubbed the reins and waited. His left hand was clenched tight about the stock of his whip.

The driver of the chaise frantically worked his reins. His fearful curses carried clearly to Michele's ears as she watched, appalled, as the still-charging team bore down upon them.

At the last possible moment the chaise swerved. The carriage came to an abrupt, inelegant stop just feet from the phaeton. The chaise driver sagged in relief on his box and his blown team stood quivering in the traces.

The horseman pulled up his mount. His face was shadowed under the hat he wore. He called out, "So you have given chase, my lord. I thought that you might, but the speed of your pursuit is astonishing. I made sure that you would be nursing a throbbing head for a few hours, at the least."

"It is not I who suffer, but Captain Hughes. I have come as his deputy," Lord Randol said.

A momentarily startled expression crossed what could be seen of Sir Lionel's face. He turned his horse abruptly so that he could reach down to unlatch the chaise door. The door flew open. There was a startled cry, and out tumbled a flurry of arms and skirts.

"Lydia!" Michele exclaimed, rising. Her wrist was caught

in a viselike grip and she was dragged back down to the phaeton's seat. She turned furiously on Lord Randol. "Let me go! I must see to Lydia at once."

"Not now," Lord Randol said in a grating voice. He did not even glance at her, but kept his eyes on the tableau before him.

The young woman disentangled herself and stood up. Her unhooded hair gleamed unmistakably pale in the moonlight. She looked up at the horseman with undisguised revulsion. "You! How dare you!" she exclaimed. Then she saw the phaeton that blocked the road and bolted toward it. "Help me! I have been abducted! Pray help me!"

Sir Lionel watched Lydia go. His gloved fingers were tight on his reins, and bile rose to his mouth. He could hardly believe that he had made such a stupid mistake.

A touch of wind caught open the cloak of the woman who had started to descend from the phaeton, and the movement claimed his attention. It was then that Sir Lionel realized who it was that had accompanied Lord Randol. "By God," he breathed. He reached into his coat pocket.

Freed by Lord Randol, Michele climbed down off the phaeton to meet Lydia. Lydia clutched at her thankfully. "Michele!" She burst into tears.

Michele held her cousin tightly. "It is all right. You are safe now," she said soothingly. She glanced up, only to stare in horror. Sir Lionel had brought out a pistol, and now he leveled it straight at the woman he had claimed to love. Fury leapt like flames in his blue eyes. His lips were drawn back in an ugly snarl. Michele knew that his finger was tightening about the trigger, but she seemed paralyzed to move.

A whip cracked. Its tip snaked tightly about Sir Lionel's uplifted wrist. Lord Randol yanked sharply on the whip, and Sir Lionel cried out in mingled surprise and rage as he was pulled from his saddle. There was a deafening report and a flash of sulfurous smoke.

Sir Lionel's horse squealed and jumped away from the origin of the noise. One of Sir Lionel's boots caught fast in the stirrup. The horse dashed across the road. The man bounced twice on the gravel before his boot slipped free.

The horse came to a shuddering stand, blowing nervously.

Sir Lionel lay on the ground, quite still. His neck was cocked at a grotesque angle from his body.

Michele shook so hard that she could hardly stand upright. Indeed, if she had not had her arms still about her cousin, she would have fallen. The brush with death left her shocked and cold.

"What happened?" shrilled Lydia. The whites of her eyes showed as she looked fearfully over her shoulder toward Sir Lionel.

"I . . . I believe he is dead," Michele said faintly.

Lydia broke away from her, hardly noticing when Michele sagged abruptly against the side of the phaeton. She took a faltering step toward the fallen man, then stopped in fearful indecision. She glanced at Lord Randol, who had jumped to the ground beside her. Clenched in his left hand was his coiled whip. "Is he truly? But how?" Lydia asked, bewildered.

Lord Randol walked rapidly over to the fallen man to look down at him. There was no pity in his eyes. "His neck is broken," he said shortly.

The chaise driver spoke for the first time. "I never seen the loikes of that, guvnor. The whip caught his arm pretty as you please, and over he went outen the saddle. I'd wager any day that ye could clip a fly's wings with that whip of yourn."

Lord Randol inclined his head with an ironic smile. "So I have been known to do. However, I think it time we decided upon a course of action. Fellow, are you familiar enough with this area that you might guide us to the nearest magistrate?"

"Aye, it be but two or three miles back. What are ye planning, guvnor? For I'll tell ye straight, I'm of no mind to be stuck with a corpse," the chaise driver said forthrightly. He added practically, "And who is to pay me fare, is wot I'd loike to know."

"I intend to give testimony, never fear. And I'll settle your account as well. But now let's get him up into your carriage," Lord Randol said. With the chaise driver's reluctant help, he carried Sir Lionel's body over to the chaise and slid it onto the floor. Lord Randol gave the driver instructions before he walked back to the two women, who had remained beside the phaeton.

Lord Randol smiled reassuringly at Michele, and she walked immediately into his embrace. His hand smoothed her windblown hair. "I wouldn't have let him harm you. You must believe that," he said softly.

Michele raised her head. Her eyes were huge in her whitened face. She said, still unbelieving, "*Mon Dieu*, Anthony! I cannot stop shuddering. He meant to kill me. I saw it in his eyes the instant before he shot."

"Yes." Lord Randol smiled down at her. The warmth in his eyes caressed her spirit. "My dear brave love, do you think that you might tool my phaeton? I know that you must wish to share confidences with your cousin, and I do not think that either you or Lydia would care to share the chaise with the body."

Lydia shivered. "Decidedly not!"

Michele managed a wavering laugh. "Certainly, my lord, if that is what you wish. But what will you do?"

Lord Randol gestured at Sir Lionel's horse, which stood with its ears pricked forward and its eyes fixed on them. "That poor fellow will do for me."

Michele shook her head quickly. "That is not what I meant at all, my lord, as well you know."

Lord Randol smiled. There was a gleam in his eyes. "Trust me in this, my love. Now, up you go." He helped both ladies to climb into the phaeton, then mounted Sir Lionel's horse. He gestured to the chaise driver, and the cavalcade started back the way it had come, though at a considerably more sedate pace.

Lydia said urgently, "What of Bernard? I saw him fall and . . . I am so ashamed that I did not ask at once! Is he quite all right?"

Michele smiled, not taking her eyes from the road. The reins moved smoothly between her fingers. "Perhaps you have not had the time to do so. Captain Hughes was suffering from concussion, I believe, but otherwise he appeared quite lucid.'' She glanced at her cousin with a flash of a smile. ''Your beloved Bernard has a rather hard head, I think.''

Lydia smiled even as she shook her head in relief. ''All I could think of when I awoke was Bernard and how much I wished for him to come. I did not even know who had attacked him, or why I had been abducted. The chaise was locked from the outside. It just bowled along forever. I was in absolute terror.'' She reached out to squeeze her cousin's arm. ''I am so thankful that you came after me, Michele. And Lord Randol too. I haven't thanked him properly, but I shall. It . . . it has ended rather badly for Sir Lionel, hasn't it?''

Michele was silent a moment. The cool wind brushed her face. ''Has it? I wonder if Sir Lionel was not so twisted by hate that in the end he felt he had little to lose.''

Lydia was startled. This view of Sir Lionel's state of mind had not occurred to her. ''I understand what you mean, of course,'' she said.

The magistrate was not best pleased to be hauled from his bed in the small hours of the morning. But when he realized that there was a body involved in the business, he was able to set aside his irritation. It was not every night that a gentleman died in peculiar circumstances. And the circumstances must have been very peculiar, he thought, glancing disapprovingly at the concealing silk dominoes of the ladies.

But Lord Randol was able to reassure the magistrate that it had all been an unfortunate accident. The party had been guests in the neighborhood and had decided to leave for London that night instead of in the morning. Sir Lionel had been in his cups and had foolishly attempted to jump a fence before he was set. The resulting tumble had broken his neck.

''I completely understand, my lord. An unfortunate gentleman, indeed. But these things must be expected when one imbibes too freely,'' the magistrate said. He glanced again at the dominoed ladies and shook his head over the vagaries of the Quality. He would never voice his suspicions, of course, but it was his opinion that the dead gentleman had tried to impress one or other of the females of the carousing party and thus had met his untimely end. He agreed to see that the gentleman's belongings and horse were gotten to the proper place.

The unpleasant duty was soon done with and the chaise driver was paid off. Lord Randol took up his place in the phaeton. He flicked his whip at the leader's ears and the team started up. He glanced at his passengers. The scar on his face accentuated his devilish expression. "We are off to London, unless either of you wishes to avail herself of the hospitality of the neighborhood. I understand from the magistrate that there is a fairly respectable inn called the Huntsman's Prize. He said we would know it by its sign of a garroted lion."

Lydia grimaced in distaste. "Thank you, no!"

Michele laughed throatily. "My lord, your suggestion is untimely in the extreme. Pray attend to your driving. Lydia and I wish to end what is left of this night in our own beds."

"As do I," Lord Randol said in a low voice. There was a warm light in his eyes as he raked a glance over her soft curving figure.

Michele flushed, fully aware of the significance of his lingering gaze. She glanced quickly to see if Lydia had caught it as well. But Lydia seemed completely absorbed in the passing vista, which was undeniably breathtaking by moonlight. Michele was grateful for her cousin's inattention, but still she threw a fulminating glance at the viscount. "You are abominable, my lord!" she hissed, earning her a deep laugh from his lordship.

On returning to London, Lord Randol drove at once to the Davenport town house. As he had anticipated, Mr. Davenport and Lady Basinberry anxiously awaited them. Lydia was welcomed thankfully by her father and her aunt. Mr. Davenport wrung his lordship's hand, expressing his deep gratitude. When he heard of Sir Lionel's unfortunate end, he merely grunted and offered his opinion that the gentleman had come by his just deserts.

Lady Basinberry informed the arrivals that Captain Hughes was at that moment settled comfortably upstairs. A doctor had been in to see him and said all that was needed was some rest before the captain would be back on his feet. "It will not do to have Captain Hughes under this roof for his entire convalescence, of course, but we may talk of his removing to his own rooms later. We sent around for his valet so that he would be comfortable while he remains with us, however. I am persuaded no gentleman cares to appear less than his best, whatever the circumstances,'' Lady Basinberry said.

Lydia had listened to her aunt with an anxious air, casting several glances toward the drawing-room door, as though she wished to be gone. ''Oh, aunt, do you think that I might visit with Captain Hughes? Only for a moment?'' She faltered before her aunt's upraised brows. ''I feel so . . . so responsible, you see.''

Lady Basinberry exchanged glances with Mr. Davenport. ''If your father has no objection, Lydia, I am willing to accompany you on your visit to Captain Hughes.''

Lydia turned beseeching eyes upon her parent. ''Go ahead, my dear,'' Mr. Davenport said gruffly. She hugged him quickly and then went swiftly from the drawing room, with Lady Basinberry beside her. Mr. Davenport turned to offer his excuses on Lydia's behalf to Lord Randol.

Lord Randol waved away such considerations. ''I fully understand, sir.'' He glanced toward the lady remaining with them and then addressed Mr. Davenport. ''I should take my leave of you now. It has been a long evening for us all.''

Mr. Davenport shot a glance at his niece's lowered head. ''As you say, my lord. If you do not mind my rude manner, I shall say good night. I must look in on Lydia before she retires. Michele, my dear, I depend upon you to say all that is proper.'' He ignored his niece's startled expression as he walked out of the drawing room and firmly closed the door behind him.

Michele could scarcely believe that her uncle had left her unchaperoned, but her amazement was forgotten when Lord Randol held out his hand to her. She walked quite willingly into his waiting arms and lifted her lips in invitation.

Lord Randol kissed her lingeringly. Finally he said, ''I must go. The servants will be talking.''

''Let them.'' Michele slid her hand behind his head to urge him close. She kissed him slowly, again and again.

Honor-bound to behave the gentleman, Lord Randol uttered a feeble protest. "My cattle must be seen to," he said hoarsely.

Instantly Michele released him, slipping free of his warm embrace. Her dark eyes laughed at him. "Then definitely you must go at once, my lord."

Lord Randol was staggered by her abrupt abandonment. "What?"

Michele held out her hand, all formality, and out of ingrained habit he bowed over her fingers. "Until tomorrow, my lord," she said primly, stepping away from him.

Lord Randol hesitated, but when she made a shooing gesture, he went reluctantly to the door. With his hand on the knob, he bethought himself of an important question. "When are your parents due, Michele?"

"In a few weeks' time, my lord," Michele said demurely.

He smiled at her. A wicked gleam entered his eyes. "Then soon there will come an evening when you will not be so easily rid of me, mademoiselle," he said meaningfully.

Michele felt her face warm under his ardent gaze. "That is true, my lord. I shall not wish it then, even as I do not wish to be rid of you now." With one swift step Lord Randol left the door and attempted to sweep her back into his arms. She eluded him, laughing, and took refuge behind a chair. "*Non, non*! Go away, my lord!"

"You are a tantalizing witch indeed." His low voice made a caress of the words. He left then, quickly, before he succumbed to the temptation to give chase to her.

25

The wedding was a surprisingly small affair. The guests numbered a scant hundred and consisted only of family and close acquaintances. The ceremony was held at St. George's, Hanover Square, and the small gathering lended an unusual air of intimacy to the proceedings.

Michele appeared breathtakingly lovely in a wedding gown of Belgian lace over white satin that was cut with a low décolletage and a short train. The gown's puff sleeves were short, ànd she wore long white gloves. Her dark hair was covered by a cottage bonnet with a lace veil attached to the brim. When she turned her head to smile up at her lord, her dark blue eyes shone like stars through the filmy veil, rivaling the sparkling sapphires and diamonds in her ears and about her neck.

Lord Randol himself was resplendent in a dark blue dress coat over a white velvet waistcoat and frilled shirt. His cravat, tied in an intricate style that won envy from more than one attending gentleman, was fastened with a jeweled stickpin. His pale-colored pantaloons smoothly fitted the length of his well-formed legs and strapped under his shoes. He also wore gloves.

Miss Lydia Davenport was the bride's maid of honor, and the exceptionally dignified Honorable Ferdinand Huxtable-Taylor stood in the capacity of best man. Monsieur du Bois proudly gave away his daughter while Madame du Bois watched through smiling tears as Michele plighted her troth to the gentleman that she had steadfastly refused to put out of her heart. In an aside to Lady Basinberry, Madame du Bois whispered brokenly, ''It is just as I always envisioned it, Beatrice.''

Lady Basinberry nodded regal agreement, well-pleased. It was not the original match planned, but one did not quibble when one had more than one young miss to settle. Her eyes traveled to Captain Hughes, who was seated nearby and appeared to admiration in his gleaming regimentals, and she pursed her lips. She had heard that the captain had recently done very well for himself in the 'Change. That was a decided point in his favor, especially when Lydia had proved so disobliging as to turn down every other offer made for her that Season, thought Lady Basinberry. Really, she had no notion how the girl could have come to possess such an obstinate streak. But she had not been too displeased to discover that her flighty niece had more backbone than she had previously given her credit for. Lady Basinberry began planning for a second wedding, and anyone who chanced to glance at her at that moment would have discovered an expression of unusual contentment upon her countenance.

With the end of the ceremony, Lord Randol slowly lifted up the veil and settled it over the brim of Michele's bonnet. He bent his head to kiss her in a reverent manner that caused a sigh of satisfaction to go through the assemblage. The bride and groom left the church in their own carriage and the wedding guests followed in a veritable caravan of vehicles.

The reception was held at the Davenport town house, to which open invitations had been sent out. Besides the original wedding guests, upwards of five hundred personages came to pay their respects to the newly wedded couple. Michele had left her veil draped over the back of her bonnet so that she could better greet the guests. The receiving line was lengthy and she felt ready to collapse before she felt her husband slip her arm through his and they began to mingle with the company. She glanced up, a happy smile lurking about her lips. ''I do not think that I could uphold my duty without you at my side, my lord,'' she said.

''I should hope not,'' he retorted. There was a devilish light in his eyes. ''I have my own surprise for you, dear lady,'' he said. He made an imperious gesture. Instantly the unmistakable first strains of a waltz floated on the air. Lord Randol held out his hands. ''May I have the honor, my lady?'' he asked softly.

Tears glimmered in Michele's eyes. She could not speak and could only nod her joyful acceptance. Lord Randol took her into his arms. The guests parted around the wedding couple, retreating with many astonished exclamations and approving laughter. Lord Randol and Michele started to whirl in solitary splendor about the floor that had been cleared for them alone. The waltz was enchanted, its golden magic to be treasured for a lifetime.

It was late when at last Lord Randol and his bride were able to depart London for his lordship's country estate. Michele put on a white satin pelisse trimmed in swansdown over her wedding gown. With the shouted good wishes of family and friends still ringing in her ears, she leaned back against the squabs with a weary sigh. She felt her husband's arm slide about her as he pulled her snugly against his side. His hand came up to lightly encircle her breast. Michele started up, pushing him away in blushing confusion. ''Anthony!''

He laughed and firmly pulled her back to her former half-reclining position. His breath was warm against her face. ''My dear love, certain conventions may be relaxed between husband and wife. Have you forgotten already the ring on your finger?''

''I think that for a moment I did.'' Michele regarded the thin gold band on her finger with wonder. ''It is still all a dream.''

He tipped up her face with his hand. ''I assure you, it is no longer a dream.''

He lowered his head and kissed her with such tender passion that it brought tears to her eyes. ''Oh, Anthony.'' Michele brought up her fingers to place against the side of his face, unconsciously caressing the slash of scar that accentuated his face. She was startled when he caught her wrist and took away her hand. ''Anthony, what is it?'' she asked.

For reply, he gave a laugh and put her hand about his neck. His arms tightened about her and he kissed her with greater urgency. Even as Michele melted into his embrace and wholeheartedly responded, there was an uneasy question in her mind. But the answer to it would have to wait for a better moment than this, she knew.

Lord Randol finally released her. Michele shifted her position, and the hard brim of her bonnet connected with his nose. He gave an unhappy howl. She turned her head swiftly, voicing instant concern, and he yelped again. Protectively covering one eye, his lordship glared balefully at the bonnet on her head. "Do you know, as delightful as that contraption is, I shall do it injury if it is not immediately gotten rid of."

Michele laughed and undid the ribbons to her bonnet. "*Oui*, my lord. Naturally your every wish is my command," she said demurely, tossing aside the offending headgear.

Lord Randol flashed a sudden grin. "I am most happy to hear it," he growled in mock severity. "For I mean to be a most exacting husband."

"I do not doubt it in the least, my lord," Michele said, laughing deep in her throat.

The newly wedded couple passed the journey in the making of happy plans for their future. They sat close, their hands clasped, occasionally sharing a sweet kiss, but always content in one another's company. Michele at some point dropped into a light doze. She was drowsily aware when Lord Randol gathered her closer so that she could rest with her head on his broad shoulder.

Dusk began to fall. When the carriage stopped, Michele wakened immediately and peeked out the window. She was surprised when she did not see the manor house, as she had expected. The carriage was opened and the driver invited them to step down before a small hunting lodge set within deep woods.

As Lord Randol handed her inside the door of the hunting lodge, Michele looked around in some puzzlement and curiosity. She turned from her contemplation of the rustic comforts. "What is it you have planned for us, my lord?" she asked.

Lord Randol smiled. Walking forward, he placed his arms around her. "I have merely obeyed to the letter your wishes, dear wife. You shall not be required to share me with society or even with my extensive household. This hunting lodge is on the estate grounds, but it is a perfectly private retreat for our honeymoon."

At the warm teasing note in his voice, Michele blushed. She felt his hands moving slowly along the curve of her spine. Over his shoulder she saw that the other carriage, containing their baggage and the valet and her maid, had arrived. She pushed urgently against his chest. "We are not entirely alone, my lord," she said, warning him.

Lord Randol looked at her with the glimmer of a smile in his eyes. The scar down the right side of his face made him appear dangerously rakish. "We soon shall be," he promised.

Michele discovered that the lodge was to be staffed only by Lord Randol's valet, her own maid, and the cook. That evening she and her new husband dined in solitary splendor. Their conversation flowed easily, broken only by occasional comfortable silences. Afterward she and Lord Randol together ascended the stairs and he showed her to a bedroom. A massive four-posted canopied bed dominated the center of the room, and Michele realized that she stood in the master bedroom. She noticed that the coverlets and sheets had been turned down. The pulse began to beat more rapidly in her throat.

"I shall leave you to your privacy now. I will be next door in the dressing room," Lord Randol said as he bowed her inside the bedroom. Michele moved past him with her eyes lowered in sudden shyness. She heard him laugh softly as he shut the door.

Her maid was waiting to help her out of her pelisse and gown. Michele bathed leisurely in the large tub before the warm fire. Afterward the maid drew a thin lawn gown over her head, followed by a lace negligee that could be tied by satin ribbons under her full breasts. Michele laced the ribbons herself while the maid brushed her soft curls to gleaming black. When Michele's toilette was complete, the maid quietly withdrew. Michele stood before the grate, contemplating the flames of the fire.

The door opened softly, then closed again. Michele turned, her heart beating hard. She watched as Lord Randol walked slowly toward her. His dark hair glistened with tiny droplets of water. He had put on a quilted satin dressing gown over his pantaloons and he was barefoot. He stopped within touching distance of her and they regarded each other solemnly. Each was acutely aware of how much they had wrested from the ashes of hatred and revenge to arrive at this moment.

But Michele knew that before anything else was said, there was still one more question, one more fear, to be set to rest. In a low voice she said, ''I want to see your wounds.''

Lord Randol regarded her with pained hesitation. Then without a word he freed his right arm of the dressing gown. He had taken off his shirt, and the firelight played over ragged scars that twisted over his shoulder and his lean ribs. His eyes were inscrutable as he watched her face.

Michele reached out. With gentle fingers she traced the ravaging furrows. She knew that the remaining angry color would fade completely away to silver with time. It was symbolic somehow of their relationship. Their shared passion, born out of the urgency of war and tested by misunderstanding and adversity, would over the years come to shine as brightly as polished silver.

There were tears in her eyes when she looked up to meet his dreading and waiting gaze. ''You do not know how very much I love you,'' she whispered.

Lord Randol reached out with a shaking hand to frame her face. ''My dearest sweet wife,'' he said huskily. With her simple words, all his uncertainties were finally and completely laid to rest.

Michele wound her arms around his neck, a throaty laugh emphasizing the happy light in her eyes. ''Kiss me as you never have before, Anthony!''

"Gladly, my lady." Lord Randol crushed her to him and bent his head to kiss her with all the passion demanded of him.